THE BELFAST CASE-F

THE DETECTIVE INSPECTOR TAYLOR COLLECTION

Vol. 1

PHILLIP JORDAN

FIVE FOUR PUBLISHING

GET EXCLUSIVE MATERIAL

GET EXCLUSIVE NEWS AND UPDATES FROM THE AUTHOR

Thank-you for choosing to read this book.

Sign-up for more details about my life growing up on the same streets that Detective Inspector Taylor treads and get an exclusive e-book containing an in-depth interview and a selection of True Crime stories about the flawed but fabulous city that inspired me to write, *all for free.*

Details can be found at the end of **THE BELFAST CRIME CASE-FILES Vol.1**

THE DEVIL'S ELBOW

A DETECTIVE INSPECTOR TAYLOR CASE-FILE

PHILLIP JORDAN

FIVE FOUR PUBLISHING

PHILLIP JORDAN

Chapter 1

"GIVE IT ANOTHER minute will you, woman?"

Detective Sergeant Doc Macpherson gave an imploring look before tugging his jacket sleeve down to rub a porthole in the steamed-up driver's side window of the old Volvo.

"Are you frightened the ghouls are going to get you?"

Macpherson snorted in reply.

A westerly wind was driving the rain down the street in sheets but it was doing little to deter a coven of tiny witches going door to door in the annual search for coin and confectionery.

"It's not Halloween until the weekend for God's sake," he added with another grunt of derision and a shake of his head.

Macpherson reached forward and tweaked the control of the Volvo's heater in an attempt to clear the windows. It responded with the gasping gurgle of an asthmatic on eighty a day.

"Ack, come on, will you?" He thumped a palm on the dash, his huge paw at odds with the rest of his stature which had earned him the moniker of one of Snow White's famous friends.

"It's easing off. Let's get this over with and I'll shout you a Maharaja on the way back," said Detective Inspector Veronica 'Ronnie' Taylor, wielding the knowledge that naan bread and lamb biryani were more effective than carrot and stick in motivating the man who, since the death of her father, was much more to her than subordinate and colleague.

Before he could answer, the boom of impact caused them to jump in their seats, the heavy metallic thuds striking from the rear quarter panel to the driver's door sending their hearts into throats.

"Trick or treat!"

Macpherson heaved his door open.

"Get away home, you wee bastards!"

The scurry of feet and a riot of laughter drifted in the wake of the disguised youths as they sprinted away, black capes and devil horns disappearing into the gaping black mouth of the entry that ran behind the row of old Victorian terraces and down to the footpath cutting along the edge of the Stranmillis Embankment.

"You alright?" said Taylor, stepping out into the mizzle to join her sergeant.

"Near gave me a bloody heart attack."

He wasn't wrong. It wasn't too long ago two police officers, in this part of town, would have been a target for the local gunmen.

Taylor closed the Volvo's door and turned towards number seventy-four. Inside the bay window was framed with ominous black drapes and the soft scarlet glow of candlelight.

"Trick or treat," said Macpherson with a tut, following his inspector across the road and up the broken tile path.

Taylor reached out and thumped a brass goat's head against scratched paintwork.

Trick or treat, she thought, eyes coming to rest on the children doing their rounds. Their sing-song requests ringing out as each door opened to spill light onto doorsteps and eager outstretched hands.

The simple tradition and rhyme brought darker thoughts to the forefront of her mind. Memories of her father out on the beat and the worry of her mother. The echoes of television bulletins and the scent of newsprint. The shadow of Northern Ireland's troubled history was never far away, and with only a few days to go until the anniversary of the Greysteel massacre, those three simple words conjured up images of carnage and cruelty.

Her mind was still preoccupied as the door to number seventy-four Brunswick Street creaked open.

Inside the house, the heat was stifling.

Three gas bars grinned from the grate and there were enough church candles burning in close proximity to voile and velvet that even the usually composed Taylor felt the creep of anxiety.

Macpherson was sweating bullets. He dabbed his brow with the cuff of his jacket, trying and failing not to look aghast at the menagerie of mismatched furniture, Celtic idolatry, crystals, and the wall-mounted lamb's skull.

Their host it seemed was oblivious to his shock.

"Please. Sit yourselves down, can I get you tea? Are you not soaked."

"We're grand, Mrs Meehan," said Taylor.

"You can call me Luna," she said, waving away Taylor's formality and ushering the two police officers towards a sofa covered in gaudy throws and a coating of pet hair.

Taylor eased onto the edge while Macpherson resisted, his eyes scanning the room for the beast responsible.

"You've a cat?" he said.

"I've a few." Luna nodded, her eyes wrinkling ahead of a sage nod. "I can sense you're not a cat person."

Macpherson sat hesitantly beside his inspector, drawing up his cuff to show a ragged scar.

"I'm not a fan of anything that sinks its teeth in for no good reason. Give me a goldfish any day of the week."

The householder gave another bob of the head. "There's always a reason," she said cryptically.

Luna Meehan was probably pushing sixty but looked younger. She had clear skin and her straw-coloured hair was tied back from a pale narrow face. In contrast, she wore dark eyeliner and lipstick which gave her a slight air of theatricality when combined with the purple taffeta skirt and a long frock coat. As she moved nearer the hearth Taylor noted she was barefoot. At first glance and with the addition of a pointy hat, the woman wouldn't have been too far out of place going door to door with the kids outside.

"You reported some suspicious activity by the river?" prompted Taylor.

"I did. I did." Luna held up a palm and then retreated out of the room into what Taylor presumed to be the scullery.

"Ack, she's a spacer," mumbled Macpherson.

"Shhhh." Taylor nudged him with her elbow.

"Have you seen thon?" He stabbed out a finger to make his point.

"Yes." Taylor had seen the sideboard with its collection of crystal balls, bones and Ouija board.

"And she's a soup merchant."

A bottle of gin was tucked discreetly beside the room's only armchair. Empty glass by its side.

"Here we are." Luna breezed back into the room and presented a small wooden trinket box inlaid with Mother of Pearl.

Taylor's brow furrowed in confusion.

"I got it at the charity shop," Luna gestured vaguely out the bay window. "Across the bridge, beside the surgery."

Taylor nodded, aware of the row of shops but unable to recall exactly which one Luna referred to. Luna thumbed a switch, illuminating the room's big light to better appraise the piece.

"Were you on your way back when you saw something?" said Macpherson.

"Oh no." The woman gave an emphatic shake of her head.

"No?" Taylor gripped her knees so as not to run an impatient hand through her hair.

"Not in that way." The woman caressed the box solemnly.

"Mrs… Luna," Taylor smiled. "What exactly do you need us to look into?"

"A death, inspector. An untimely death."

"I'm sorry, I—" Taylor began, eyebrows rising at the sudden revelation.

"I've seen her every night since I brought this home."

"You've seen a ghost?" breathed Macpherson, unable to keep the scepticism from his tone.

Luna gave a patient nod.

"It's easy to mock what we don't understand," she said, offering the box to Taylor.

It was in good repair, the hinges glistening as though they had been recently oiled.

"Her name is Julie, or Jenny," said Luna. "Or Judy?"

"Jesus, at least you've narrowed it down to an initial…" Macpherson's words were barely audible under his breath.

"How do you know that?" said Taylor, ignoring him and looking up.

Luna shrugged.

"I see her in the water, by a bend in the river near a bridge. She's calling out her name."

"Luna, I appreciate you might think that you've—"

"I know what I see, inspector. My abilities and the prejudices of those who can't comprehend them are not new to me." She knelt and placed her hand on Taylor's. Her touch was warm and oddly comforting. "I'm not asking you to understand, inspector. I'm asking you to open your mind because somewhere out there a mother is wondering what became of her daughter."

Taylor looked again at the box but there were no distinguishing marks. She clicked open the lid.

And the lights went out.

Chapter 2

"IT SMELLS LIKE the devil's armpit," said Detective Constable Chris Walker, trying and failing to mask the stench with the crook of his elbow.

"It can't be that bad." DC Erin Reilly shooed her partner away from the trash heap.

"Have you been into the gents the morning after Doc's been for an all-you-can-eat?" Walker took a step back, taking a deep cleansing breath. "I have and I'll tell you what, this comes in a close second."

Reilly swatted away a squadron of bluebottles. It stank right enough.

"I'd have thought the constabulary had more pressing matters to attend to. Do you want me to dig you out a couple of shovels and you can lend a hand?"

Reilly rose from her haunches and nodded a greeting to the council worker plodding through the fly-tipped pile of split bin bags, rotten garbage, household junk and general wanton waste.

"A criminal offence is a criminal offence," said Reilly as he stopped a few paces short and nudged a pile of broken bathroom tiles away from the kerb with his boot.

Morning traffic rushed past, buffeting them in the slipstream. There was little of interest to the commuters, the waist-high mound not gratuitous enough to warrant the slow creep of rubberneckers.

"Ever since the depot started limiting what goes to

landfill this carry-on has been on the increase. Norman Murphy." Murphy gave a polite nod of introduction to both officers, leaning on his shovel and surveying the mess.

"Did you report it?"

Murphy bobbed his head. He was a small man, five foot five and slight in stature, his head bullet shaped with a covering of steel grey fuzz.

"To the office, like. I didn't phone nine, nine, nine."

Reilly brushed off her hands and sighed. There wasn't much more for them to see, and there was no more they could do other than log the location details and keep an eye out for any witness reports that came in. The council would inform them if anything incriminating was found in the contents.

"Not as bad as last time," said Murphy. Reilly raised a questioning eyebrow.

"Waste fuel and oil drums."

"Where was that?" said Walker, taking a quick step into the detritus to avoid the wing mirror of an onrushing bus. The council worker gestured over his shoulder.

"Up near Drumkeen Forest. We had the environment agency and fisheries involved too. They thought it might have contaminated the water." He thudded his shovel into the pile. "My boss is spitting nails over the head of this."

"Yours and ours both," said Reilly.

Illegal dumping was on the rise and it was impacting the crime statistics for the quarter which in turn meant the chief super was on the warpath over the league tables, and like the garbage spilling across the embankment, his anger also rolled downhill.

"Are you taking it back to the depot?" she said.

Murphy gave a grunt.

"Eventually. We'll have to wait on a supervisor before we sift through it and see if we can identify where it might have come from but there's that many cowboys it could end up being from all over the city, further maybe."

"Someone got it lifted," said Walker. "Probably paid for it too. "

"Aye, and if there's anything to identify them, and they point the finger, then it'll be over to you to track down the culprits." Murphy smiled but without confidence anyone would be caught. His expression changed.

"Davy, be careful. There could be syringes or anything in there. What are you doing?"

Ten feet away his younger colleague who had been carefully circumnavigating the heap had bent from the waist to dig his hand through a pile of what looked like old clothes, sweat-stained pillows and crumpled bedsheets. Davy was tall, rangy and pale as a corpse. He couldn't have been more than late teens, very early twenties.

"I just thought…"

Murphy excused himself and tramped over, face reddening.

"Get out of it. Leave looking for anything until George gets—"

Reilly and Walker had followed and now watched as Murphy knelt and plunged a gloved hand into the waste at the boy's feet.

"Not quite a diamond in the rough, but…" He offered his open hand to Reilly.

"Distinctive," she said.

In his rough gloved palm, the council worker held a

pendant on a snapped chain. The decorative charm was silver and fashioned to resemble an ornate mirror with a black cat perched on the lip.

"Not the sort of thing you'd turf out." Walker peered over Reilly's shoulder, then to the boy. "Good spot."

Davy blew his jet-black fringe from his eyes and shuffled, staring at the ground towards the spot from where his treasure had been seized.

"Flip it over?" said Reilly, not really sure what she hoped to see. Murphy nudged the piece over. The back was smooth with a hallmark stamp below which was an engraving.

Just the two letters, J.W.

Chapter 3

THE CID SUITE at Musgrave Central took up a section of the building's eastern facade, the blast-proof windows overlooking Ann Street and across to the Queen Elizabeth Bridge, the Lagan Weir and beyond that the dome of the Odyssey Complex and the famous Belfast shipyard, birthplace of the Titanic and home to its twin cranes, Samson and Goliath.

The area was divided up like any modern office space with blue fabric acoustic screens marking out workspaces, rest areas and meeting zones, each territory distinct and yet, as Taylor walked towards the area which housed her small team she noted someone had been busy adding a touch of spooky adornments to all.

Decapitated pumpkin heads lined the sills and artificial cobwebs clung to the corners of windows. Among the cubicles, cardboard skeletons rattled their chains and at least half a dozen rubber bats dangled from the suspended ceiling tiles.

Cutting across the central aisle she caught sight of Macpherson outside the rest area of section two.

"Here she is. Doc's telling us all about your encounter with the 'Witch of Brunswick'." Detective Inspector Phillip MacDonald dropped a set of bunny ears around the description, his expression creased in amusement.

"And you weren't to know Sergeant Harris would have us out chasing ghosts, I suppose?" said Taylor, swinging her bag from one shoulder to the other.

MacDonald laughed again and swept his chair around to face the other man in the room. Tall, tanned and immaculately groomed, Detective Constable Samuel 'Slick' Simpson offered her an embarrassed shrug.

"You're not the first if it's any consolation," he said.

Taylor waved the apology away. In the past, she had dismissed the DC for his egregious oiliness and his enthusiasm to impress superiors and those of the opposite sex. The frost had thawed though when they worked a domestic violence case together.

"What's her story?" said Taylor. MacDonald slid his chair up to his desk and leaned on his elbows.

"Fruit cake. Every major enquiry she's on the phone wanting to lend her 'services'." He dropped the bunny ears for a second time.

"She's a medium," said Simpson.

"You should be in tailoring with an eye like that, Slick," said Macpherson.

Simpson smiled. "A psychic."

"What was it this time?" asked MacDonald.

"Spirit of a dead girl needing justice," said Taylor, ushering Macpherson towards their own desks.

MacDonald waggled his fingers and gave a wavering woo, his laughter following them as they left.

"It's not like you to turn your face up at buns?"

Detective Constable Carrie Cook pulled back a Tupperware box of iced cupcakes topped with ghosts, pointed hats and pumpkins.

Macpherson raised a steadying hand. "Hang on now, not

so fast there, DC Cook." He beckoned the box back and Cook relented. "I'm still feeling a bit ropey from last night's kebab but one of these should sort me out." He didn't look certain and Cook shook her head as half the cupcake disappeared in one bite.

"Guv?" she said, offering the box.

The DC had initially been seconded to the team during the investigation to a domestic slavery ring but with a workhorse ability to get the job done and an inherent aptitude for investigation Taylor had managed to keep her on board, much to Macpherson's delight due to her endless supply of home-baked cakes and savouries. Cook was a feeder.

"Thanks." Taylor plucked one out and placed it on her desk. DCs Reilly and Walker approached bearing tea and coffee.

"Thanks," Taylor echoed accepting her coffee from Reilly. Walker deposited his drinks to Cook and Macpherson, taking his own from Reilly. He lowered his nose to his shoulder and sniffed.

"Run out of Right Guard or something?" said Macpherson, washing the second and final bite of cupcake down with his tea.

"I can still smell that crap from this morning." Walker gave a shudder, then self-consciously reached up to brush his hair forward as all eyes looked at him.

"More fly-tipping?"

"Along the embankment near the Lockview and the forest park."

"Shitting in the same place twice. That's not too far from the fuel spill," said Macpherson.

He nodded up at the map of the city and surrounds pinned on their display board. Twenty coloured pins had been jabbed through the printout into the cork marking different sites.

A red pin skewered a section of the River Lagan near the Belfast Boat Club and the fringes of the Lagan Meadows nature reserve and Drumkeen Forest Park. It marked a lethal section of fast-flowing water known locally as The Devil's Elbow, a spot which had claimed multiple lives from thrill-seeking canoeists to those foolish enough to think it could be forded on foot.

"They're getting bolder," observed Cook.

"CCTV in the area?" asked Taylor.

"Down. There was a power cut last night," said Reilly

Macpherson spluttered a mouthful of tea. "Don't talk," he said mopping a splash from the desk with his cuff.

"What happened, did you get lost on the way to the bathroom?" said Walker with a grin. Macpherson pulled a face.

"The power went off in the middle of an interview, and then I had to drive around for half an hour to find a kebab shop still open. The Maharaja had to close early," Macpherson's head wobbled in irritation as he thought back to missing out on a visit to his favourite takeaway restaurant.

"You could do with skipping the odd midnight snack, sarge." Reilly lunged forward and prodded him in the midriff.

"You can't fatten a thoroughbred, Erin," he scolded, batting her hand aside.

"I'm surprised you were still hungry after your scare,"

said Taylor, easing back into her seat and peeling the cupcake case off.

"What scare?" The three DCs said in unison.

"Ack, don't you be encouraging them, Ronnie."

"Is this about the wicked witch of the west?" said a voice.

All heads turned to face the newcomer rounding the cubicles. Constable Leigh-Anne Arnold gave a cheery smile. The TETRA radio attached to the lapel of her hi-vis jacket warbled and she turned it down.

"Brunswick is more south than west, Leigh-Anne. If you'd stayed in school you would know that," grumbled Macpherson. Arnold's blue eyes twinkled in her baby face.

"We were responding to a call about suspicious activity; let's say the lady had a flair for the dramatic and the power cut added to the theatre of the evening," explained Taylor. Arnold chuckled accepting a cupcake from Cook.

"She sees dead people," said Arnold.

"Piss off," said Walker, eyes widening.

"I'm just telling you what they say."

"The only spirits she sees are supermarket own brands," said Macpherson, crooking a finger at the box of buns.

"Guv?"

Taylor gave Walker a dismissive wave. "I think the spirit of the season is getting to everyone," she said. "What can we do for you, Leigh-Anne?"

Arnold balanced her cupcake over the case, nibbling icing off the top.

"Sergeant Harris says the council have turned up some stuff might be of interest on the fly-tips."

"Okay, thanks. Erin, can you and Chris see if it's a viable

lead so we can report some progress to the chief super?"

Reilly nodded and gave a thumbs up.

"There's something else too, guv. I'm just back from a call-out reporting a historic domestic incident."

Taylor nodded and dug out her notebook.

"The reporting party is Helen Broadbank. Her friend hasn't shown up to their last two arranged meetings and she thinks she may be a victim of coercive control."

"So it's out of character?"

Arnold nodded then gave a little wince. "They are part of a paranormal society."

"You must be joking me," said Macpherson, letting his forehead slump to the desktop.

"Have we a name for the friend?" said Taylor.

Arnold was skimming through her notes.

"I have it here somewhere…" she said, mumbling as she chewed the last of her bun. "Josie, Jamie, Jacqui…"

Chapter 4

"HUBBLE, BUBBLE, TOIL and trouble, huh?" said Macpherson, clipping in his seatbelt.

Taylor pulled the Volvo's door closed and waved out of the window at the three chalk-white faces staring from the doorway of the student accommodation that doubled as home to Pentangle Paranormal.

"They seemed sweet enough."

"They want to tell their faces will. Between the make-up and the metal, they'll scare the bloody ghosts away, and your woman in the middle? Did she have fangs?"

Taylor chuckled.

"Takes all sorts, Doc."

"There's something in the bloody water this week," he huffed, nudging the Volvo into traffic.

The girls had been welcoming although certainly, they were unique in their physical appearance and hospitality.

All were dressed resplendently in blacks and deep purples, Marie did indeed have fangs, and Helen Broadbank had enough piercings in her ears and face to sink the Titanic, but to Macpherson, the cranberry tea served in skull-design mugs on a coffin-shaped coffee table had definitely upped the ante from odd to borderline cuckoo.

Broadbank had explained to the two detectives that not all of her 'sisters' could attend but that the three of them; herself, Marie Faux and Caroline Duggan could vouch that

Jane Morrow who was a founding member of their group had disappeared and cut off contact just after their last "summoning", the evening culminating in an altercation between the girls and Jane's boyfriend, Maxwell Parker.

"They probably wanted to use him as a human sacrifice," said Macpherson, swinging the Volvo across traffic and onto Ormeau Embankment.

The road was hemmed in on one side by skeletal branches overhanging the wrought iron railings of Ormeau Park, the oldest municipal park in the city and former home of the second Marquis of Donegall until mounting debt saw the land sold off to the Belfast Corporation.

On the other side, the grey-green waters of the Lagan silently continued their journey from the slopes of Slieve Croob out to Belfast Lough.

"It'll do no harm hearing his side," said Taylor as Macpherson turned right across the Ormeau Bridge and then left into an avenue of three-storey red-brick terraces.

"Aye, I just hope as he doesn't open the door dressed as bloody Dracula."

"I've give him a shout. He'll be down in a minute. Just grab a…"

The young man who'd identified himself as David Black and had granted them access to eighty-eight Cairo Street paused and had the courtesy to blush as he gestured towards a rickety sofa and two beanbags.

"Was anybody killed in the explosion?" said Macpherson, surveying the damage.

"Sorry, got a bit carried away last night." He shrugged. "Just sit wherever you can find a spot," he said, pulling on a dark parka jacket with a fur-lined hood. "I'm running a bit late for work here." He gave an apologetic smile and picked up an armful of the dozen or so empty pizza boxes, and moved to crack open the blinds and the window.

"I'll let a bit of air in," he said by way of apology for the fug of body odour and the less than wholesome fragrance of the morning after the night before.

"No problem," said Taylor moving to wait in the middle of the small lounge for Parker to make an appearance.

"Students," said Macpherson doing a three-sixty as the letterbox rattled declaring David's departure. "Might as well be Dracula we're visiting. The wee shits sleep all day and wreck all night."

Tobacco and the scent of Class Bs clung to the fabric in the room. So did the smell of stale lager and fried onions and the decor did little to deter the stereotype of student lads more keen on excess than education. A pyramid of beer cans was stacked on the hearth, the grate itself packed to the gills with discarded fag packets, sweet wrappers and junk mail. Separating the lounge from the kitchenette, a glass-topped table was topped with mug ring marks and an overloaded ashtray, alongside a pack of playing cards and scattered copper coins.

The kitchenette wasn't in a much better state. The sink overflowed with crockery and cutlery, while sat on the worktop was the obligatory stolen traffic cone and a mug tree festooned with mismatched underwear.

Macpherson huffed out a breath and prodded one of the beanbags with his toe.

Taylor watched Parker's housemate dump the boxes into a wheelie bin and then cross the street, glancing back as he walked away.

Cairo Street, like its neighbours, Damascus, Jerusalem and Palestine made up a section of the lower Ormeau known as The Holy Lands. Built by the Victorian developer and former Lord Mayor of Belfast, Sir Robert McConnell, the names had been inspired by his travels to the Middle East.

The rows of red-brick terraces once housing working-class families had now largely been snapped up by property speculators, sub-divided, and then given over to student accommodation. The result during term time was a wild riot of endless parties and anti-social behaviour.

The thump of a baby elephant hammering down the stairs drew her attention away from the window. The young man who entered was wiping sleep from his eyes with one hand and wrestling his hair into shape with the other.

"Hi," he slurred, fighting the effects of a rude awakening from a hops and barley induced slumber.

"Maxwell Parker?" said Taylor.

"Max," he nodded at Macpherson who stood at parade ground ease with a stern expression. "Dave said you're the police. Is this about the party?"

Parker negotiated the room's mess to search the kitchen countertop and then a cupboard for a clean glass. Not finding any he rescued one from the muddy waters of the sink.

"It's about Jane Morrow."

"Oh."

"Do you want to sit?"

"I'm alright here," he said testily, setting down the glass

and folding his arms.

"Is Jane here?" said Taylor.

"Pfft, what would she be doing here?"

"You're her boyfriend aren't you?"

Parker shook his head. "Not anymore."

"Not after you hit her a slap in front of her mates, eh, son?" said Macpherson.

"I didn't hit her—"

"Three eyewitnesses say different."

Parker pointed a finger, his voice rising.

"If anyone was in the wrong it was those crazy bitches, she—"

"Easy, Mister Parker, that's quite a temper you've got there," said Taylor.

Parker dropped the finger and eased into a non-threatening stance. Two seconds later he was barricaded behind folded arms.

"Do you not care about what her mates were up to? You should be looking into that?" he said.

"We are interested in Jane's whereabouts as there has been a concern raised regarding her safety," said Taylor. She remained in the centre of the lounge, tempering her annoyance at Parker's belligerence with the knowledge he was dying with a hangover.

"If you think it's just charms and chants for the craic, I'm telling you different, that Helen one is twisted."

"Just focus, sunshine," pressed Macpherson "What about Miss Morrow? Do you know where she is?"

"When I went round, the crazy bitch was boiling mice! Boiling them alive and making Jane join in for Christ's sake!" Parker had become agitated and pushed off the counter, pacing the kitchenette in obvious distress at the memory.

"You don't look like the stereotypical animal rights activist," said Macpherson. He raised a hand up in a measure of Parker. The young man was pushing six feet, probably close to fifteen stone and was built like the wall. The Ulster rugby shirt he wore strained at the biceps and shoulders and there was no doubt that he was well accustomed to a T-bone steak.

"It's just wrong. She's sick," he mumbled.

"Max," said Taylor. "Rather than lash out at Jane's friends can you just tell us if you know where she is or the last time you saw her?"

Parker rubbed his face. There was a creak in the hall that was impossible to miss.

"Sorry." David Black walked sheepishly into the lounge, crossing to the sofa and shoving his hand down the side of the seat. "Van keys, I didn't mean to interrupt."

Taylor gave a small shake of her head to say he hadn't and then Black retreated, the slam of the letterbox once again declaring his departure.

She watched him walk away. This time he didn't look back.

"I don't know where she is, honestly," said Parker.

"And the last time you saw her?"

"Look, after… after what happened, she stayed away for the night. The next morning she came back to gather up what stuff she had here and left. She didn't even speak to me. She just left."

"You didn't try to get in touch?"

"Not right away, I thought she was with…" He stopped,

face reddening and unable to speak the name of the Pentangle Paranormal Society.

"But you tried later?"

"Yes, to apologise, but she must have blocked my number."

"Did you try other friends, her parents?"

"No, she didn't have many mates before those girls got their claws into her and she told me she didn't really get on with her folks, Bible bashers according to her. Tried to keep her wrapped in cotton wool. We weren't together long enough for me to ever meet them."

"How long?"

"A couple of months."

Taylor took a breath and cast an eye around. Observing him in his home environment, she thought she had the measure of him. Big guy, sporty, popular with the lads and the lasses alike. The house was obviously party central and was unquestionably a male-dominated lair. Booze, booty, and the PlayStation all confirming her initial feelings that university for Parker was more social than scholarly.

A few months wasn't long enough to count as a serious relationship but had he been drowning a broken heart or had he sailed on with a clear conscience.

"What are you studying?" she said, turning her attention back to Parker.

"Structural engineering with architecture."

"Was Jane at uni?"

"Biological sciences," said Parker nodding.

"Okay, Max." Taylor nodded, indicating that the questioning was over for the moment. "We'll be back in touch. You're not planning on going anywhere are you?"

Parker shook his head and she placed a business card on the marked surface of the table.

"If you have any sudden recollections or insights as to where Jane might have gone, give me a call."

Chapter 5

APPROACHING THE CID suite, Taylor and Macpherson found that the entrance was now guarded by four foot long, skull-faced grim reapers suspended one on each side of the door.

The puppets' red eyes were illuminated and their haunting moans and the rattle of chains followed as they pushed through the doors. Macpherson paused to plunge a hand into a disembodied plastic pumpkin head to retrieve a fistful of roasted monkey nuts.

"Best thing about bloody Halloween," he said with a grin, offering one to Taylor.

Cook and Reilly were sat at their desks, each busy at their respective keyboards, and Walker was pulling printouts from the copier.

Macpherson wrinkled his nose as he sat down.

"What's that smell?" he said through a mouthful of nuts, dumping the shells on the desk.

Walker's eyebrows rose and he gave his arm a long sniff.

"What's it smell like?" he asked tentatively.

"That smell is hard graft, sarge," said Reilly, rising to her feet and pulling a face.

"Come off it, Tinkerbell, you two wouldn't know hard graft if it hit you up the hole."

Reilly flicked a broken shell across the table, hitting Macpherson on the chin.

"On the contrary," she said. "We might have our first

firm lead on the fly-tippers."

Walker presented the contents of the copier with a flourish.

"Two hours of my life I'm never getting back spent poking through a council tip comparing piles of garbage." He shuddered. "To think some people choose that as a job!"

"You're a copper, Chris. Dealing with other people's crap is your job." Macpherson spun a couple of nuts across the table at his two juniors. Walker considered his words as he cracked open the shell.

"What do you have?" said Taylor, accepting the offered printout.

"The council stored the last three dumps and the effects from The Devil's Elbow fuel spill at their Blackstaff compound. In summary, they identified comparable material from each dump site, mostly commercial but also some domestic."

Taylor looked at the snap-shots of garbage piles and then individual items and finally several rows of documents that had been carefully laid out on a workbench.

"We canvassed the people at those addresses and each confirmed they had paid for waste removal. Two are from the south side of the city and a third was out near Newtownabbey and the dates match the tipping to within twenty-four hours," said Reilly.

"None of them admit to knowing it would be fly-tipped but all of them used the same contractor, Junk It. They found him on Facebook."

"Happy days, well done." Taylor gave a nod of gratitude for the effort and then Reilly grasped the nettle of bad news.

"Unfortunately the Facebook page no longer exists and the phone number associated is dead. We do however have a partial plate for a white van with a distinguishing mark on the rear driver's panel."

"Okay, I take it you're running the partial for a match."

Walker nodded. "We've put in the request and it's running now."

"Okay, good. What about the mark?"

"Ghosting," said Reilly, widening her eyes and waving her fingers at Macpherson.

"I'll ghost you in a minute," he grunted mid chew, one cheek puffed out like a squirrel with toothache. Reilly snatched another nut from his pile.

"The previous decals have been removed and the paint underneath the vinyl stands out against the remaining sun damage," said Walker. "We don't know what it says but the fact each of the people we spoke to mentioned it, narrows down our suspect vehicle."

"And with more than sixty per cent of used vans being white, you may get that crackpot medium back on the phone for a bit of help," said Macpherson.

Walker looked a little deflated after the appraisal.

"It's a start," said Taylor. "More than we had this morning. Good work."

Macpherson harrumphed at the approval and swept his shells into the wastepaper bin. He gave the two juniors a grudging nod; praise for doing the job you were paid to do wasn't included in his old-school handbook.

"Any joy on your side, Carrie?" said Taylor. She handed the printouts back to Walker and eased back in her seat. Cook gave an eager nod and then tucked a flyaway strand of mousey hair behind her ear.

"Yes, actually," she said. "It seems Miss Jane Winifred Morrow is safe and sound and back in the arms of Jesus."

"It's a wonder he took her after the shenanigans she was up to."

Taylor waved Macpherson down and gestured for Cook to continue.

"When I got your text I contacted the admin department at Queen's University. The girl was really helpful and told me Jane Morrow transferred to the Ulster University Campus at Coleraine."

She tapped a few keys and read from her screen.

"Cited family issues and was able to shift and continue her studies closer to home. The family property is Ballymena, slap bang in the middle of the Bible belt. She gave me contact details and I spoke to her father. He's an evangelical pastor."

"One extreme to the other," said Macpherson.

"Shush your jaws a minute, will you," admonished Taylor. Cook continued.

"I got the sense he wasn't keen on her going to the big smoke in the first place so when she came back with her tail between her legs he was able to issue a bit of righteous admonishment."

"But she's okay?" said Taylor. Cook nodded.

"Oh yeah. She fell in with a bad boy and a badder crowd and she's been welcomed back into the arms of the Free Presbyterian community to repent her sins and atone for not listening to Daddy in the first place."

"So either Jane isn't the one haunting loopy Luna or she may hang up the crystals and get a real job," said

Macpherson, his face a mask of faux shock.

"Actually, I did a bit more digging," said Cook, beckoning them over so she could share her screen.

"Teacher's pet," muttered Walker, eliciting a smirk from Macpherson.

"One year ago another student was reported missing in the same area after a night out. She had separated from friends and the last sighting of her was captured by CCTV as she crossed the Ormeau Bridge on her way home. Search and rescue were deployed to dredge the Lagan between there, the King's Bridge, and along the embankment but nothing was recovered. She's never been seen since."

"I vaguely remember that. We were working the Brookvale baseball bat murder at the time," said Taylor recalling events. "Apart from a missing girl, possibly drowned, what else have you?"

"Her name begins with a J. Josie Wyatt."

Macpherson blew out a breath. "You're reaching there, Carrie."

Cook started to protest.

"Doc's right," said Taylor. "If I take this to the DCI given it's based on a call from the local crank medium she'll laugh me out of the station."

Chris Walker was spluttering, the struggle to get his words out equal to his eagerness in searching through the pages of his printouts. Reilly beat him to the punch. She held out her phone.

"What about if you show her this?"

Taylor peered at the snapshot of a pendant on Reilly's phone. The DC flicked to the next picture showing engraved initials. Walker spread out a page on the desk showing the location of the find.

"We found it here." Walker prodded the contour lines. "At a recent dump site not a mile from where she went missing."

Taylor's phone rang before she could consider the coincidence further.

"DI Taylor?"

She listened, nodded, replaced the handset and then stood quickly.

"What is it?" said Macpherson.

"Luna Meehan has been assaulted in her home."

Chapter 6

LEIGH-ANNE ARNOLD gave a small wave as Taylor and Macpherson exited the Volvo.

It was too early in the evening for the covens of witches or warlocks to be touring Brunswick Street but just like the last time they had attended, parked cars narrowed the small street like an Ulster Fry narrowed the arteries. The situation was exacerbated by a rusting, yellow builders' skip abandoned half on, half off the kerb on the left-hand side.

"Is she okay?" said Taylor approaching along the pavement.

Arnold nodded, mumbling into her TETRA and receiving a clipped affirmative in return. The door to number seventy-four stood open behind her.

"She fine. Just shaken," she said.

"Does she know who it was?"

Arnold took a slow breath and stood aside as Macpherson trundled up behind Taylor.

"I think you better just go on in."

Macpherson's quizzical look was met with an eye-roll from Arnold as he stepped into the house.

A draught swept up the short hallway and as they entered Luna's living space the eclectic order she had previously maintained was in disarray. The lamb skull lay broken on the hearth. Crystals, vessels and furnishings were strewn about, and the throws and cushions from the sofa lay scattered on the floor.

The lady of the house had rearranged the armchair by the bay window and was sat quietly nursing a glass. A footstool had been righted and on its surface sat the Ouija board.

"Are you okay?" said Taylor as she entered. The draught continued to cut through the room from the open kitchen door.

"It's not the first time. I'll be fine." Luna Meehan gave a stoic smile.

"Miss Meehan," said Macpherson. "Do you mind if I…?" he motioned towards the kitchen.

"Go ahead, sergeant. They're long gone."

Macpherson disappeared from view and Taylor took a knee beside the homeowner.

"Are you hurt?" she said, eyes searching for the physical signs of assault; abrasions, scratches, bruising.

"The damage is to the spirit not the flesh, inspector." Luna peered at her with rheumy eyes. "She needs us to find her."

"She?"

"The girl in the water."

Taylor took a breath and stood, she could hear Macpherson wrestling with the keys and the lock of the back door.

"What exactly happened here, Luna?" said Taylor.

"Her spirit came in the night. Restless. Raging. I woke and she was over the top of me; red eyes and wrapped in a burial shroud. When I couldn't quell her pain she lashed out." Luna gestured around the small room and to the door beyond. "She wanted her box back."

"Okay," said Taylor, steadying her voice and keeping her expression neutral. "I'm going to check on how my sergeant is getting on. Just give me a second."

Luna eased back in her armchair and took a short sip from her glass, then closed her eyes, her lips moving silently as if in prayer.

Macpherson was on the back step when Taylor entered.

"Did she see the wee bastard that did it?" he said.

The kitchen had been ransacked as violently as the living room. Cupboards were open, contents spilt out, and one door hung like a broken wing. In the middle of the floor was a pool of spoiling milk.

"It was the spirit of our missing girl," said Taylor, peering at the smashed glazing of the window. Large pieces of glass lay in the sink and on the countertop, with smaller shards and fragments littering the floor nearby.

Macpherson took a step down into the yard and beckoned Taylor forward.

"The only spirits here are the ones you tip down your throat."

On the rough concrete path leading to the entry sat a toughened plastic recycling box. It was filled with the empties of more than a dozen cheap gin and vodka bottles.

"I told you she was a crackpot from day one," he said.

"Maybe so," said Taylor, her gaze pausing on a patch of moss and mud under the window sill. "But I'll take a punt that neither our lady indoors nor the Lady of the Lagan wears a size ten work boot."

Macpherson followed her gaze to where a distinctive tread pattern and muddy smear marked the ground.

Chapter 7

THE DRIVE UP the coast had been pleasant for Reilly and Cook even though the thought of what lay at the end of the road was not.

It was a bright autumn day, the skies were clear, and sunlight dappled the windscreen as they travelled along the A2, first skirting the small town of Holywood and then, as they travelled a little further, past the signage and slip road leading to the Ulster Folk and Transport Museum and Ballycultra Townland. The museum's old buildings and dwellings had been preserved from across the island of Ireland and painstakingly rebuilt on the hundred and seventy-acre site.

Six miles later and with the dark smudge of Dumfries and Galloway visible against the glistening Irish Sea, Cook dabbed the brakes and eased the car off the dual carriageway and into the outskirts of the seaside commuter town of Bangor.

Their destination was a pretty chalet bungalow at the end of a short cul-de-sac. The property was rendered in pink pebbledash and surrounded by a white picket fence, the twisted stems of a magnolia bush threading through the slats.

A car was parked outside the house and as they got out the driver's door opened.

"DC Cook?"

"That's me, Chrissy is it?"

Chrissy Glover nodded, swapping handshakes with the two detectives.

"Thanks for arranging this," said Reilly. Glover waved a hand.

"No problem. I'll admit, it was a surprise to hear of a new development. I've been family liaison since Josie disappeared but obviously, time passes, the trail goes cold and you get new assignments."

Peter Wyatt was waiting at the open door as the visitors crunched up the gravel path.

"Hello, Peter," said Glover.

"Thanks for seeing us, Mister Wyatt," said Cook.

Wyatt gave a small nod and beckoned them in. He was late-forties, with red-blond hair and an oval face, and as Reilly followed him along a neat and tidy hallway she thought to herself that he bore a striking resemblance to the lead actor in a TV series but she couldn't place which.

Wendy Wyatt sat on a two-seater in a kitchen that opened into a sunroom. She was pretty but prematurely grey and had the haunted expression of someone living on their nerves.

A picture of her daughter sat on a nest of tables beside her.

"Have you found her?" she said. The tone of her voice was calm but the whiteness of her knuckles gripping a tea towel betrayed her tension.

"I'm afraid not," said Cook before Glover extended introductions.

Wyatt offered them tea which they accepted along with a seat.

"We're following up on Josie's disappearance and have a

few questions about how she was at the time, her friends, anything that might have seemed insignificant then but could help us now."

"We told Chrissy and the team everything," said Peter over the rumble of the kettle boiling in the background.

"Josie wouldn't run away," said Wendy. "She was a home bird. Something happened to her. Someone took her away."

"What's prompted this, detective." Peter Wyatt set down the cups and a plate of chocolate-covered oat-flake biscuits. His tone wasn't confrontational, but it was frank.

Cook shared a glance with Reilly. Glover spoke into the silence.

"The detectives are involved in another case which has turned up an item they would like you to look at."

Reilly took out a picture of the recovered pendant. Both sides of the charm and chain were set against a dark backdrop with forensic measurement markers framing the piece.

"Could you tell us if this belonged to Josie?" said Reilly.

The words were unnecessary, Wendy's reaction more explicit than anything she could have said. She snatched at the picture, tears in her eyes.

"Yes." Her voice was a hoarse whisper. She looked up at Peter who was also fighting back tears. The photograph was the first tangible link to their little girl in a year.

"She was wearing it the last time she was home. I teased her about it." Peter wiped his eyes, giving a terse laugh. "She's a Harry Potter nut. I think she liked it because it was witchy."

"How was she the last time she was home?" said Cook

gently.

Peter blew out his cheeks and Wendy sniffed. Glover passed over a tissue and squeezed the mother's hand.

"Josie and I had a couple of days away. Just up the coast to Newcastle," said Wendy, blowing her nose, eyes fixed on the photo. "Her exams were coming up and she hadn't been home in a while. I wanted to spoil her before she started a new term."

"Was she in good spirits?" said Cook.

"She was in great form, although when I think back she could have been putting on a brave face."

"There had been a bit of stress over the exams," explained Peter. "And some angst over an admirer."

"Okay," said Cook with a nod. "Is that who gave her the necklace?"

"Possibly," Wendy shrugged. "She only ever referred to him as *this fella* so I don't think she was taking any of it too seriously. Josie was always one for letting exam pressure build up so I know, for her, a relationship at that time was a no-go." Wendy gazed at the image. "She could have bought it herself. Peter's right; she loved those wizard books and she was never out of St George's Market."

Wendy gestured to a windowsill of photos that captured Josie's short life. Images from childhood through to teenager, the last was of a grinning young woman in striped scarf and witch's hat at a house party. Beside her beer bottles lined a countertop and ghostly white faces behind were blurred in the glare of a disco ball.

Clasped around her throat was the mirror and cat pendant.

Chapter 8

"…AND CHRISSY GLOVER confirms no boyfriend was ever traced during the initial inquiry," said Cook, summing up the trip to Bangor.

Taylor rubbed the knot forming between her eyebrows.

Somewhere in the background Michael Jackson's 'Thriller' was playing too loudly and there was a distracting bustle of activity as cleaners began to do the rounds and the shift change progressed, one lot eager to get off and begin a weekend of creepy celebrations and eerie activities, the other half bemoaning they would be missing out and would be left with the fall-out of the looney long weekend.

"What's your thoughts on the necklace turning up now?" said Macpherson.

"It's not it turning up now, it's the manner in which it did." Taylor rotated her shoulders. "We found Josie's pendant at a fly-tipping site. We now need to go back to the council and have the rubbish examined for any other personal items: clothes, shoes, underwear. I'll request help from the dog section and if they pick up any traces of cadaver amongst that…" She gave a grim twist of the lips. "Then it's the call to Seapark to get the SOCOs involved."

Each of them could see the investigation picking up pace and spiralling exponentially in cost and manpower.

"What we need to consider is, that by accident or design, someone used the illegal dumpers to get rid of evidence that's been missing for a year. Were they holding it as a trophy? Why the sudden need to get rid of it now, like this?"

"Are we anywhere closer to finding this white van?" said Macpherson to no one in particular.

Both Cook and Reilly replied with short shakes of heads.

"So we make it a priority to get a lead on that, however unlikely it is that the driver will be able to identify who gave him what to dump?" he added

"Not necessarily," said Taylor, standing and making her way to the board pinned with dump sites. "We know it was found here, near the boat club, and that section is impounded at Blackstaff council depot. So A, we identify any householders we haven't already from the rubbish and then run them through the system for previous form; history of violence, domestic abuse, the sex offenders register. Then B, when we find the driver we push him to recall details of that particular dump. How does he take the collection in, who loads the van, does he remember any wee details that might rip a few pages out of the book that we'll be throwing at him?"

Neither Macpherson nor the two DCs looked overly buoyed at their chances and Taylor knew it too; more than that she understood that an opportunist could have just added Josie's trinket to the pile.

"What else is there to do but start there?" she said.

"Guv?"

Taylor twisted away from the pinboard towards Chris Walker. The DC's face was red and he carried his jacket over his arm.

"Guv, I've got a witness for the night Josie went

missing."

"Didn't I tell you it was worth keeping him?" said Macpherson with a clap. "Don't you listen to what these girls say about you, Chrissy boy, you're alright in my book."

"What have you got?" said Taylor.

"I visited campus and got speaking to a few tutors and classmates. The general consensus was that Josie was very bright but also very anxious about her upcoming exams,"

Macpherson rolled one hand over the other.

"Details, Christopher, get to the details." Walker sped up, words tripping out nineteen to the dozen.

"Josie was a regular at the McClay Library. She spent hours in there and one member of staff knew her well enough to talk to. The girl's called Hannah Crawford. Anyway, Hannah had a boyfriend who also did Chinese deliveries for a restaurant at the time of the disappearance."

"While I've still got all my own teeth will you get to the point, fella?" snapped Macpherson.

"Hannah's boyfriend had picked her up that night when she got off and they saw Josie and an IC1 male walking together in the direction of the Holylands."

"Did she have a name?" said Taylor. Walker nodded.

"The social scene is pretty incestuous so she did recognise him from a house party. I got an address too."

"We got there in the end," said Macpherson with a sigh. He stood, crooking a finger at the DC's notebook. "Give us a look. You've either got the last person to see the wee girl alive or the mystery boyfriend; or for a bonus point, both."

"Here you go," said Walker.

"Ack in the name of God, are you serious?"

Macpherson handed the notebook, containing the neatly printed address, to Taylor.

❖❖❖

"When you said you'd be back I didn't think you meant so soon."

"Can we come in, Max?" said Taylor.

Max Parker deliberated for half a second and then turned and walked up the hallway, leaving them to follow.

"Another wee soirée planned, eh?" said Macpherson.

The devastation of eighty-eight Cairo Street had been repaired to a degree. The lounge was rubbish free and the kitchenette tidied. A selection of beer and wine was on the floor and Parker bent down to lift a twenty-four pack of cider and set it out on the back step.

When he turned back he gave a shrug.

"Halloween isn't it."

"But you don't need that as an excuse to party, son."

Parker chuckled. "No, I suppose not." He eased up against the worktop. "If you've more questions about Jane I've nothing else to tell you."

"We're not here about Jane," said Taylor; neither detective had made a motion to sit.

"So?" Parker drew out the question. "What can I help you with?"

"Did you know Josie Wyatt?"

Parker was quick, but not quick enough to hide the recognition.

"Not really," he said at length.

"But she was here." Taylor gestured around the space. "Parties, social get-togethers, whatever?"

"She might have been once or twice."

"What did you think when she went missing?"

"I don't know. That it was terrible?"

"You asking or telling, son?" said Macpherson.

"It was terrible. No one wants to hear of something bad happening to somebody they know."

"Something bad?" said Taylor. Parker pulled a face, shrugged and raised his hands.

"Going missing. Snatched. Fell in the Lagan drunk and drowned. Whatever happened that night?"

"But other than what was reported, you've no idea of what might have transpired that night?"

"None," said Parker empathically.

"Did you and her ever..." Macpherson let the query hang.

"No."

"What about your housemate? David, isn't it?" said Taylor.

"Davy?" Parker huffed out a laugh. "Davy's not that way inclined I don't think."

"You don't think?" said Macpherson.

"I've never known him to bring anybody back after a night out, never mind any girls," said Parker.

"Maybe he's just paranoid they'd fall for your charms," said Taylor. A small cock of the head as she saw she had struck a nerve.

"He's your mate but I'm pretty sure I know where your priorities lie, Max. You'd sell your granny for a quick tussle between the sheets and it wouldn't matter who you stepped on." She turned, lifting a picture off the mantlepiece. It showed a raucous crowd of young men in a club, arms around each other. On the periphery, almost in the background was David Black.

"Josie's parents say she had a boyfriend."

"Well, it wasn't me." Parker took a step forward. "What is this? First Jane and now Josie? Are you trying to fit me up?"

"Do you recognise this?"

Taylor pulled a picture of the mirror pendant from her pocket. Parker took a quick look.

"No."

She nodded, seemingly satisfied with his answer.

"You're sure?"

"I'm sure," said Parker.

"Could we ask David?"

"Davy?" Parker's tone was incredulous.

"We've had a witness come forward who saw David and Josie walking near here the night she went missing. We just need to establish where they parted ways. If he noticed anybody suspicious in the area? Does he remember her wearing that necklace?"

"Davy?"

"Yes. Is he here?" Taylor's voice was clipped and seemed to jolt Parker out of his thoughts.

"He's at work still."

"When's he usually home?"

"There's a few of us going for drinks at the Rugby Club. Davy was meeting us there and giving lifts back for the party," explained Parker.

Taylor nodded at the crest on his tee shirt.

"Sports Association Club near the Lockview?"

"Aye."

Taylor knew the spot. Manicured sports pitches, a

clubhouse and bar sat on open ground on the edge of the forest park. The Lagan towpath ran along the fringe to Lockview, a tourist lookout point where the River Lagan swelled before channelling into the deep vicious bend at The Devil's Elbow.

"Okay, Max. Thanks." She put down the photo, noticing her card still on the mantle. She tapped it.

"Tell Davy it's in his best interests to call and not to have me come look for him."

Parker nodded mutely and Taylor gestured for Macpherson to lead the way out. Parker flipped the hall light switch as they made their way towards the front door.

Taylor stopped.

"Are these yours, Max?"

Parker followed her finger to a pair of work boots nudged under a radiator cover. She stooped to peer at the soles and the scummy residue smeared on the leather upper.

"Are you hard of hearing, son?" growled Macpherson.

Taylor, having pulled a latex glove from her inside jacket pocket had carefully lifted one boot, examining the sole to find mud and moss mashed into the tread. Near the heel were several chunks of glass.

"Max?" she said again. Parker blinked twice before he answered.

"They're Davy's."

Chapter 9

"SAY AGAIN, ERIN?"

Reilly's voice had cut out as she shifted the call to hands-free.

"A white Renault Kangoo. Registration matches the partial we received," she repeated much more clearly.

"Okay, great. We're about five minutes from the sports grounds," said Taylor.

She gripped the overdoor handle as Macpherson thundered the Volvo along Stranmillis Embankment heading for Lockview and the sportsplex. Her phone was connected to Bluetooth so Macpherson could listen in.

"What about the connection to Josie?" she said.

The three DCs were gathered around a conference phone back at Musgrave Street. Taylor had informed them of developments at Cairo Street and requested uniformed back-up to the house, both to keep an eye on Parker and in the event she missed Black at the clubhouse. His boots were bagged and would be analysed against the soil and glass samples from Luna Meehan's house.

Parker, having discovered a long-overdue sense of loyalty to his housemate found his resistance crushed under Macpherson's blunt persuasion, the DS intimating that the lack of assistance was tantamount to the aiding and abetting of an offender. Adequately subdued, Parker guided them up to David Black's room.

Careful that she wasn't about to jeopardise a potential

future case, Taylor had a look inside, the snoop yielding little other than Black's taste in music which leaned towards gothic and alternative rock, a selection of art prints by H.R. Giger, and a shelf of sci-fi fantasy literature.

Walker's voice came on the line with Cook accessing the central database and putting the documents relating to Wyatt's disappearance up on a display screen.

"David Black was routinely questioned along with others who were with Josie on the night she went missing. All interviewees say she left the bar early on her own. No reason why. There was no mention of Black or anyone else leaving to walk her home and they all alibied each other for the duration of the night afterwards."

"Doesn't mean to say Black or anyone else didn't slip out unnoticed," said Reilly, her voice losing clarity as the Volvo passed through a spotty patch of coverage.

"Chris, speak again to the girl in the library and narrow down a timeframe of when she saw Josie and Black together. We can press Parker and revisit the other statements if she can give us a window to work in," said Taylor. Macpherson slowed the car as the sports pitches loomed ahead under floodlights.

"Guv," Walker confirmed his instruction.

"And Carrie, check ANPR in and around any of the sites of the fly-tipping and see if we can't pick up Black's vehicle now we know what we're looking for. Actually, extend that to yesterday evening in the vicinity of Brunswick Road too. We're here," said Taylor. "I'll check in with you again shortly."

She closed the call as Macpherson bumped the Volvo down a rutted lane in desperate need of resurfacing. To the left and protected by a row of stakes and a low chain were the pitches. Several scattered groups were involved in drills or practice matches which even the thud of the Volvo's sump tank striking the lip of a deep pothole didn't distract from.

The right-hand side was rough gravel car parking, skirted by a barriered walkway leading up to the squat clubhouse and changing facilities. Signage pointed to the various pitches and towards the track that ran into the wooded area behind the buildings and onto the Lagan towpath beyond.

Macpherson pulled up, the two detectives seeking out a white Renault Kangoo van in the collection of cars and other vehicles.

"There," said Taylor. A white van sat on its own at the end of a row of spaces. Macpherson nudged the Volvo into gear.

As they approached from the passenger side their headlights swept across the bodywork, a ghostly swooping pattern and the remnants of a phone number were visible where exposure had burned the images of old decals into the side panel.

Macpherson pulled up behind. Close enough to make exiting the space difficult. A quick visual scan confirmed the plates matched the partials.

The van's interior light illuminated as a figure emerged. Male, dark haired, rangy and dressed in working clothes. He made to pull the back door open, then squinted into the glare.

Taylor stepped out.

"David Black?"

Black let go of the door handle and ran.

❖❖❖

"….suspect is on foot travelling in the direction of Lockview and the Lagan towpath. Officer in pursuit."

Macpherson wrestled the TETRA handset from its charging unit on the console, and ducked back out of the car, looking east.

Black led Taylor by a good fifty yards, his arms pumping furiously as he sprinted in a straight line for the gloom of the pines.

"Why couldn't the wee bastard have just stood apiece?" he grumbled to himself, wrenching open the rear door of the Kangoo.

He slammed it home almost instantly and blew out a disgusted breath.

The stink of decomposing food waste, fuel and rot was overwhelming. The single glimpse he had managed had shown an interior packed with plastic bin liners and loose household waste material.

"Right, you wee shite, you're for the high jump when I get my hands on you for making me run."

Macpherson wrangled the earpiece of the radio into position and joined the chase.

Chapter 10

THE PATH WAS treacherous.

Underfoot, the gravel track which had skirted the sportsplex car park had transitioned into the towpath, the surface soaked as rainwater ran off the higher ground and down a winding slope and steps cut into the bank leading to the Lagan walkway. The path was covered in a carpet of perilous, slimy leaves and Taylor lashed out a hand to steady herself from slipping.

Out of sight, but not too far distant she heard Black curse as he stumbled, losing the delicate balance of speed over safety.

The harsh barks of competition and training still echoed from the pitches, but each ragged lungful of air and the banks of foliage passing with every stride deadened the shouts.

Taylor slipped and slid the last few feet onto the hard-packed towpath, two feet of grass and bullrushes separating her from the black surface of the Lagan's waters.

The gloom was sudden and complete. The glare of the pitchside floodlights continued to blink through the swaying branches of the treetops but did nothing to illuminate the path.

She could see Black ahead, a strip of luminous material on his work jacket marking him out as he fled, heading for a small iron and wood bridge that crossed the narrow end of the big pool beside the tourist lookout of Lockview. The small coffee shop and tourist information office was closed and offered no light to guide hunter or prey.

The building sound of rushing water took over from its lazy lap against the banks of soft vegetation as Taylor made the footbridge in time to see Black step off the other side and descend the path towards The Devil's Elbow.

The route zigzagged through the tree line alongside the narrow channel where the calm flowing water was suddenly forced down and funnelled into a deep gully that cut ninety degrees through a V of limestone.

"Ronnie!"

Taylor turned to see a wobbling beam of torchlight mark out Macpherson as he made the towpath behind her. She looked back, seeking Black's shadow moving through the gaps of the trees but not finding him. She took a deep breath and plunged down the slope in pursuit.

The rest of Macpherson's shouts were drowned out by the surge of water.

❖❖❖

"Don't boke. Don't boke. Don't boke."

Macpherson chanted the mantra as he pushed the sensation of vomiting down and urged himself forward. After half a mile racing to catch up, his short arms and legs were moving like misaligned pistons.

"Ronnie!" The shout was more a gasp as he threaded his way across the narrow footbridge, the roar and motion of the water rushing underneath disorienting as he peered down past his rubber legs and between the planks.

Reaching the far side, he paused, heaving in breaths and aiming the torch beam towards the slope of The Devil's Elbow.

The first few passes caught nothing, and then he saw her.

His partner had reached the end of a switchback and had paused to either catch her breath or reorientate on the fleeing David Black.

Macpherson took another shuddering breath and started to move, his guts freezing as the torch beam bounced through the branches to catch movement rushing in from her blind side.

"Ronnie!" he screamed.

❖❖❖

Taylor never heard the warning over the roar of the water but she felt the sudden impact.

For several seconds she hung suspended in thin air, then suddenly her stomach flipped, a wash of spray misted her face and she plunged into the icy water.

Her immersion was sudden and terrifying.

The rage of the water flipped her over and her head struck a rock but before she had time to register the impact, the torrent whipped her away.

Shock and the freezing water held the pain at bay but its grip dragged her deeper into the darkness.

Taylor flailed, hands desperately searching for a way to arrest her momentum but her fingers found nothing but slimy rocks and tree roots. The cold and the constant flipping around was disorientating and, kicking wildly, she sought the surface, her lungs screaming for oxygen but unable to tell which way was up or down.

Finally, her head broke through and she gulped a half breath of air and a mouthful of water. Choking up the latter and caught in a fit of coughing she battled the eddies, vainly sculling for the edge but only finding sheer sandstone, earning another bruising battering as she careered against the rocks to then be thrust back into the surge.

The roar was deafening and her limbs were losing feeling and mobility as the cold sucked the life from them, her central nervous system battling to redirect heat to her core at the expense of her extremities.

Another rock slipped past, another overhanging branch remained tantalisingly out of reach and then she caught hold of a jagged crevice.

Taylor felt her shoulder scream as the force of the water tried to break her grip, the torrent hauling her deeper into the churning depths of The Devil's Elbow. She howled in anger and frustration, reaching her free hand around to assist her tenuous hold and earning another lungful of water in the process.

Two feet away, rising like a spectre from the bubbling water, the pale face of David Black broke the surface. His face was set in a grimace as he barrelled into her.

Taylor's fingers broke free and the two were dragged under the water.

❖❖❖

"Code Zero. Code Zero. Officer in need of assistance. Devil's Elbow at Lockview. Officer in the water."

Macpherson's breath came in shallow, panting gasps as he made his report on the hoof. Continuing his slip, slide, shuffle along the rutted path he began to consider that with the throbbing in his head and the crushing band beginning to encircle his chest, if he didn't quit the running soon he'd be needing an ambulance of his own.

David Black had rushed from cover amongst the trees to

shove Taylor off the path and into the raging river. Unfortunately for Black and to Macpherson's surprise, the suspect lost his footing as he pivoted away, toppling sideways to bounce down the steep rocky bank into the water.

Macpherson searched the raging current tearing through the deep narrow canyon of The Devil's Elbow. The torch beam danced back and forth to no avail. There was no sign of either Taylor or Black.

The TETRA warbled and he pressed his earpiece, struggling to separate the violence of the rapids from the confirmation units had been despatched for assistance.

"Ronnie!" he shouted.

Taylor's head broke the surface, her mouth open, gasping for air as the malevolent figure of Black clambered over her seeking buoyancy.

Both disappeared below the black surface once more, Macpherson's torch beam left dancing impotent circles on the waves.

❖❖❖

Black's hands were wrapped around her throat, and Taylor grunted as his knees dug into her back as he kicked and thrashed.

All the while she held her breath, biting on her lip to keep the impact of his feet scrambling up her shins and thighs from knocking out the last of the valuable oxygen the fight was using up much too quickly.

They spun and twisted in the violence of the rapids, each strike of rock and root trying but failing to split them apart or stop their freefall through the deep-water canyon, the impact on occasion causing more sunken vegetation to join them in the swollen cascade charging downstream.

Taylor gouged at Black, her fingers seeking the soft tissue around his eyes and mouth, scratching and writhing to gain some kind of purchase.

Black, although willowy, held on with a vice-like grip and with the pressure on her larynx tightening, Taylor convulsed. She coughed, immediately inhaling but the reflex only serving to let more water in.

The gloom of the water darkened as her grip loosened, the battle against hypoxia lost.

She had never really considered dying in the line of duty. If she had, she doubted it would have been drowning that offered the fateful way out. Shot or stabbed probably; blown up like her father? Less likely now, but you could never rule it out.

The cold of the water began to fade, a feeling of near euphoria slowly seeped up from the nape of her neck and her vision prickled with flecks of light.

Something touched her hand and instinctively she grabbed it for buoyancy, but the cascade crashed them once again against the rocks. Black released his grip, his feet kicking her deeper into the dark.

Taylor was limp. Lifeless.

Her hand gripped what felt like a thin branch flowing alongside, and she focused the last of her consciousness on the touch.

Her thoughts were with Macpherson on the riverbank, of the pain she knew he would endure at her loss but also of the contentment she would feel at re-joining the parents so cruelly snatched away in her youth. Would they be proud? Would they be glad to see her?

The branch was wrapped in flimsy sacking and as Taylor gripped it tighter she let herself ride the currents, suddenly propelled upwards and out of the whirling depths.

Breaking the surface she voided her lungs and stomach of brackish water, thrashing at the loose material that was coiling around her limbs.

The branch, she realised was an arm and thinking it was Black, she recoiled, but the face she looked into was serene.

❖❖❖

David Black gagged as he broke the surface of the raging water, spewing what felt like a gallon of the Lagan mixed with bitter bile. Each effort was more tiring than the last, and now he had lost the slight advantage he had held by using the woman for buoyancy, he felt weaker.

Cold, alone, and at the mercy of The Devil's Elbow, he suddenly felt a stab of guilt and regret at the situation he was in.

On the right-hand bank, a beam of torchlight flitted across the water. Indecipherable shouts carried across the night; calls that he knew weren't out of concern for him.

A sudden clarity descended as he continued to be buffeted around in the water. Long lost sermons from a restrictive childhood reverberating around inside his head, coupled with images of a sour-faced man with skin the pallor of death and nicotine breath. His message: Be sure your sins will find you out.

As the years passed David had come to realise his sins were not those of the flesh but of silence. A silence that had enabled the preacher to continue his reign of abuse until cancer delivered the long-overdue judgement.

He hadn't meant for it to happen. He hadn't woken that

day and thought to murder, but when she laughed in his face all the pent up feelings of shame and defilement, of rejection and rage, bottled up over the course of his life, erupted in violence.

Who was she to speak to him like that, to judge him? Why had the preacher singled him out? Why was it fair that the Neanderthals like Parker and the others could tempt women to their beds as easily as fruit falling from the forbidden tree.

Black's hands twisted into fists, he smashed them impotently into the water as flashbacks of Josie Wyatt's last night coursed through his mind. Her struggle, the unexpected weight of her body as he shoved it into the van, the exertion of wrapping her in old sheets and then the welcome release as he dumped her off the bridge into the very waters that were now trying to drag him to his fate and a reckoning of his own.

A metre away the police officer surfaced, vomiting and thrashing. She was caught in some of the industrial detritus that found its way into the river, struggling to free herself from the pale sacking that was sucking her back under.

Black was buffeted away, salvation appearing in the form of a broken tree and the fork of fallen branch which dipped into the water. He stretched out a hand, the thick trunk holding as he pulled with the last of his strength against the surging waters. Struggling to drag his head from the bow wave created as the torrent swept against his body, he saw the woman break free from her binding, the material caught in the maelstrom swirled away at speed.

Black hooked his arm under the branch and caught his breath, exhaustion and the cold as dangerous now as when he had battled the current.

He watched the police officer swoosh past but made no attempt to reach out, her face was peaceful, her expression resigned.

Shifting to secure his grip, he looked back upstream. A shudder tore through him as he realised what he was looking at and then he gave an involuntary cry as the ghoul rose from the water.

He let go of the branch and at once he was snatched up by the water, but not fast enough to avoid the clutches of the horror that embraced him.

Black's blood-curdling screams echoed over the roar of the water as he stared into the face of Josie Wyatt.

Her lips were pulled back in a grimace of decomposition and the patches of hair that remained stuck to what was left of her scalp were thin and lank.

Sightless sockets glared in accusation as Black battled to free himself from her thin arms; limbs that, although they were more bone than flesh, now held greater strength than in life as they pulled him under the water to face judgement.

Epilogue

TWO WEEKS LATER

Macpherson pulled up the collar of his raincoat to ward off the wind sweeping across the exposed cemetery. The patter of rain beat a gentle tattoo on the canopy of his umbrella to accompany the solemnity of the coffin lowering.

His gaze lingered on the weeping relatives for a few more seconds before searching downhill beyond the rows of granite headstones to a plot shaded by a pale golden canopy of silver birch trees.

While it could be classed as uncommon, it wasn't without precedent for victim and violator to find themselves interred in the same consecrated ground.

David Black lay far enough away to be out of sight, and as Macpherson watched the rooks begin to roost in the thin branches of the treetops, he knew from grim experience that his crimes would never be far from the minds of those now living with the consequences.

For Peter and Wendy Wyatt, while the return of their daughter was not in the manner they had hoped, they were grateful to have a body to bury and a place to finally mourn. Even if they did have to share it with her killer.

"Are you alright?" he said to the person sheltering under the cover of his umbrella, squeezing the arm entwined through his own.

Taylor nodded. The scabs on her face were healing but

still told a story of a narrow escape.

"I'm fine," she said. And she was, now, but it had been a rough couple of days directly afterwards.

Pulled by Macpherson from the calmer waters at the mouth of The Devil's Elbow it had taken uniform and the paramedics time to negotiate the path to the riverbank and by that time hypothermia had set in. Rushing her to the Ulster Hospital for treatment, it had taken doctors the first two days to gradually warm her and even two weeks later she was still more susceptible to the cold, but the worst of the injuries that remained were cuts and bruises.

Not that it was just the physical preventing her return to work. Her mental health required assessment and sign-off and it would be another week before she returned to duty and only after a referral to occupational health had been agreed with time scheduled to talk and come to terms with her experiences under the eye of a service professional.

She still hadn't spoken to anyone about the minutes where she believed she would die, nor the vision of Josie Wyatt.

"Damn thing, eh," said Macpherson into the keen of the wind.

No one had as yet been able to explain what exactly had occurred, other than speculate that their plunge and desperate wash through the rapids had somehow dislodged the previously sunken body of Wyatt.

"Two birds with one stone," said Taylor.

After the initial frantic commotion to rescue Taylor and get her to hospital, attention had turned to Black's van which had contained another consignment of illegal waste. Working to the adage that where there was muck there was brass, Black had begun private waste collection as a side hustle to his job with the council, his endeavour hitting the skids when a new manager reprimanded him for skirting regulations and permit controls by bringing van loads of rubbish to landfill, and for not having a waste carrier's licence. With his initial plans foiled it left him looking at the back alleys, quiet beauty spots and the side roads of the city to offload.

A follow-up search of Cairo Street produced Josie Wyatt's handbag and some of her jewellery, the evidence damning Black when coupled with Hannah Crawford's now official statement naming him as the last person to be seen with the victim.

Taylor shifted her weight to ease the pain in her back which still hadn't fully recovered from her rollercoaster descent through The Devil's Elbow. In the end, she guessed, it was a tale as old as crime itself. Spurned love. Rage over rejection. A crime of passion.

The service was wrapping up with handshakes and hugs.

"It's good to see you looking better, inspector."

Taylor released Macpherson's arm and they both turned to face the voice.

Luna Meehan had left the pointed hat and broomstick at Brunswick Street but still managed to maintain an air of witchery.

"I've been reading in the newspapers about what happened," she said.

Macpherson scoffed and gave a shake of the head.

"Sure you know reading that twaddle only encourages them to write more," he grunted.

"Are you keeping okay yourself, after everything?" said Taylor.

Luna smiled, raising her chin to point down the hill towards the unseen mound of mud and flowers that marked Black's grave.

"The dead will do you no harm, it's the living you need to watch out for."

"Isn't that the truth." Macpherson gestured back towards the car park and the shelter and dodgy heaters of the Volvo. "Ronnie?"

"Actually, inspector, I hoped you would do me a favour before you get off?" said Luna.

"Christ, this better not be another one of your ghost hunts?"

"Away and get the car," said Taylor, laying a placating hand on his arm.

Macpherson gave the medium an arch look. "I'm fine," said Taylor.

He nodded, handing over the umbrella and then trundling off up the hill with a limp, not quite fully recovered from his own exertions.

"He's a character," said Luna.

"He is that." Taylor smiled as she watched the man who had stepped into her parents' shoes walk away, his lips moving in a silent grumble.

"What can I do for you?"

Luna reached into her large shoulder bag and pulled out the charity shop trinket box.

"I wondered if you could give it back to her parents?"

"Luna, we don't even know if—"

"It's hers," said the medium.

Taylor nodded, taking the box and not wanting to make a scene. Conscious of what had happened in the river, she paused, thinking of a way she could frame her question and understand her belief it was Josie Wyatt who had guided her to safety.

"Coincidence is just the dead leaving us breadcrumbs, inspector," said Luna. "I believe we go on existing in this place after we've gone. That maybe we have more to do when unburdened of the physical." She paused, looking to the funeral party. "To those like me that brings comfort, but I understand others need more tactile memories."

"I'll give it to them," said Taylor.

"Thank you, inspector. I'm glad you're okay."

Taylor smiled her thanks and shook the woman's hand, turning then to walk down the narrow path between the headstones to intercept the Wyatts.

Luna Meehan watched her go, then nodded a greeting to a couple paying their respects under the shade of an ancient elm. They were about the same age as the Wyatts and their gaze followed the young detective inspector as she wound her way down the path.

Luna Meehan smiled and stepped onto the grass to walk amongst the dead.

Sometimes parents lost their daughters, and sometimes daughters lost their parents but death was no more the end of love than the horizon was the end of the earth.

When she glanced back the couple was gone.

❖

BEHIND CLOSED DOORS

A DETECTIVE INSPECTOR TAYLOR CASE-FILE

PHILLIP JORDAN

FIVE FOUR PUBLISHING

PHILLIP JORDAN

Chapter 1

"THERE'S NO CLOCK in here."

It was an accurate observation. The absence of a clock meant there was no way to pinpoint and measure the passage of time and served to ratchet up the acute anxiety Jimmy Harding was feeling.

He slammed a balled fist against the thick plexiglass panel of a door that had no lock yet couldn't be opened. The door remained unyielding.

"I need to know about Julie! Is she OK? For God's sake, tell me something!" he shouted.

He slammed his fist home again, half-heartedly this time. Resting his head against the opaque glass, tears fell down his face.

"You can't keep me locked in here not knowing." He slumped against the door and rubbed the heels of his hands into his eyes. "Please, what about wee Tommy? He wasn't breathing. Jesus, he wasn't breathing."

Jimmy stalked across the room. He stared at the beady black eye set in the wall at head height above the only other furniture in the room. A table and four chairs. Ensconced in the smooth dry-lined ceiling, covered panel lights hummed overhead.

"Can you hear me?"

He looked into the lens. Red eyed, hair askew and hanging on his last ragged nerve.

Chapter 2

Detective Inspector Veronica Taylor scanned the charge sheet and glanced up at the large screen that dominated the wall of the observation suite and displayed Interview Room 3.

"Jesus, he wasn't breathing."

The voice captured by the AKG boundary microphones in the Interview Room was relayed in total clarity through the FAP-40T in-ceiling loudspeakers above her head. The voice that filled the observation suite was strained and creaked on the verge of breakdown.

"I still can't see why they dragged you in? I'm perfectly capable of handling something like this myself. It's hardly one for bloody Inspector Morse, is it?"

Taylor ignored the comment from the man standing behind her. She confirmed that at least the initial paperwork was in order, which was something. The suspect's face loomed in the screen.

"Can you hear me?"

Taylor slipped the charge sheet into the document folder on the desk beside the mixing equipment and the digital video and voice recorders that monitored the room next door.

"Where's DI MacDonald again?" she said.

"Majorca," said Samuel Simpson. Resentment that his DI was sunning himself in the Balearics while he remained stuck in an unseasonably wet and miserable Belfast was evident in his tone. His body language suggested that having his interview gate-crashed was also an affront to an equal power.

Taylor looked at her watch and then to the subordinate officer leaning nonchalantly against the door frame.

If CID didn't work out for him, he'd be a good snake oil salesman. Detective Constable Samuel Simpson liked to believe that his nickname, Slick, was due to his sharp dress sense and the suave sophistication he reserved for superiors and colleagues of the opposite sex.

Taylor knew, however, that behind his back any self-respecting female police constable and her own Detective Sergeant Robert Macpherson put it down to his egregious oiliness and the half tub of hair ointment that slicked his hair into a style he thought gave him a debonair look.

"Well, have you read enough?" Simpson pointed at the document folder. His enthusiasm to impress those further up the chain of command did not extend to her.

"Yes. I think it's time Mr Harding explained his version of events."

Simpson scoffed. He smoothed his narrow spotted tie and adjusted the ostentatious pin that held it in place.

"What's to explain? Creep shot his wife and child. Had the gun on him when he was lifted and kept telling anybody who would listen that he was sorry. No brainer, Veronica."

Taylor pursed her lips.

"Guv will do, DC Simpson. Make sure any additional reports from the scene or the hospital are legible and accurate when I ask for them. Can you manage that?"

Simpson glowered and then took a seat at the recording console. He hitched up his skinny-fit suit trousers to reveal an inch of sun-bed tanned leg and paisley patterned socks.

"I still don't see why they dragged you in. This is a hole-in-one." Simpson tossed a biro onto his spiral notepad.

Taylor tightened the bobble and pulled her shoulder-length chestnut hair into a sleek ponytail.

"It's tunnel vision like that got me involved, Slick," she said. "No-one wants your lazy thinking turning this into an albatross around our necks."

Chapter 3

Detective Sergeant Doc Macpherson's face was flushed and his teeth were bared in a grimace resembling a snarling bear. This was odd considering his moniker derived from his uncanny likeness to one of Snow White's famous friends.

"Jesus, I'm sweating like a priest in a primary school. Here, Tinkerbell. Pull this bloody suit off me."

Detective Constable Erin Reilly shook her head in dismay at the spectacle. The battle to extricate himself from the clinging Tyvek oversuit was more akin to wrestling an angry octopus than the simple task it should have been.

She stowed her used suit, her overshoes, and finally her nitrile gloves in the boot of the pool Vauxhall.

"You want to cut down on the sausage rolls, Sarge. It'd be easier cutting you out of this."

"You're a cheeky wee witch, Erin."

"Call it as I see it."

Macpherson blew a long breath as he was finally freed. He groaned as he bent to pluck off his blue overshoes.

"You can't fatten a thoroughbred," he said, nodding sagely as Reilly held open a paper bag for him to deposit the plastic shoe covers into.

"Or a mongrel." Her eyes sparkled with mirth. Gymnast-lithe and sharp as a whip, all five foot five of her was a bundle of excited energy. With her enthusiasm, ever-present toothy smile and pixie cut, it looked like she was barely out of school. A mistake Reilly could rectify with her acerbic wit and a look that Macpherson had seen only once and determined never to have visited on him again.

"That's some day."

It was. In the sense that it was something awful. The wind whipped across an expanse of open farmland broken only by the wicked spines of a hawthorn bush and the rickety fence that surrounded the property but did little to protect it from element or intruder. Rainwater glugged as the gutters and downspouts attempted to carry the deluge of a brief but violent shower from the roof to the overflowing drains, the greedy mouths of which were covered in a moult of slimy autumn leaf.

"God, that's gone cold." Reilly winced as she swallowed the dregs of a coffee.

"Not as cold as that wee soul."

Macpherson had slid into the passenger seat. He pulled a bag of sticky pear drops from the glove box, his eyes on the blacked out undertaker's van pulling out of the driveway.

"What possessed him?" said Reilly, tipping the last of the coffee onto the pebbled drive.

Macpherson looked up at the house. Every window was illuminated by lamplight and she could see the stirring of strangers within.

It would have been a peaceful scene a few hours ago. The glow of Belfast City and glimpse of the Lough as you approached over the hill in the late afternoon light. Nice winding country lane. A house of whitewashed stone. A pretty country cottage with a rough pebble drive and slightly overgrown lawn. A simple hand-tooled sign on the gate: 'White Cottage'. A wooden playhouse atop a climbing frame and swings plopped in the centre of the grass with a well-trodden path leading from the side stable door to the old outhouses set further back in a wildflower meadow.

Now, though, it was a crime scene.

Chapter 4

"ARE THEY OK? Is my son all right?" Jimmy Harding had aged ten years in the two hours he had been in custody. He sucked at a bloody rag nail, then rapidly changed tack to chew the skin at the edge of his index finger.

"If you could take a seat, Mr Harding." Veronica Taylor gestured to the seat. A smile and nod.

Harding swept his fingers through his hair, giving them a break from the feasting. The sleeve of his grey sweatshirt rode up to reveal red scratches on his wrist and forearm.

"Can you…" His voice died away as Taylor shook her head.

"Please. Take a seat and a deep breath."

"Mr Harding, the inspector needs you to calm down and take…" The duty solicitor jerked back in his chair as the enraged face turned on him.

"Calm down! Calm fucking down! I need to know if my son is dead and neither of you are telling me a damn thing!" The bitten finger waved between Taylor and the brief, Harding's ire rising in waves.

Taylor pulled out her own chair and sat, unfazed. She'd seen it all before. There was a knock at the door, followed by a series of short beeps. Harding's attention strayed. A nervous twitch, expecting perhaps the heavy mob. The door opened and a woman entered wearing a high street skirt suit and sensible flats, a tablet under her arm. She smiled, even though the tension was treacle thick.

"This is Detective Constable Cook. She'll be sitting in. Mr Harding, please. If you'll just sit, then we can get started and get you up to speed."

Harding dropped into the chair. The adrenaline of his arrest and the fight for news cut from under him. His arms dropped to his sides. He stared at the ceiling, a tear escaping the corner of his eye, which he wiped away.

The duty solicitor rearranged his notebook to make right angles with the desk and swapped the pen in his hand for one in his pocket.

Taylor waited a second, allowing a moment for all to compose themselves and for Simpson to prepare, note the time and ensure the system was recording.

The dual tone was clear when it sounded. Flat, then a higher pitch.

"Interview commences at 7:47 P.M. Present in the room, Detective Inspector Veronica Taylor, Detective Constable Carrie Cook and…"

"Henry Scott, solicitor for Mr Harding."

"And?"

Harding was a million miles away.

"Could you state your name, please, Sir," said Taylor.

"Jimmy…. James Harding."

"Thank you. Jimmy, we've arrested you for the incident that took place this afternoon at 179 Dunregan Road, Belfast, contrary to the Firearms Order of 2004. Do you understand?"

"What about Julie? And Tommy?" said Harding. He was nodding but not listening. He sat up, seeking an answer.

Taylor looked him square in the eye.

"Jimmy, your wife is in theatre. The prognosis isn't good

and by the time the night is out there's every likelihood you'll be facing serious charges in connection with her injuries and possibly even her death."

Harding didn't blink. No emotion registered on his face. Beside her, Cook shuffled in her seat and crossed her ankles under the chair.

"Your son, Tommy." Taylor slid a six-by-eight glossy image of a farmhouse kitchen from the document wallet in front of her and flipped it around so Harding and Scott could take in the aftermath. Better to have it up close and in their face rather than put up on the wall-mounted hi-res monitor. A picture from Country Home and Garden, it wasn't.

"Tommy died at the scene, Jimmy. I'm sorry for your loss but I have to inform you we are now re-arresting you for assault occasioning actual bodily harm. We expect that the PPS will pursue a charge of murder. DC Cook?"

Cook pushed the formal paperwork across to the solicitor, whose face had blanched as the chain of misery Harding had unleashed wrapped tighter around him.

Taylor had seen plenty of tougher men than Harding dissolve when faced with the prospect of life imprisonment. What she hadn't expected was for him to resign himself so quickly. He looked at the image, reached out, then retracted his hand as though stung.

"…do say can be used as evidence? Do you understand?" said Cook.

Jimmy Harding sighed and sat back.

"I'm sorry," he said.

"Do you understand the reason you've been arrested and your rights as DC Cook has read them to you?" asked

Taylor.

"Yes. Yes I do. I didn't mean to do it."

"That's OK. We'll come to that. We'll give you a few minutes to compose yourself and consult your solicitor. Would you like another room, Mr Scott?"

"This is fine, Inspector. It would seem my client wishes to assist in matters. Is that right, Jimmy?"

Harding said nothing. He stared at the grotesque parody of what had been his kitchen. The heart of his home. That heart had now been ripped out.

"Detective Inspector Veronica Taylor. Interview suspended." She checked her wristwatch. "8:01 P.M." She stood and picked up the document wallet, but left the six-by-eight where it was.

"Five minutes."

Chapter 5

"Cat and dog they were. Anytime you came past that lane you'd hear her screeching. Couldn't for the life of me understand why they stayed together. I suppose it was for the little one. That's what they say, isn't it?"

Macpherson poked candy out of a molar and nodded.

"You pass most evenings then?" he asked, sucking the offending gooey glob off his fingernail.

"Oh, aye. Walk Tess here thrice a day. Keeps me fit and healthy."

"So I see." Macpherson looked up at the house, feeling Reilly shoot a glare that burned into the back of head.

"Mr Reynolds?" said Reilly.

"George, please." George Reynolds was ruddy faced. A stubble resembling beard rash crowned his head, and he scratched at an impressive red beard. His belly hung below a John Deere sweatshirt, modesty just about preserved by the oversized shirt beneath. By his ankles, head cocked in observation, was a black Labrador.

"George, you didn't hear anything this afternoon, did you? See anything out of the ordinary?"

"No, Constable. I was walking back home when I saw the ambulance. Terrible. Just terrible. Julie being a nurse herself, too. She's a good neighbour. My mother had an operation, and she called in often enough to help us with the dressings. Jimmy was a quiet sort. Until he got a drink."

Reynolds mimed sinking a glass. "Still, not the kind of thing you expect." He shuddered. The dog stood and shook itself.

"You ever have any bother with Jimmy?" asked Macpherson. He stroked the dog's neck and accepted the lavish attention she returned.

"Me? No. Like I said, quiet fella until he gets a drink."

"Finds his voice, does he?"

"And the rest." A low chuckle. "Look, I'll not speak ill of the wee lad. He's had it tough with work and the wee one lately, but I'll tell you this." Reynolds looked about, a surreptitious glance to confirm he was not being observed from the hedgerow.

"You'll have him on your records, you know? Previous, as they say. He battered one of the other boys in the local a few months ago. Haven't seen him in since but…"

Reilly looked at the big farmer and nodded for him to continue. Reynolds glanced towards the house.

"Nothing to say he wasn't still knocking it back indoors, is there?"

Chapter 6

"OK, RUN THROUGH what we know for definite," said Taylor.

Carrie Cook sat on her right. Sam Simpson remained at the recording console, laptop open. He dragged windows across onto the screens of two larger monitors, his expression not hiding his belief that they should have charged, and had Harding in the cells by now.

On the large observation screen, Henry Scott was talking. Harding was slumped over the table, leaning on his elbows, head in hands. Carrie Cook read out the summary.

"Call centre receives a triple nine call at 5:05 P.M. The caller, later identified as Harding, states there has been an accident at 179 Dunregan Road, Belfast. Confirms ambulance requirement and also police. Someone was accidentally shot."

"Do we have the recording?" asked Taylor, looking to Simpson.

"Yes," he said.

"Cue it up. I want to play it to him."

The DC nodded and set about the task.

"Carrie?"

"Armed response unit confirm no threat to life, and ambulance crew find Julie Cosgrove and Tommy Cosgrove in the kitchen. Gun shot wounds to both. Julie transferred to the ambulance and taken to Ulster Hospital. Tommy Cosgrove declared dead on scene. Shotgun secured by first responders. Licensed to James Harding. Same address. Twenty-eight years young. One conviction for driving without due care, which has expired, and a current suspended for assault. Six months ago. Bar brawl."

"Not married?"

"Kept her maiden name," said Cook. "Harding treated for shock. Didn't resist. Arresting constable confirms he was adamant it was an accident. He didn't mean it. Etcetera. Etcetera."

"Forensics?"

"Pathologist verbally confirms death as result of GSW. Diane Pearson and the scene of crime team are still at the house. Harding swabbed and clothing seized. All been sent for analysis."

"Good."

"I told you it was a hole-in-one," said Simpson.

Taylor pursed her lips and stood.

"Hold the celebrations until we confirm if it was an accident or not."

Taylor's mobile phone rang, a dull buzz from her inside jacket pocket. She let herself out of the observation room and answered.

"Doc?"

"Ronnie. Is that wastrel behaving himself?"

Taylor huffed a chuckle.

"You're not my dad. I'm a big girl. I can look after myself."

"Aye, well. Tell him if he's at his antics he'll be needing a dentist to remove my boot from his sphincter."

"Lovely image."

"What's your man like?" said Macpherson.

"Depressingly normal. I just told him the kid was dead."

"How'd he take it?"

"Calmly. He knew already."

"We had a nosey around the house. Frigging bloodbath. Short range. Twelve gauge buckshot. It's a mess."

"He's saying it was an accident."

"What do you think?"

"I think why would you be cleaning your shotgun at the kitchen table at tea-time?"

"There wasn't any sign of that, but there were a few broken cups and glasses in the kitchen bin and bits of furniture that have seen better days in the yard. Do you know what I'm saying?"

"All was not rosy in the garden."

"I've just spoken to a neighbour who says they were partial to a barney."

"Interesting." Taylor pushed off the corridor wall, nodding to a uniform constable who was passing.

"Reckons Harding has previous, too."

"Bar fight. He got twelve months suspended."

"This neighbour also says he likes a drink."

"He seems OK to me. I'll check if anyone has done a blood and alcohol."

"No bother. Anything you need from us?"

"You could touch base with the family. Break the bad news about the youngster and see if they knew of problems in the marriage?"

"Do you save all the best jobs for me on purpose?"

Taylor smiled despite the circumstances and the stark similarities that could soon exist between herself and Harding. Child dead. Wife likely to follow. Whatever crimes he would be charged with, he would face the rest of his life without a family. A victim of violence.

Her own father had died when an under-car booby trap exploded one sunny March morning. Her mother followed a year later. They couldn't put broken heart on the death certificate, but Taylor knew the truth.

"Ronnie, are you still there?"

"Yes. Sorry. Look, I'm going back in here. Let us know if you find anything I can squeeze him with."

"You sure you're OK?" said Macpherson, concern in his voice. Taylor could picture the two lines between thick bushy eyebrows and felt the warmth as her surrogate parent placed a big hand on her shoulder. Robert Macpherson had been her father's best friend and colleague. The man who stepped into the missing role and guided her through the brutal years of orphaned grief and out the other side as a well-adjusted young woman and exceptional investigator. She considered the question. Was she? Child deaths were one of the most difficult to face. Emotive and depressing. A life cut way too short. Light snuffed out before it had a chance to shine beyond the family fold. She wasn't a parent but she could empathise with the loss. She had waded through similar tragedy before.

"I'm grand, Doc."

"Aye, well. I mean what I said about Simpson. Any nonsense…"

"Goodbye," said Taylor, a grin creeping into her voice again.

"See you later."

Chapter 7

THE SAME TWO familiar tones blared from the hidden speakers. Harding flinched.

"Detective Inspector Veronica Taylor. Recommencing interview. The time is 8:13 P.M. Same persons present."

Carrie Cook pointed a remote at the hi-res wall monitor and it blinked to life, revealing the Police Service of Northern Ireland Logo on a rifle green background. The bottom right corner of the screen displayed a black window and a cued media file.

"This is a recording of the emergency call placed this afternoon," said Taylor.

The black window expanded, and the graphic representation of the sound flickered along the bottom of the screen.

"Emergency. Which service do you require?"

"There's been an accident." Jimmy Harding looked down at the table. The voice was his own.

"Sir, do you require an ambulance?"

"Yes, please. There's been an accident."

There was a rapid series of clicks.

"Ambulance Service. Can you tell me the number you are calling from?"

"I'm sorry. I'm so sorry."

"Sir, this is the ambulance service. Can you tell me your number and your location?"

Harding rhymed off the phone number.

"I'm at home. 179 Dunregan Road. Please, quickly. She's just...."

"It's OK, Sir. Postcode?" Harding obliged.

"What's happened?"

"Oh, my God. There's been an accident. My wife. My son. They've been shot..." There was rustling in the background. Harding was sobbing. *"I'm so sorry. I'm so sorry."*

"Sir, is there anyone else in the house?"

"No, it's just me."

"They've been shot?" The call handler's voice ticked up an octave. The click of a supervisory ear could be heard coming on the line.

"Yes!" Harding was losing his grip.

"Is the area safe, Sir?"

"Yes. For God's sake, they're bleeding."

"Try to stay calm, Sir. What's your name?"

"Jimmy. James Harding."

"OK Jimmy, the ambulance is on the way. Open the front door and leave it open. Have you any pets? Dogs?"

"No."

"OK. Switch on any outside lights so the ambulance crew can identify the property."

Harding could be heard moving, his breath rapid.

"OK."

"Good. Now, how many people are injured?"

"Two. My wife and son."

The call handler chipped away with more questions. Age and gender. Conscious or not. Breathing or not. Calm reassurances. They are bleeding. Where are they bleeding? How badly?

All the while, Harding's ragged breath hissed on the line.

He mumbled cries and apologies, the mouthpiece smothered by fabric. There was the distant sound of a siren, the scrunch of tyres on a pebble drive, then the audible slam of doors. Movement.

"Armed Police. Mr Harding? Mr Harding, please move away and towards the patio doors."

The click of the line went dead.

"Are you OK?" asked Taylor.

Harding was a man wearing the experience of torment in his expression. He wiped a hand over his eyes and nodded.

"Mr Harding wishes to assist, Inspector. I'd like it on the record that you had his full co-operation from the off."

"Noted. Can we have the next slide, please?"

The image Sam Simpson had on his monitor was duplicated on the interview room display.

"Image Alpha, double zero one. A Franchi Affinity Three twelve-gauge shotgun. Is that your gun?"

Harding nodded. The image on the screen was a wide angle scene photograph of the shotgun set upon the kitchen table. The image changed to close up, revealing a bloody palm print on the stock and another set of prints on the barrel.

"Jimmy, I need you to answer, if that's OK. For the recording, please," said Taylor. She could see distress in his eyes. He couldn't look at the screen. What composure he had gathered was unravelling.

"Yes."

"Licensed?"

He nodded, catching her supportive smile.

"Yes. I have a licence."

"Sporting gun, is it?"

"Clays. I don't like to…" He paused and looked down at his hands. A crescent of blood remained in the cuticle of his right thumb.

"Where do you keep it?"

"There's a gun cabinet under the stairs."

"That's the only weapon?"

"It is."

"Great, Jimmy." Taylor nodded, and the shotgun disappeared. A family photo replaced the firearm.

"Nice photograph of you all."

"Inspector, Mr Harding is traumatised and in some distress over the news of his son. Could we maybe dispense with the…" Scott jerked his chin at the picture of happier times. Taylor ignored him.

"Jimmy, I need you to go through what happened today. You've said it was an accident and I want to believe that. So, help me out. Was today a typical day?"

"How do you mean?"

"Was it same as any other Tuesday? Are you usually all home together at tea-time?"

"Depends."

"On what?"

"Julie's shift pattern."

"Julie's a nurse?"

"Cardiology."

"Not working today?"

"She hasn't been in this week." He hesitated. "She took a few days' leave. Tommy wasn't too well."

Taylor nodded, not pressing the point. It was hardly relevant now. Whatever ailment the child had, the point blank twelve bore shells had cured it permanently.

"Are you working at the minute?"

"I am. I'm a hand at the Dereks' Farm. It's up the road. We rent the cottage from him."

"OK. Someone will have let him know what happened. What is it you do?"

"This and that. I'm a mechanic by trade, so I keep the machines up and running."

"Arable?"

"Bit of everything. He has a small herd of cattle, but the fields out our back are all rapeseed and sunflower."

"Had you finished for the day?"

"I was home for my dinner. I'd go back out from six to after eight this time of the year. There's a cut for silage and then bailing to be done."

"OK. So normal enough day then."

Harding nodded. He took a long look at the family photo, then rubbed the sleeve of his sweatshirt.

"What happened there?"

"Nothing," he said, tugging the cuff down past the angry lesions that marked his forearm and wrist.

"Looks painful."

Harding shrugged.

"Probably pulling a calf out of the hedge or trying to muck about with the hay-rake." Harding read the look. "It's a machine to flip the grass. I was replacing the spines. Sometimes they're hard to get off and you don't notice you've scratched yourself."

Taylor nodded.

"You wife ever help? With the farming stuff?"

"Julie. No, hates the countryside. She'd rather be in the city."

"I'd have thought where you were, you had the best of both worlds. Dunregan Road is what? Fifteen minutes from the city centre on a good run?"

"You can see right over the cranes to the city centre from the edge of our back field," Harding agreed.

Taylor knew the geography well enough. Dunregan Road climbed up from the A55 by-pass that looped around the outskirts of the city into the Craigantlet Hills. It passed the Victorian edifice of Campbell College and skirted the edge of the Stormont Estate, Northern Ireland's seat of power. The Portland stone of the Parliament Buildings could be glimpsed through the tree-tops as you rounded the first bend and ascended up the Craigantlet slopes. *Stoirmhonadh. The place for crossing the mountains.* An exaggeration if you were talking about the rolling hills and lush farmland, thought Taylor. Not so much if you were talking about the peaks of division and conflict that had been conquered in the grounds of the Estate one long Good Friday past.

White Cottage was on the edge of Ballymiscaw village, a collection of small businesses, farms and a tiny housing estate skimming the outskirts of Belfast city and sandwiched in the windswept wilds of the hills between Holywood on the coast and the suburb of Dundonald to the south.

"Why the move up there?" she asked.

Harding gave a momentary glance at the picture.

"A few months after we had Tommy, the job come up for me at the farm. I'd done a bit of work for old Harry with another firm and he was looking to take someone on. Offered the cottage as a sweetener. We thought it would be good for the child. The space. The animals. The Ulster Hospital is ten minutes away for Julie's work. Should have worked out."

"Should have?"

"Julie didn't like it. Too cold in the winter. She suffered from hay fever in the summer."

"I see. There are marks on your wife's arms similar to those." Taylor pointed the tip of her pen at his own arm. Harding slipped his hands under the table.

"You said on the tape it was an accident."

"It was." He bowed his head. "It was an accident."

Taylor let the lack of explanation fly.

"I need you to tell me how it happened." Taylor put down the pen and placed both palms on the table. "I know it's difficult. I know you are thinking about your wee boy. But I need to understand how, Jimmy."

"I was cleaning the gun…" he said.

Taylor picked up the pen and sat back.

"Next image, please."

The window flicked up and the screen quartered. The top two images were scene photographs. The worst of the devastation wasn't in the frame. It was easy to establish the space, though. The bottom left showed the image of the shotgun and shell casings. The remaining image was a plan view sketched out on an imaging software package. All elements were in place: storage units, breakfast table and range. Doorways offered access to the utility room, hallway and snug. It could have been knocked up in a retail chain offering zero percent finance on a new kitchen. There was one morbid addition, though. The icons dropped to represent the position of the bodies and a reverse engineered cone of ballistic spread.

"Image Alpha, double zero, two."

Harding looked at the screen.

"Do you understand what you're seeing there, Jimmy?"

Harding was mute.

"Where were you cleaning the gun?" said Taylor.

"At the table." He hesitated.

"At the dinner table?"

He nodded, mute again.

"You're no stranger to a shotgun, so at best that's reckless, don't you think?"

"It was an accident…"

Taylor leaned in.

"Jimmy, you need to tell me the truth. The absolute truth, because you aren't at the minute and I'm the only one who can help you. That image was constructed from evidence gathered in your kitchen." She pointed the pen at the screen, her eyes not leaving his.

"That gun. Your gun. It didn't discharge anywhere near the table. It discharged there. Twice. Right where the paramedics found your family."

Chapter 8

"I ALWAYS THINK you should bring grapes or something."

"It's ICU, Sarge," said Reilly, exasperated. She stopped and turned back to where Macpherson had dawdled to read a poster.

"Aye well, she'll be glad of them if they end up feeding her through a tube for a week. If she lasts that long."

"If we had brought anything, you would have had it eaten by now. Come on. Let's get this over with."

Reilly pushed through the swing door, shoes squeaking on the polished linoleum that led to the private family area outside the entrance to the intensive care ward. Macpherson followed a few steps behind. The low voices in the room paused as the strangers entered. The conversation, like the small life a few miles away, was cut short.

"What are you doing here? You should be out making sure that mad-man is locked up for doing this to my wee girl!"

The woman didn't bother raising her voice or herself from the padding of the soft blue chairs. Her eyes were raw from crying and her face was a mask of worry and anger.

The room was small, and with the addition of the two police officers it was now uncomfortably so. The distraught woman was flanked on the seat by a younger version of herself.

"Ma. Go easy. It's not their fault," she said, giving an apologetic smile as she rubbed her mother's arm.

A man sat at her side with a few days' worth of stubble and the beady eyes and weathered features of someone used to working outside. A tall, older man stood beside a vending machine with his back to the wall. Macpherson felt a fleeting sense of recognition, as though he should know who these people were.

"I'm Detective Constable Reilly. This is DS Macpherson. You're Julie's family? Mr Cosgrove?"

"Colin." The man stepped away from the vending machine and took the offered hand.

"We're very sorry for your troubles. Have you had any news?"

"The ward sister came out twenty minutes ago and told us the doctors were working on her. That it was grave and we should prepare ourselves." Colin Cosgrove stumbled over the last words, as though speaking them aloud was tempting the faith and fate that the family were clinging to.

"What kind of animal shoots his own wee boy? His own flesh and blood. I knew this would happen. I told you letting him take her up there and away from me was a mistake. I told you!" Mrs Cosgrove broke into the wracking sobs of a broken woman, the comforting arm and words of her daughter doing little to quell the desperate grief.

"Come on, Mummy. Let's get some air. You'll call us if the nurse comes out?"

"There's a tea machine around the corner. Can I get you some?" asked Reilly.

"No, we've done nothing but drink the stuff since we came in. Thanks." The daughter helped the mother to her feet, tissues appearing from the sleeve of a cardigan. Macpherson eased to the side as they exited.

The lobby opened into a corridor and a short walk to an automatic door that offered a sheltered breath of fresh air, if fresh could be described as stinking like a week-old ashtray. As the sensor drove the doors open, the smell wafted in.

Macpherson waited until the women were clear and the door had closed. It felt like cheating.

"Mr Cosgrove, I'm afraid we have some bad news."

"Tommy?"

"He didn't make it," said Macpherson.

The man's eyes welled up, but he blinked back the tears. He looked to the ceiling as he fought the raw emotions that emerged from the grief of losing his grandchild.

"I'm sorry. I'm sure they did all they could, but…" Macpherson drifted off. But what, but the poor craiter took the brunt of the blast and was almost blown in two? If you couldn't say anything comforting, say nothing, was his mantra in these situations.

"I expected it. I heard them when the ambulance arrived. They said they had only one adult patient coming in. God Almighty, what am I going to tell Louise?" Cosgrove wiped his eyes.

"We can do it, Sir," said Reilly. Macpherson glared at her, as he a forced a sympathetic smile at the grieving grandfather.

"We've a family liaison team for times like this. They'll be in touch before the night's out."

Cosgrove nodded. The younger man rose from his seat, where he had been watching.

"Has he been lifted? Is he saying anything?"

"You are, Sir?" asked Macpherson.

"This is Dan. Daniel Wright. He's my son-in-law. Debbie's husband." Colin Cosgrove motioned a hand towards the outside lobby.

"Mr Harding is assisting our colleagues with details about the accident," said Reilly.

"Accident?"

"We're talking to Mr Harding to get his version of what happened," said Macpherson.

Daniel Wright spat a bitter laugh.

"Good luck with that. Bastard couldn't tell the truth to save his life."

"Daniel, we don't need this…"

"What's going on?" Louise Cosgrove was at the door, cheeks as red as her eyes and wreathed in a perfume of Benson and Hedges.

"She says Jimmy told them it was an accident."

"An accident?"

"Mr Harding is in custody and we will find out how this happened."

"You better because if anything happens to Julie or our wee Tommy, I'll kill him myself."

"Louise…"

"No Colin, don't be Louise-ing me! I told you the first time she came home you should have had it out with him and not let the shit sweet-talk her into going back. He's a violent…"

"Louise…"

"Bet he hasn't told you that yet? How he beat her and she had to leave for her own safety."

"We'll put that to him, Mrs Cosgrove. The team will take

allegations of domestic violence seriously," said Reilly.

"It's not an allegation, it's a fact, and it was more than the one time." She sat and then stood again.

"I made a complaint about it at the time to Chief Superintendent Law. Do you know him?" She launched the name out like a threat.

Macpherson caught Reilly stiffening at the mention of the name. William Law, chief bean-counter and pain in the arse. A man with more skill in wielding a spreadsheet than investigative process.

"I know him," said Macpherson, and gave a single nod. The woman's stare fixed on him. A sense of recognition began rising up his spine.

"Well, ask him. He'll know the history. If you had done your job the last time then my Julie wouldn't be lying in there!"

She moved away, running her hands through her hair. Macpherson worried that she might tear clumps out in rage and frustration.

He eyed the woman carefully, struggling for a minute to link the face to the name and the sense of familiarity, then it clicked. Dragged from her dinner and in obvious distress, Louise Cosgrove, former Chair of the Policing Board, wasn't dolled up to her usual polished standard. He had been witness several times to her pit-bull style in committee debate, and although she had stepped down, there was no doubt her jaws would be rag-dolling this particular case until a conviction fell from them.

"I don't know what hold he had over her, but he's a nasty wee bugger. Doesn't look it, but he is. Did you tell them about that other slut he was seeing?"

"Louise…" Colin Cosgrove was reaching out to his wife, but she batted him away.

"Connie what's-her-face." She spat the name. "Ask her what she was up to with my daughter's so-called-husband and then what he did to her when she caught them."

The bleep of electronics could be heard and the door to the ICU opened.

"What's going on here?" The ward sister stood half in and half out of her domain, identification lanyard tucked into the breast pocket of her scrubs.

"Police, Sister. We're just giving the family some news." Reilly flashed her warrant card.

"Well, do it quietly. I've seriously ill people in here." She turned her withering stare on each of them, and then, without waiting for a response, she went back inside. The door bleeped closed behind her.

Louise Cosgrove looked confused.

"What news?"

The look on her husband's face broke through her anger towards Harding, his infidelities and his attack on their daughter and conveyed more than words ever could.

❖❖❖

"I'm sorry again about Tommy," said Macpherson.

Colin Cosgrove accepted the outstretched hand.

"Thanks, Sergeant. I don't know how Louise will cope. She doted on that wee boy."

"It's tragic, right enough." Macpherson allowed the man a second to wipe his eyes and quell the rising tide of grief that caught in his throat.

"We all did. He dug in his jacket pocket for an electronic

vape and put it to his lips, exhaling a thick cloud of cherry-scented smoke.

"Family liaison will be in touch, Sir. They have your details. If you need anything, just ask them. They'll fill you in if there's anything else regarding background that we might need to know."

"Appreciate it."

The two men walked in silence through the underground car park. The rising whoop and two tones of an ambulance echoed off the bare concrete as a set of headlights illuminated ahead. Reilly gunned the Vauxhall to life. The car's exhaust fumes swirled under the glow of the overhead sodium lamps.

"Would you look at that, for God sake?" said Cosgrove.

Macpherson stopped beside him as he dropped to his haunches and examined the rear quarter panel of a white Peugeot. There was a deep scar on the paintwork and the rear brake light was shattered.

"Is this yours?" said Macpherson.

"Debbie's."

"Not what any of you need right now. Another stress."

"I just hope it's not coming in threes," said Cosgrove. "It will kill Louise if anything happens to Julie."

"She's in good hands."

Cosgrove nodded and ran a finger along the scuff marks.

"I spent last night cleaning the bloody thing. Debbie must have hit it on the way out of the drive. I'm never done telling her to park over a bit and stop reversing out."

"It'll buff up and you can swap out the light unit handy enough."

"Car mechanic in your spare time?"

"I've a daughter too. You learn to do things yourself or they'd have you bankrupt."

Cosgrove huffed a laugh, acknowledging a shared understanding. For a split second the weight of misery that was waiting a hundred yards away was forgotten.

"I'll be in touch," said Macpherson.

Cosgrove stared at the broken glass. A keen sense of its fragility and that of his daughter's precipitous situation coalesced into pinpoint focus.

Chapter 9

"How is she?"

Veronica Taylor looked across the table at the man who that morning had all the trappings of what could be classed as normality but had seen it all shattered in a single heartbeat.

She felt for him. Sam Simpson and his fraternity of close colleagues might have had a few choice names to describe her behind her back, but Taylor wasn't bereft of feeling for the suspects she chased and ran to ground. The human condition dictated that the most conservative, right-minded and right-thinking individual could snap under pressure. Yes, evil men did evil things, but the man, or woman, next door was equally capable of brutality and that was the simple truth of it. It was a sad surety that nine times out of ten the perpetrator, the killer, was known and close to the victim.

"Julie is in surgery at the minute. That's all we know. I have colleagues at the hospital and we'll be notified of any change," said Taylor.

Harding bobbed his head. The meaning was clear. If the worse comes to the worst.

"Would you like another drink, Jimmy?"

Harding shook his head, lost in his thoughts and avoiding eye contact.

"Let's just go back over this afternoon. You were home

for dinner?"

"Yes."

"What did you have to eat?"

Harding looked around the table, everywhere but at Taylor.

"Was dinner ready? Was it something she had prepared or do you cook together?"

"We were having a stew again. It was left-overs from last night. I put the hob on when I came in."

"Where were Julie and Tommy while you did that?"

"Tommy was in the snug watching his cartoons. He hasn't been well, I said that. I heard the TV and looked in. He was wrapped up in his blanket with Floppy."

"Floppy?"

"It's his teddy. It never leaves his side." The magnitude of what he was saying seemed to steamroll over him and Taylor thought he might be sick. The angelic face from half a dozen photographs she had skimmed in the observation room burned behind her eyes.

"Carrie, can you fetch Mr Harding some water? Jimmy, it's OK. Take a breath. For the tape, DC Cook is leaving the room."

Carrie Cook was gone for a maximum of fifty seconds. When she returned she placed down four bottles of spring water and plastic beakers. Taylor cracked open the lid of one and poured a half measure, sliding it in front of Harding. His hand trembled as he lifted it to his lips.

"Inspector Taylor," said Scott. "May I request a break? It's evident my client is in no physical or mental condition, given the gravity of this evening's circumstances, to be pressured into admitting responsibility for something so tragic."

"I'm not pressuring him or blaming him for anything at the minute, Mr Scott. I'm trying to establish that your client's account that this was a terrible accident is true."

"You're a detective inspector, not the Health and Safety Executive," said Scott.

"And as there has been a death, it is my duty to investigate."

"If you have evidence that this was anything other than a horrible, horrible mistake then hand it over so I may review and consult with my client."

Taylor poured herself some water. She sipped it and replaced the lid of the bottle.

"I'm aware of procedure, Mr Scott. I just have a few more questions and then we can take a break. OK, Jimmy?"

Harding shrugged. From this day on, he would have no break. He was a child-killer, regardless if the charges stuck or not. That indictment would imprison him.

"That's an interesting point that Mr Scott brings up."

Harding took another shaky sip of the water. The condensation was leaving a ring on the table. He wiped it with his sleeve, the fabric pulled down to cover the marks on his arm.

"A mistake or an accident? Two different things."

"Detective Taylor…"

"You came home, put the stew on and checked, Tommy. When did Julie come into the kitchen?"

"Julie was there when I turned around. She might have been on the chair and I missed her. She was just there."

"Did she welcome you home, ask about your day?"

"No, I…"

"Did you ask her about Tommy? If he was feeling better?"

"I went to take off my overalls and wash up."

"And then?"

"I don't know. This is so hard. I can't remember. My son is dead and you won't tell me how my wife is!" Harding grabbed the sides of his head.

"When did you get the shotgun?"

"I don't know. After I got washed?"

"You were only heating the meal. Leftovers, yes? Wouldn't it make more sense to clean the gun later? When Tommy was in bed?"

"I think it was before dinner. Maybe it was after?"

Taylor shook her head.

"The stew was still in the pot. No places were set at the table."

The screen, with perfect timing, blinked up a slideshow of crime-scene shots. Cottage kitchen. Domesticity. A large Le Creuset pot on the stove. Long-handled ladle on a plate beside. Paper and crayons on the pine table. Taylor mentally checked a box on Sam Simpson. Alert and on the ball. Perhaps he could be moulded after all.

"Did you argue?"

Harding dropped his hands to the table, fists bunched, eyes screwed shut. The muscles of his jaw clenched tight.

"How would you describe your relationship, Mr Harding? Loving? Volatile?"

"I loved my wife," said Harding.

"Loved?"

"I love my wife," he said, drawing out each syllable.

"Are you a violent man, Jimmy?"

"No."

"Never?"

"Are you going to bring up Freddie Moore now?"

Taylor opened the manila file tucked under her left elbow.

"Frederick William Moore. Twenty-five. Victim of a sustained and serious assault. Broken nose and jaw. Hairline fractures to the skull. Treated for severe concussion. If it hadn't been broken up…" Taylor left the obvious potential hanging between them.

"It was…"

"Don't say an accident, Jimmy," she said.

Harding glared. For the first time, there was hostility towards her in his expression.

"What was the fight about? Banter gone bad? Spilled drink?"

"He was upsetting Julie."

"Oh, I see. Very chivalrous."

"He was accusing me of things. Calling her names."

"What was he accusing you of?"

"He was drunk. Chatting a load of rubbish. I told him to back off, and he came at me. I was defending myself," Harding protested.

Taylor slid a copy of a hospital report and accompanying photograph of the injuries to Freddie Moore.

"That's a big step over the line of defence, Jimmy."

Harding looked at the broken, bruised and bloody face.

"What was he accusing you of?"

"He told Julie I was sleeping with his sister."

Chapter 10

"Is this the place?"

Reilly pulled into one of the small car parks that bookended the Bucks Head. The public house was set back twenty feet from the main road that cut across the hills. A few benches were placed under a Guinness harp and an awning which had both seen better days. A cigarette bin adjacent had a grin of ash stamped on its face, and a carriage lamp illuminated the front doors. From inside warm light and dull conversation spilled out.

"Bit out of the way, but I've been in worse," said Macpherson, clicking off his seatbelt and reaching for the door handle.

Reilly blipped the locks and followed, side-stepping a pot-hole and acknowledging the nod from a smoker sheltered in the lee of the old farm building's gable wall.

"Ah, I can see why the booting didn't put him off." Macpherson held the door as Erin followed him inside.

They both unzipped their jackets as they entered the public bar. Logs sparked in an open grate, a pile of hand-cut turf was stacked on the hearth and the smell of polish, beer and food service was heady in the air. The porch had opened directly into a seating area, with half a dozen round tables enjoying a brisk trade. The left and right sides mirrored each other: small open snug, raised banquet seating and dim lights. The bar itself was on the left-hand side. Polished oak and a long brass foot-rest. Optics gleamed and pumps offered a selection of local and popular transatlantic fare.

"Oh, smell that? I'm starving." Macpherson rubbed his belly as he negotiated a couple tucking into two juicy steaks and sharing a platter of thickly cut chips.

"Do you ever give your jaws a rest, Sarge?"

"That's why you've no man in your life yet, Erin. You haven't worked out that the way to our heart is through our stomach."

"What can I get you?" The bar steward was in his fifties, with close-cropped sandy hair and a genial smile. He carried the broad shoulders of a man who had spent his days in manual labour and was either making a few quid on the side or had decided he'd given enough to the fields and was closing time in less strenuous toils.

"Freddie Moore?" Macpherson held up his warrant card. The bar-man turned up his lower lip.

"Not yet, Officer." He glanced at the clock on the wall to his right. "Regular as clock-work, mind you. Give it twenty minutes?" A wary look. "Has he done a mischief?"

Macpherson shook his head and offered his hand.

"No. Just a few questions he might help with. Do you know him well?" The barman's hand dwarfed even Macpherson's massive mitt.

"Bobby. Pleased to meet you. I know him as well as any of the regulars." He cast a vague look to the end of the bar and the snugs where drinkers supped and swapped the spoils of the day's gossip.

"Pint of Tennent's then gets a Vodka chaser when the shutters are coming down. Usually takes the lasagne if he's eating. Works the quarry over by the crossroads. He's a bit boisterous but not a bad lad. Is this over the beating?" Bobby frowned as though an unpleasant smell had wafted in.

"It might be. You here that night?"

"I was. Pulled that bloody nutter off him. I heard the police were up at the cottage. Has he been at it again?"

Macpherson tutted. "Can't really get into it." The barman nodded, accepting the brush off.

"Drink?"

"Aye, go on. We'll wait. Erin?"

"I'll have an orange juice, please." Reilly scanned the crowd, spotting two seats tucked in an alcove by the front porch. Macpherson nodded his understanding as he caught her eye.

"I'll bring them over. I'll have the same, please. And a couple of packets of bacon fries."

"I'll get you a menu, if you want?"

Reilly, now seated at the table rearranging beer mats, overheard and raised her chin. Macpherson humphed.

"Crisps will do."

"It's on the house. I'll bring it over," said Bobby.

"Here, keep the change. Appreciate it but you wouldn't believe the antics of anti-corruption these days." Macpherson put a ten pound note on the bar and collected the crisps, threading his way to Reilly.

"Excuse me?"

Macpherson paused his step and met the outstretched hand of a small balding man. The arms of his navy overalls were tied around his waist and he was wearing a check Tattersall shirt and brown wool tie.

"Can I help you, Sir?"

"I'm Harry Derek."

Macpherson nodded as realisation dawned.

"Mr Derek. DS Macpherson." He offered the man a refill.

"No thanks. A half is the limit for me, Sergeant. May I join you a minute?"

Macpherson ushered Derek to the table and introduced Reilly. On his heels, a waitress delivered the drinks and excused herself.

"Terrible business." Derek looked like he meant it. Macpherson nodded in agreement.

"There's quite a bit to get through but chances are you'll have the cottage back by this time tomorrow, Sir," said Reilly. Derek waved a hand.

"No rush. Take the time you need. If it's true, I can't believe it."

Macpherson took a sip of his orange but said nothing.

"We can't discuss it, Sir," said Reilly. "But, if there was anything different about Mr Harding's temperament, state of mind or general demeanour of late it might help us piece together a picture. You sure you won't take a tea or something?"

"Have you tasted Bobby's tea? There's better to be found in the roadside shuck." Derek smiled, but it pained him. Events at the cottage and the outcome for the young family seemed to be weighing on him.

"Jimmy's a quiet wee lad. A very diligent worker. Never late. Doesn't skive. I just can't believe it of him."

"How long has he worked for you?"

"Good three years now, although I know him this long time."

"Generally, he's no trouble?"

"If I'd another couple like him, I'd be a happy man."

"Reliable?"

"Oh aye," Derek nodded. "The odd day here and there. Plays a bit of rugby. Has had a few black eyes and the odd knock but it has never stopped him coming to his work."

Macpherson gave a sharp nod. Qualities he admired. It aggrieved him how many of the new generation of coppers seemed to swerve a day and take advantage of the generous sick package available. Reilly braced for his 'In My Day' speech, but it never came. Instead, "Nothing seemed on his mind?"

"He was a bit distracted today. Took off early. He'd cleared up his work, though."

"Did he give a reason?"

"I never asked. I'd an idea something was bothering him. Christ, if I knew it would lead to this…"

"He didn't say what the something was?" asked Reilly.

"I think it was more someone."

Macpherson nodded in understanding, jerking his head towards the bar.

"You heard me asking about Freddie Moore."

Harry Derek's eyes narrowed. He clicked his tongue. "I did. That's part of the reason I wanted to speak with you."

"Oh? Sounds ominous," said Macpherson.

"I had to let Freddie go from the farm. It wasn't long after Jimmy came on. I'll be frank in saying there's some animosity between the two."

"I'd say that's an understatement by the medical records."

Derek spread his palms.

"I agree that in black and white it looks bad."

Macpherson, unable to resist any longer, snapped open the bacon fries, offering the packet around. To his delight, neither Derek nor Reilly accepted. He plunged in, popping three in his mouth, and crunched.

"Jimmy's lucky he didn't go down for it," he said, around a mouthful of the reconstituted corn snack. He dipped his fingers in for seconds.

"Freddie thinks Jimmy had something to do with me dismissing him, but that's not the case. He was a liability. Nothing grand. There was no one incident and I gave him the benefit of the doubt, but the fella just wasn't a worker."

"Do you think Freddie started on Jimmy Harding that night?"

"I was here. I know that's how it was. He was shooting his mouth off about him stealing his job. I gave him short shrift and told him to pack it in. Then he got personal." Derek blushed.

"Jimmy told him enough was enough, but Fred wasn't having it."

"The eyewitness reports say Jimmy had to be pulled off him?"

The old farmer gave a resigned shrug.

"That he did."

"What did he say that riled Jimmy so badly?" asked Reilly.

"He told him stealing his job was bad enough, but he wasn't having him knocking off his wee sister into the bargain?"

The two detectives shared a look.

"His sister?"

"Connie Moore. Freddie told the entire bar, including Julie, that Jim and Connie were having it away. Jimmy went mad after that."

"This was months ago. What's going on now?"

"Freddie's been hassling Julie again. In the shop. On that social media." He gestured to Reilly's phone. "Telling her they're still at it and there isn't a damn thing Jimmy can do to stop him or he'll find himself banged up."

Chapter 11

"IS THAT WHAT you argued about?"

"We weren't arguing."

"Jimmy, something happened this afternoon that has resulted in us meeting like this. You've told me it was an accident but I don't believe you," said Taylor.

"What you believe isn't relevant, Inspector. You have a burden of proof to establish and if you don't start presenting your case, I'll be advising my client to reserve his right to silence." Henry Scott sniffed and rearranged himself, smoothing a Hugo Boss marine blue and rouge silk tie.

Fair enough, thought Taylor. She could appreciate that Scott was playing his cards as they fell. He wasn't the most pugnacious brief she'd ever faced, although obviously adept given the high end clothes and the hundred and fifty quid Parker pen he was scratching notes with.

Julie Cosgrove was in surgery, little Tommy was dead, and in the absence of any other living witnesses she was going to have to crack Harding. It looked bad for him. He could call one discharge accidental. But what was that but gilding the lily of recklessness? Or gross negligence. Two discharges were nothing short of deliberate.

Scott knew one very simple key point. One that Taylor was acutely aware of. The clock was ticking.

"How long have you been married, Jimmy?"

"Six years."

"Generally speaking a happy one?"

"I already told you I love my wife."

"It isn't a trick question."

"I suppose it's happy. We've had our ups and downs," he said.

"Who doesn't? Moving jobs, house, raising a child. They all add degrees of pressure."

"Are you married, Inspector?"

It wasn't a question she normally faced from suspects, and was one that wasn't touted out too often. Those in her limited social circle knew her marital status, and those who moved through the periphery of her life that didn't were colleagues, both legal and enforcement, usually asking another question in a roundabout way.

Taylor was single. Not through lack of suitors, but she made a stand not to date within the job and didn't have the patience to put up with the sly looks and innuendo that would slip in when her profession came up with those outside.

She was committed to her work, dedicated to following in her father's footsteps and exceeding the expectations she imposed upon herself. It required tunnel vision and a lack of distraction, and she guarded her spare time fiercely. When she thought about it, she would accept that watching her mother's grief and subsequent decline following the death of her father had had a detrimental effect, skewing her view on the social norm of pairing up, having children and seeking the happy ever after. The experiences of ten years in the job also highlighted reasons that put paid to the reality of that fairytale.

"I'm not," said Taylor.

"We loved each other, but we fought from time to time. Stupid stuff."

"Like who was supposed to take the bins out?"

"Yeah. Like that." Harding's expression softened. A memory from the past.

"Did you have much of a social life together? I know it must have been difficult lately if Tommy had been ill, but you had family to lean on, right?"

Harding's wistful expression darkened.

"My folks are dead."

Taylor felt a sharp stab under her ribs. The spark of a kindred spirit.

"I'm sorry, Jimmy." A mental flash of a little body in the morgue blinked once in her mind's eye. "Times like this you need your parents."

Harding shook his head. He sniffed and scratched his nose with the back of the hand.

"God, I hate to say this. I sound like a broken record." He looked at Taylor. "It was an accident. They were on a caravan holiday in Scotland. Head on with a lorry. It was a while ago, but it never really leaves you."

Taylor regarded the sorrow in his eyes. She felt the pain of having loved ones snatched away.

"I know."

The hum of the air-con and the click of the thermostat were the only sounds in the room for several moments.

"What about Julie's family?"

Harding puffed out his cheeks.

"We didn't get on. They didn't like Julie coming out to the country."

"Really?"

"Yeah. You'd think we were moving across the world, but they're so tight knit. Her parents, aunts, sister. They all lived practically next door to each other. Latch-key. I hated it. Someone would always just walk in and it would be a job to get them to leave."

"You felt you'd no privacy in your own home?"

"Something like that. They didn't understand what the problem was. Her mother went mental when we moved up to the cottage."

"Not regular visitors?"

"No, Julie would run down into the town with Tommy for a visit, but it was rare they came to us."

"Did you never join them?"

"I wasn't all that welcome. I'd do Christmas Day. That was about it."

"OK."

"Look, there's something else."

"Uh-huh?" Taylor was scribbling in her notes.

"You'll find out soon enough. I'm surprised Louise hasn't been on to you already, baying for the noose to be brought back."

Taylor sat back. He'd tell her in his own time. Head shaking, he leaned forward suddenly, stabbing a finger on the table.

"I loved my wife. OK? But they're going to tell you all the problems we had and how she ran back home. That's true. She did for a little while, and she took Tommy. But we worked through it. We sorted it and she came back of her own free will."

"OK, Jimmy. Sounds normal to me. Couples fight, need a bit of space."

"They said I beat her. I didn't. I swear I never laid a hand on her. Fuck, it was an accident. I walked out of the barn with a plank to fix up Tommy's playhouse and hit her on the nose." He threw back his head, sighed and splayed his arms wide.

"We laughed about it, for God's sake and then we had some stupid fight and she ran home. Next thing Louise is on the phone threatening all sorts. She has connections. You know? To the police. She made complaints at the time."

Cook thumbed the tablet on her lap, dabbing passwords to databases.

"When was this?"

"A while ago."

"A month? A year?"

"Not quite a year."

"Not quite a year," said Taylor. "About the same time Freddie Moore told Julie you had been sleeping with his sister?"

"I wasn't shagging his bloody sister!" Harding jumped to his feet, then his anger deflated like a burst balloon. He looked around as though lost.

"I wasn't. I loved my wife." A tear bloomed and broke free.

There it was again, thought Taylor. Loved. Past tense.

Chapter 12

Another drink each and a further packet of crispy treats for Macpherson, and true to form Freddie Moore made his regular appearance through the doors of the Bucks Head. It was more of a stumble than a grandstand entrance, but as regular as they'd been assured, nonetheless.

They recognised him straight away.

In the intervening time since they had bid Harry Derek a good evening, Reilly had scoped Freddie Moore out on his social media. Why he believed hiding behind an avatar and running out a diatribe of abuse against Jimmy Harding, the Dereks and Julie Cosgrove for the crime of remaining with her husband, offered any form of anonymity or excuse was beyond her. They had both watched dumb-founded as his audacity intensified, posting videos of verbal abuse from the window of his car or in the supermarket aisles. Others showed him doing a drive-by of the Hardings' cottage and setting off fireworks over the roof of the house.

"See, Harding knocked no sense into him," said Macpherson, then rose from his chair as Moore walked past.

"Freddie Moore?"

"If this is about the hedge clippers, I took them back. Jesus, have you people nothing better to do?"

Moore was a good foot taller than either detective, but Macpherson doubted he weighed half as much as the diminutive Reilly. Whatever Derek had employed him for, his obvious talents had been overlooked. Jam a bucket hat on the fella's head and you could stake him out in a field to scare the birds.

"We don't know anything about hedge clippers, Mr Moore," said Reilly, brandishing her warrant card and a disarming smile.

"You're cops though?" He glanced over Reilly's shoulder. He was stranded between the door and the bar.

"Aye, son. We are. Hoped you might have five minutes."

"What about?"

Macpherson tilted his head towards the vacant table. From the corner of his eye he noticed Derek pulling on a gilet and searching his pockets for the means to settle his bill.

"Jimmy Harding."

A gleam appeared in Moore's eyes, along with a self-assured smugness.

"Oh, aye? What about him?"

"Can we sit?"

Moore shoved his hands in the pockets of his coat and considered it, accepting the offer after a beat and following Macpherson's outstretched hand.

"Drink?"

"Pint of Tennent's," said Moore, unbuttoning his khaki military-style jacket.

Reilly gave the order at the bar and re-joined them, setting the lager in front of Moore, who grunted a thanks.

"Who's he give a kicking to this time?"

"What makes you think that?"

"Because he's a psycho." Moore set down his pint and

tilted his head to the right. He parted the hair above his left ear. "See that? That's what Jimmy Harding is capable of. Nutter."

A jagged line of old stitch marks scored an angry welt across his skull.

"What happened that night, then?"

"This happened." Moore pointed at his own head. Macpherson nodded to him to continue.

"I told him to stay the fuck away from my sister."

"Connie, right?" said Macpherson, receiving a grunt of acknowledgement. "How did you know there was something between them? Did she confide in you? Did you catch them on?"

"I didn't need to catch them on. I've eyes in my head, don't I?"

"To be clear, you saw Jimmy Harding and your sister in a compromising situation?" said Reilly.

Moore pulled a face as he downed a draught of his lager.

"Christ, no!"

"So how did you know?"

"Jimmy was never away from the shop. She works in the Spar, the garage. Down the road?"

Reilly nodded at her sergeant. They had passed the Maxol signage and the small forecourt that fronted the convenience store, off-licence and chip shop on the way up the hill to the Bucks Head.

"Aye, well. Every night she's on, he's hanging about. Fawning over her. Buying her a bar of chocolate. Having a wee coffee. Laughing his bloody balls off at me." Moore stabbed a finger into his chest. His face was darkening as he played it all back in his mind.

"Maybe they were friends?"

"She's twenty-one, and he's a grown man with a wife and child. What would she see in him?"

"Age is just a number," said Macpherson, seeing where this was heading.

"He's a bloody predator is what he is. I told him to back off one-too-many times. He didn't, so I told his wife what he was up too and he done this. Scarred me for life. Could have killed me." Moore pointed to his head again.

"It stopped after that?"

"He was heart scared he'd get in any more bother, so yeah. Until lately and he's back pushing the boundaries."

"Which is why you are hassling him again?" asked Macpherson.

Moore's expression turned stony.

"Hassling him? You're saying that like he's the bloody victim."

"What my colleague is saying, Mr Moore, is given the history between the pair of you, why are you still content to pressure Julie Cosgrove about her husband's alleged relationship with your sister?"

"You don't think she should know her man's running around after a wee girl half his age? She should fucking ditch him and take the child. That would sicken his happiness."

"And this has nothing at all to do with you getting the bump from the Derek farm and Jimmy taking your place?"

Moore choked as he swallowed a sip of the Tennent's. His eyes watered as he cleared his throat.

"Is that what the sly wee bastard's told you?" he said.

"Mr Moore, harassing a member of the public at home or

in the shops and posting it on-line could be viewed as breach of the communications act. If you don't knock this vendetta on the head, it will be you who ends up in the courts."

"I'm doing a bloody service making sure everybody knows that sicko is preying on wee girls."

"Your sister's a grown woman, son."

Moore set down the remains of the pint. Lager was sloshing from lip to lip like an angry amber ocean.

"I'm done here."

He pushed off from the table and the glass fell. Reilly snatched for it, but it was too late. It spilled. She righted the glass. Picking up a dry napkin, she wiped her fingers then dropped it to soak up the worst of the mess.

"Julie Cosgrove could've had you done for harassment. So could Jimmy, for that matter. Have you any idea what might have happened if one of those rockets had hit the house?" she said.

"Piss off." Moore was unapologetic for the mess and unrepentant for his actions.

"Where were you at half five today?" said Macpherson.

"What?"

Macpherson shrugged. "Where were you at half five?"

"Why? What's happened?" Moore was suspicious. His eyes darted to the door, then to the lager dripping off the table.

"I didn't say anything happened."

"Christ, has somebody took a pop at Jimmy?" He looked down at the upturned faces of the two detectives.

"Were you anywhere near White Cottage at half five?" asked Reilly. She could see the cogs starting to freewheel.

Panic? Hope?

"I didn't do anything."

"You sure about that?" Macpherson, aware of Reilly's look, dropped the wind up.

"Did you see anything?"

Moore may have towered over the detective, but the steely look and the air of authority radiating off the smaller man made him feel as tiny as a field mouse. He also knew at that point that something had happened. And he wished more than anything that he could answer in the affirmative and have been there to see it.

"I was at the quarry. You can check with my foreman. We had a problem with one of the conveyors and I ended up getting away late."

"You weren't stalking Jimmy or his missus, then?"

Moore for once looked shame-faced.

"No. No, I wasn't near them."

Macpherson pushed back his seat and stood. His hope for an eyewitness pooled around his feet like the dribbling remnants of Moore's lager.

Chapter 13

JIMMY HARDING PACED the room and then, as realisation dawned that his nightmare would have to continue for some time yet, flopped onto the seat and put his head in his hands. He stared at the floor.

Carrie Cook dabbed the tablet on her lap as Taylor watched the observation screen. Her attention wavered as Henry Scott scowled on the monitor that showed the landing lobby. He had paced in parade square for the last few minutes with his phone clamped to his ear. The pained gestures and slump of his shoulders suggested he was trying to explain why he was still stuck in a custody suite and not home enjoying a TV dinner or a restaurant date. The phone disappeared inside the tailored wool-blend jacket, and his expression wasn't dissimilar to the one Macpherson had when Diane Pearson was explaining the trigonometry and quadratic equations of a ballistics report or Professor Thompson was extolling the different physiological impacts of smothering, choking, strangulation and asphyxia.

"Does someone want to help Mr Scott with his coffee?" she said.

Sam Simpson glanced up at the screen.

"I'll go." He jumped up, then paused when he reached the door.

"Erm, would either of you like one?"

Taylor looked to Cook, who had started. Her eyebrows

arched.

"I'll have a tea please, Sam. Black. No sugar," Cook said.

"Guv?"

"I'm fine, thanks," said Taylor. An amused smile curved around the corners of her mouth as the door closed.

"You must be a positive influence, Carrie."

"I'd say your reputation precedes you, Guv."

"It hadn't an hour or so ago." Taylor turned. "I'm not that bad. Am I?"

Cook tucked a lock of hair behind her ear and re-crossed her legs.

"Have you not heard the stories Doc tells us?"

Taylor chuckled.

"Half aren't as interesting as he makes out and the other half aren't anywhere near the truth."

"It's the way you tell them," said Cook. Her tablet beeped, and she dabbed the screen.

A Detective Constable for two years, Cook had been seconded to Taylor's team for what should have been a brief period of support during an investigation into a domestic slavery ring. She had fitted in like she'd always been there and shown both an ability to get the job done and an inherent aptitude for investigation. She was also an excellent communicator and a dream to put out in the field to deal with witnesses and family liaison in what had been a sensitive case. Taylor had petitioned to keep her, and it delighted everyone when the transfer was approved. Especially Macpherson, who she indulged with Tupperware boxes full of home-baked cake and savouries.

"Hospital update, Guv."

"Good or bad?"

"Julie Cosgrove is out of surgery. Next twenty-four hours are crucial but prognosis is better than it was three hours ago."

Taylor nodded. Jimmy Harding could have been freeze-framed. He hadn't moved position since she last looked. Only the slight rise and fall of his shoulders confirmed he was breathing.

"You going to tell him?" said Cook.

"Yes. I think he deserves to know. At the very least it might focus his mind on the fact that there's going to be another version of events than just his."

"Maybe not for a while though."

Taylor nodded.

"Do you think it was an accident?" Cook asked.

Taylor had been thinking the same thing. She could nail down guilt straight off the bat normally. A combination of gut and psychology. Unconscious tells, deliberate untruths and hours locked in small rooms with bad people.

Harding sat somewhere in the middle of the Venn diagram. She wouldn't say he was bad to the bone. He was guilty. She could feel it coming off him in waves. But guilty of what? Was it infidelity? Spousal abuse? The unbearable grief of killing his own son?

The chirps of the access code being entered pulled her from the thoughts of pity that even though Julie Cosgrove would survive, Harding would nevertheless find himself alone.

"One tea. Black no sugar and two Kit-Kats." Sam gave a trademark smile as he put them on the table.

"Figured you could use the sugar hit," he added to Taylor, his earlier frostiness thawing.

"Thanks, Sam."

"I miss anything?"

Harding had shifted position and looked down the barrel of the camera. A man facing his executioners.

"Julie Cosgrove will probably pull through," said Cook.

"Good. Well, isn't it?" He noted Taylor's expression.

"Would I want to wake up and find my only wee boy was dead instead of me?" Taylor shrugged.

The atmosphere in the room cooled. Cook sipped her tea and Sam booted the laptop back up.

"Carrie, give the hospital a nudge and request an opinion on the injuries to Julie Cosgrove's wrist and chest. I want to know the probability they were defence wounds."

"Guv."

"And chase up Diane Pearson. SOCO will have their hands full at the scene, but anything they have that puts Jimmy Harding on the trigger of that gun I need to know ASAP."

Cook nodded, moving her tablet and phone to the small alcove behind the door. Her tea was balanced on top of her notebook.

"Sam."

Simpson's fingers rattled across the keyboard as he launched internal network and browsers. He looked up expectantly for Taylor's instruction.

"Let's see what else we can dig up on Julie Cosgrove. If her mother used her connections they'll be recorded. Any previous callouts to the cottage or any previous addresses. Reports of domestic violence, withdrawn statements. Hospital visits. Jimmy Harding is hiding something and I need to know what it is so I can hang him with it."

THE BELFAST CRIME CASE-FILES Vol.1

Chapter 14

Reilly swung the tail of the Vauxhall into a parking space and clicked on the handbrake. There were half a dozen pumps in the forecourt that fronted the Spar convenience store, and she had found a bay in the thirty or so that skirted the small shopping complex. A workman in orange coveralls collected cash from an ATM a few bays down. He glanced in their direction, tucking his wallet back in his pocket as he entered the store. Traffic zipped by on the main road, headlights sweeping over the Maxol sign displaying fuel prices and an offer on meal-deals. Macpherson had perked up at that as they drove in.

The first waft that hit Reilly as they exited the Vauxhall was the warm, enticing embrace of fried potatoes and battered fish. A smell from childhood. Seasides and smiles, car journeys, amusement arcades and the bracing wind of the north coast.

"...fish supper. Portion of chips. Two battered sausage and a curry sauce?" The door to the chip shop was ajar, and the voices of the counter staff drifted out on the tide of heady scents. Reilly watched as a server handed across a weighty paper bag to a female customer. Office clothes, hair scrapped back and seeking an easy fix for dinner. The woman smiled wearily as she exited to find Macpherson standing in the path. She skirted around him, juggling the bag under one arm and fussing in her handbag for car keys with her free hand.

"No," said Reilly. "I can see what you're thinking. Let's get this over with. I swear I don't know where you put it. You must have worms or something."

Macpherson stood in front of the large glass window like a child peering longingly at a Christmas display.

"I've worked through my dinner break, Missy. You can shout me chips when we come out for being so insubordinate."

"Insubordinate?"

"Aye. Here's me teaching you the benefit of a lifetime's wisdom and you, barely out of the training college, have the front to be telling me I've an eating disorder."

"Come on. You're not getting chips. You'll stink the car out."

"You're getting as bad as bloody Ronnie. Do you hear me?" said Macpherson, quickening his pace to catch up to the young DC, who had already disappeared inside the store.

The shop was relatively busy. Commuters between Belfast and the outlying towns of the North Down coast were stopping to grab ingredients for their tea or a few snacks and other confectioneries for a night in front of the television. Reilly approached a young man knelt stacking a fridge full of yogurts and brightly labelled milkshakes.

"Excuse me? Hi, can I have a word with the manager?"

The young man had to focus a second as he looked up at her, adjusting his thick glasses.

"Is there a problem?"

"No, son. We just need a word with the boss." Macpherson stretched out a meaty mitt with his warrant card on display. "Police."

"Oh, right. This about the drive-offs? Come on up to the tills. I'll page her."

Nathan, as his badge identified him, stood and beckoned them to follow. They negotiated a few dangerously driven trollies and a queue of customers elbow to elbow at the reduced-price shelf before he ushered them into a small space beside greetings cards and a rack of magazines. Macpherson plucked one out and began thumbing through.

"You seen this?" He waved a picture of a celebrity luxuriating on the white sands of a Balearic beach.

"Would you put that back?"

"I mean, what the hell was she thinking? She was a pretty wee lassie before she done that to herself. There should be a law against it."

"It's the in thing."

"She looks like a bloody duck," said Macpherson, incredulous that a syringe full of collagen might achieve anything resembling enhancement.

"It's harmless."

"Oh. Thinking about it, are you? I can picture you." He puckered his lips into a pout.

"God help your wife, Doc," said Reilly. Macpherson flapped the magazine closed and replaced it on the shelf.

"I swear I'm waiting on our Moira telling me she's going for some. She never has that lot off the TV."

Reilly chuckled. She shook her head, considering whether a drop of Botox or fillers might in any way be more damaging than being Macpherson's long-suffering spouse.

"Hi. Thanks for coming. Nathan said you're here about

the drive-offs?"

The young woman who had appeared from the double door behind the till was bright-eyed. She wore her blonde hair up in a mop on the top of her head and was fresh-faced with an attractive smile. Her green fleece, company logo resplendent on the breast, was easily two sizes too large and made her head look too small for her body. Macpherson clocked her name badge.

"Connie Moore?"

"Yes. I'm the assistant manager. I called it in," she said. Straight white teeth. Bright green eyes. Flawless skin. Reilly saw why Jimmy Harding would be attracted. She was beautiful without trying.

"Miss Moore, we aren't here about the drive-offs."

She raised manicured brows, caught on the hop.

"Oh."

"Is there an office where we could talk? Somewhere private?" said Reilly. The line of customers were trying not to look at the two police officers and the petite assistant manageress.

"God, it's not Freddie, is it? What's he done?"

"If we could just…" prompted Reilly.

"Yes, of course." A roll of the eyes. A been-here-before look. "Come through."

Connie Moore thumbed a mechanical code-lock and led the two detectives along a short corridor. Trollies of goods to be stocked were on one side, with bundled stacks of discarded packaging ready to be recycled on the other. She paused at the last door on the right, which was wedged open. The room beyond smelled of burned toast.

"Can I get you tea or something?"

"I'm fine, thanks," said Reilly, picking the one seat which didn't have crumbs or stains on it. Macpherson looked around.

"Was anyone killed?"

Connie laughed. It was a sing-song lilt, and again Reilly could see what Harding might have seen in the girl.

"In the explosion? I know. They're no better than children, honestly. Look at this!" Connie plucked a polite notice to clean as you go from the waste bin.

"Tea? Coffee?"

"I'll give it a miss, thanks," said Macpherson, looking at the sink full of muddied cups, stained tea-spoons and soiled cutlery. Connie dragged a seat across the floor and stood up to reach a large plastic container.

"Clean. For visitors." She settled the box on the worktop, clipped off the top and produced two clean white mugs.

"Aye, go on will. Coffee. Black. No sugar. Oh, none for me," said Macpherson as Connie fished out a packet of shortbread and plated a few. He caught Reilly's arched brow.

"She's only after saying I need to lose weight."

"She did not?" said Connie.

"Aye. She did."

"You're in fine form. Don't be letting anyone tell you different." Connie laughed as she passed across a cup of instant coffee. Macpherson blew across the surface and took a sip.

"You sure?" she said. Reilly nodded.

"So, what can I help you with?"

Macpherson tilted a red seat and tipped the crumbs and a foil biscuit wrapper to the floor. He repositioned the seat before sitting down.

"It's about Jimmy Harding."

Connie gulped down the mouthful of tea. Her eyes flew wide.

"Freddie hasn't…"

"No. Your brother hasn't done anything untoward," said Macpherson.

"Has he hurt himself?" Connie asked. Each word wavered with an edge of emotion.

"No. No, Jimmy Harding is fine."

"Thank God." She sat, not bothering to check the state of the chair. She clamped her hands around the warmth of her mug.

"Can I ask the nature of your relationship with Mr Harding?" said Reilly.

Connie's face twisted in a scowl that still didn't touch her soft prettiness.

"Don't tell me? My brother has sold you some story along the lines of I'm being groomed by Jimmy Harding. Well, I'm not. We're friends. That's all."

"How did you meet?" said Reilly.

"I met him at the farm. Harry Derek introduced us. I did casual work there when I was finishing my A-Levels. We got to talking. I met Julie through Jim. Did some child-minding the odd weekend. Not that there was much to it. Tommy was always asleep. Didn't peep. It let the two of them get out to the pub for a couple of hours."

"Did Jimmy ever make a pass at you?" said Macpherson.

"Christ, no!"

"We've had a few people mention that your relationship maybe stretched beyond platonic?"

"Why? Because we got on? Had a laugh? Just because a fella and girl enjoy each other's company doesn't mean they're rolling around together," Connie said, her face flustered.

"There was nothing more to it?"

Connie took a sip of tea, wary eyes on each detective.

"Should there be?"

Macpherson watched her put the cup to her lips. He was hopeful she would never feel the need to cosmetically augment the fine Cupid's bow. He looked to Reilly, who was watching the girl with rapt attention too.

"When Jimmy put your brother in hospital, did it not sway you off him?"

"Freddie deserved it." She looked at Reilly as she answered. "Almost every sinner in the bar at the time comes in here. I got the full account. Freddie never could let me make my own decisions."

"Still. A bit extreme?"

"Jimmy is... was under a lot of pressure."

"We spoke to Harry Derek. He didn't strike us as the sort of boss you couldn't talk to if you were having problems," said Macpherson.

"It wasn't work. Sorry, I thought this had all been sorted. Jimmy had his day in court and is on a suspended. If you're looking for someone to put the boot in and get him a custodial upgrade you're talking to the wrong person."

"Did you ever speak to Julie Cosgrove about Jimmy?"

"I tried." Connie's lips tightened, and she gave a brief shake of her head.

Macpherson let her have another drink. He took a sip of his own coffee and considered how much he was about to tell her.

"Mr Harding was arrested earlier today."

"What?"

"I'm afraid so. We've seen the social media stuff your brother has posted. Was it causing animosity between Jimmy and Julie again?"

"Again?"

"She left him for a time after the assault."

"She was never happy he turned to me instead of her." Connie stood. She sloshed her tea into the sink and dumped the cup on top of the others, then leaned against the worktop with her arms crossed.

"Turned to you about what, Connie? The court case? Julie leaving him?"

"No," she tutted. "Jimmy was depressed. He was hurting himself."

Macpherson blinked. He hadn't expected that. Reilly flipped a page in her notebook.

"Hurting himself how?"

Connie shrugged.

"Cuts. Burns. I caught him in the outhouse at the back of White Cottage. He'd been drinking. I saw him put a cigarette out on his arm." She tapped a spot below the line of her shoulder.

"Why?" said Macpherson.

"He was just down. His own folks are dead, you know? Julie's ones wouldn't give him the time of day."

"Did you ever meet the Cosgroves?" asked Macpherson.

"No. I saw Julie's mummy on the TV. She was something to do with the police?"

Macpherson nodded.

"Jimmy said she wasn't one bit happy when the two of them got back together. I think she might have been pushing behind the scenes."

"Pushing for what?"

"Julie was giving him a hard time over moving back to the town. She could be a real hard case. Always on his back about something. It was hard to watch sometimes. Jimmy said she was wild for the first six months they moved up here."

"Wild how?"

"She had went through a bad time. Post-natal. It sort of dragged on. Jimmy said there were days you couldn't look at her."

"That's quite an intimate thing to be sharing," said Reilly.

"I suppose, but he needed someone to talk to. I never judged him. I like to think it helped. I offered to break the ice with Julie about it but…"

Macpherson saw deep empathy in the young girl's eyes. Whatever feelings she had for Harding, whether genuine friendship or a misplaced crush, he had no doubt they were heartfelt and well intentioned.

"Are you a trained counsellor, Connie?"

"Me?" She laughed again. "No. Jesus, I work in a Spar shop."

"Julie Cosgrove is in hospital. Jimmy shot her."

Connie's hand went to her mouth.

"No, he wouldn't. He couldn't."

"You see why we need the unvarnished truth about your relationship?"

"Oh my God. Poor Tommy."

Macpherson caught Reilly's stare. Flip you for it. He

paused a beat.

"I'm sorry, but little Tommy was hurt too," he said.

Connie stared blankly, not comprehending what Macpherson was skirting around.

"Tommy died, Connie."

"No."

"I'm sorry..."

"No!" she roared, backing away from them. Tears bloomed and her face was caught in an ugly grief-stricken rictus.

"He wouldn't. He loves that wee boy. There's no way."

"When did you last see Jimmy Harding?"

"He wouldn't."

"Connie?" Reilly moved towards the woman. She seemed to have shrunk further into the oversized fleece jacket.

"Connie? When did you last talk to Jimmy?"

"Earlier. He was here after lunch." Connie was on the brink of hyperventilating. Reilly sat her down and squatted beside her, placing a comforting hand on her back.

"How was he? Did he say anything?"

"He asked to see me after work. Wanted to talk."

"What about, Connie? Did he say why?"

The tears flowed unbridled. Her words were distorted by sobs.

"What was that?"

"She told him she was leaving for good and taking Tommy with her."

Chapter 15

"SO WE ARE explicitly clear. You are aware this isn't the first time?"

Chief Superintendent William Law twirled a pen in his fingers for want of having a moustache to play with, but the effect remained eerily reminiscent of a Bond villain ready to cut loose the rope and deposit someone to the sharks.

Bunkered behind his roll-top walnut desk, he refused to blink until Taylor had the temerity to furnish a reply.

"DC Simpson has just pulled the records," she said.

"And?" Law had removed the spectacles over which he would normally fix his gaze, and had placed them on an A4 pad of scribbled notes. His left ear was red and his immaculately groomed hair was ruffled. The mobile phone responsible was face down beside the glasses.

"I've gleaned the basics, Sir. I was about to take a deeper dive when you requested to see me."

"This Harding. He's guilty? Yes?"

"He doesn't deny it."

"Good. Get on with charging him then. You're aware who the victim's mother is?"

"Yes, Sir."

"I know the woman personally, and while she no longer holds a position on the Policing Board, she has enough clout with the Executive and in the press pool to throw this under a very bright spotlight. I don't agree with trial by headline, Veronica, but if Harding is admitting to this, it's in our best interest to charge him and get him off our hands. Am I clear?"

"Crystal."

"Keep me appraised. You're dismissed."

Taylor nodded her understanding and stood. Law had already replaced his spectacles and was returning to strategise on how to keep his own and the service's reputation intact by stage managing the coming storm whilst spinning the facts of how a domestic abuser, with a history of violence, had been free to murder his child and almost succeed in killing his wife.

❖❖❖

"She's positive about that?"

"As far as believing what Harding was saying was true, yes," said Macpherson.

"What did you make of her?" Taylor put out her foot to hold open the door for a passing uniform and brief making their way up from the custody suite. She smiled in recognition as the solicitor gave a jaunty wave and mouthed a greeting. She shifted the phone to her other ear as Macpherson answered.

"Nice kid. The wee girl is fond of him. She's adamant he doesn't have it in him. Was in bits about the child, too."

"Where is she now?"

"We dropped her home. They called in a manager to cover. She was in no state to work, and she's shocked to be at the centre of something like this. I told her we would send someone to the house for a full statement."

"I'll get Carrie to ask Sergeant Harris to get one of the

section crews over," said Taylor.

"How's she doing?"

"Grand. Slick is proving useful too. Believe it or not."

Macpherson answered with a grunt.

"Doc, if Harding was on the limit and she was about to walk out with the kid, he could well have snapped."

"Aye. It's possible. It also clouds the water if his brief goes down the line of diminished responsibility by way of mental illness."

"I'll have Simpson pull his medical records to see if he is under treatment."

"Connie Moore told us he had struggled since his parents died. Julie Cosgrove also suffered post-natal depression and I think he found that hard to deal with too."

"I guess the in-laws didn't help."

"Aye. I met them in the hospital."

"I've just been in with the Chief Super. Mrs Cosgrove has been through her Filofax and he's getting his ear bent by those on high," said Taylor.

"Did you ever meet her?"

"No. She'd stepped down by the time I came along. You?"

"Saw her in action a few times. Rottweiler, but she was straight enough," said Macpherson.

It was a distraction that Taylor didn't need, and one that might easily derail impartiality in a heartbeat. Especially if the person rattling the sabre was known as a straight shooter. Great strides had been made to remedy incest and nepotism within the halls of criminal justice, but fear and favour could still be brought to bear. Particularly with something as emotive as a child's death and a desperately ill mother.

"Where are you now?" she said.

"Heading back to White Cottage. We'll have a look for any medication in Harding's name and take a snoop around the outhouses. If he was hiding out there to booze and self-harm, we might find something to hit him with before the doctors come through on your end."

Taylor took the final few steps to the landing of the interview suite and drew a deep breath as she keyed the code-lock to the observation room. It was better than doing nothing.

"OK. Let me know if you find anything."

Chapter 16

TAYLOR CLICKED THE door closed behind her and looked at the big screen.

Harding looked as though he'd been in the chair for forty hours instead of four. Henry Scott was also beginning to lose his own polished veneer. His jacket hung over the back of the chair and his neck-tie was loosened an inch. Client and brief were in a one-way conversation driven by Scott. His questions were answered with a simple nod or half shake of Harding's head.

"Guv." Carrie Cook stood, sliding her tablet across so Taylor could view it. "Preliminary forensic reports from the doctor. Jimmy Harding's blood alcohol is negative."

Hadn't been drinking then. Taylor mentally checked the box. "Any other drugs?"

Cook paused. She cocked her head to one side and flicked back a few screens, then winced apologetically.

"We didn't ask for a specific screen. Do you want me to get it run again?"

"No. I do need you to request access to Harding's medical history, though."

"Specifics?"

"Treatment for depression. Stress. Doc has a statement saying he was suffering badly and may have been self-harming to cope."

"Jesus."

"Yeah. I know. We need to find out if he had ever

presented for treatment or had a diagnosis for psychosis or similar behavioural traits," said Taylor.

Cook nodded. She dabbed the tablet to bring up a new window.

"Doctor McCall's office emailed over the death certificate for Tommy Cosgrove." She paused. There was a moment of silent reflection as the grim document loaded up.

"Professor Thompson also sent his initial brief from the scene. Death consistent with gun-shot wounds from close range. This backs up his previous verbal, and he has scheduled in the autopsy for first thing tomorrow. Usual time."

Taylor nodded. Just another indignity on the family and for little Tommy Cosgrove to endure. Cook briskly moved on.

"Diane Pearson's report. She told me to tell you to take this section with a pinch of salt until she has it corroborated at the lab." Cook had highlighted a selection of paragraphs.

Di Pearson was the Forensic Science Service senior crime scene investigator and the site team lead. Taylor had a long and trusted relationship with her and she knew Pearson well enough on a professional level to understand that her comments were a humble attempt to downplay her near psychic skill in the deciphering and analysis of the evidential patterns she picked up at the scene. Cook drew up a picture of the shotgun lying on the terracotta tiled floor. Two little yellow evidence markers were positioned uncannily like a McDonald's arch.

"She's sure the palm prints here and here will be Harding. Compare them to the size of this one here, which is smaller and more likely to belong to Julie."

"She tried to grab the gun?"

"That's what it looks like. There are fingerprints on and around the trigger guard, but she's warning they may be too smudged for use."

"OK. Anything else?"

"The lab has returned analysis from the clothes we seized. Blood from both Julie and Tommy Cosgrove and a significant quantity of gun shot residue. Probability is high enough to put Harding behind the trigger. They need to carry out some more tests but it's looking good."

"Good work. Get onto the doctor's report before we go back in."

"Sure thing."

"Sam." Taylor smoothed her hair back. Law's insistence that she get this one over with was niggling at her as the thought of sitting through little Tommy's autopsy haunted the back of her mind. "What have we got?"

"You were bang on with the mother." Simpson launched a new window and dragged up what he had uncovered, listing it chronologically.

"No incidents at the couple's previous address but Mrs Cosgrove placed fifteen calls through switchboard, reporting her concerns, within the first two months of the move to White Cottage. It was followed up on the first half dozen occasions, but Julie Cosgrove told them her mother was overreacting and she was fine. The officers attending were granted access to the dwelling and reported no signs of disturbance."

"Get those reports anyway and find out who it was. Have Sergeant Harris pull them in if need be. I want to run it through with them face to face."

"Yep. No problem."

"Is that when she escalated things?"

"Yes. She cornered the Chief Inspector's secretary at a Policing Board lunch and got an audience. His office pushed it back down to Inspector Kinning, and he got the same dead end."

"It's hard to know whether it was maternal concern or just plain nuisance," said Taylor.

"Sounds like she was sticking her nose in. Any wonder Harding didn't get on with her."

Taylor watched over Simpson's shoulder as he pulled up a copy of Julie Cosgrove's medical history.

"The mother provided this, but again Julie Cosgrove denied anything untoward and made no complaint."

Taylor looked at the diary entries of attendances to medical services, then a second batch of reports recording injuries sustained by Julie Cosgrove over a period of months. They began with the move to White Cottage and continued up to a week before Jimmy Harding was arrested for the assault on Freddie Moore. The visits started innocently enough.

An investigation into bouts of severe asthma and migraine. A diagnosis of stress related to the move and coping with a young child in an unfamiliar environment. A prescription for back pain and a torn anterior deltoid. They became more overt from there. X-rays for a broken arm, which turned out to be a severe strain, and treatment for cuts and abrasions. Julie Cosgrove put the injuries down to domestic mishaps or horseplay in the grounds of the cottage.

At the bottom was the referral report from social

services, who had attended on a number of occasions and reported that Julie Cosgrove, Tommy and Jimmy Harding were managing well and met the threshold to sign off with no further action being required.

Someone's dropped a bloody bollock here, thought Taylor, as she scanned the dates and plotted the escalation of the injuries alongside the course of Freddie Moore's vendetta against the family.

As she made to speak, one comment caught her eye. The description of a wrist injury. Running to a paragraph, it detailed the patient presenting and passing it off as a gardening accident. The physician had noted the treatment plan, but what was perhaps more incendiary, had commented that the welts and damage to the dermis and significant bruising to the wrist and forearm were consistent with defence wounding. Taylor took Simpson's mouse and clicked on the jpeg file attached. She took a step back to better take in the picture. She'd seen those marks before, on Harding's arm a short time earlier, and on the photographs of Julie Cosgrove sent across from the hospital.

Harding's insistence that the day's events had been a horrible accident was now looking more unlikely than it ever had.

Chapter 17

Reilly took the proffered clipboard and scrawled her name, then passed it over for Macpherson to do likewise.

"Thanks," she said, handing the scene log back to the constable on the gate of White Cottage.

"You can pull up over there," he said, indicating a spot beside one of the SOCO vehicles. "If you park on the verge, you'll get side-swiped, the speed they come around that corner."

"You should set up a speed camera, son. Earn yourself a wee bonus," said Macpherson. The constable pulled a face.

"That's likely right enough, Sarge." He pointed to a spot beyond view further down the winding road. "The inspector had us on one down the hill this afternoon. Where the national meets the thirty? Wish I was on a commission, I can tell you that."

"The bean-counters always like to see a lift in revenue this time of the month. Somebody has to pay to have me ferried about in this luxury." Macpherson offered a wink and tapped the roof of the car through the open window.

Reilly thanked the young constable again and negotiated the cattle grid, pulling up in the turning circle outside White Cottage beside an overgrown pedestrian gate. It was the same spot she had parked at earlier. All the lights were still on.

"Do you need me to get out the crow bar?" she said,

opening the door and already halfway out. The headlight warning tone pinged.

"You need to learn to respect your elders," grumbled Macpherson.

Reilly popped the boot. She slid across the trunk of Tyvek oversuits, booties and gloves.

"What are you doing back? Are you looking for tips on how to do proper police work?"

Diane Pearson shaded her eyes from the headlights. She pulled her face-covering off, allowing it to hang over one ear as she dropped her hood and shook out a bob of ash blonde hair.

"You must have a big holiday booked, Di. You're fair eating through the overtime budget today," said Macpherson, fighting to shake out his overalls.

Pearson laughed.

"How do you stick him?" she asked. Reilly shrugged.

"He's not that bad as long as you keep feeding him."

Pearson chuckled and zipped the front of her suit to her navel. She huffed a breath.

"What's the craic with you right enough? Something come up?"

"We had some unconfirmed on the suspect's medical history. We were going to snoop the bathroom cabinet. That sort of thing."

"Well, we're practically finished up. Not much more we'll glean that isn't already on its way back to the lab."

Macpherson paused in his battle with the polyethylene oversuit.

"Does that mean I can skip this rigmarole?"

"Are you going anywhere near the primary crime

scene?"

He shook his head, giving a nod to the upper windows and then across the wildflower meadow.

"Bedrooms, bathrooms, and over in the outbuildings. Did your lot have a look in there?"

"Yes and no. We scouted the house, but there's nothing to suggest anywhere other than the kitchen is the primary. Booties and gloves, and if anything is out of place, you tell me straight away. Gun cabinet under stairs is OOB."

"Did you notice much booze about the kitchen?"

"You having that sort of day?" said Pearson. Macpherson chuckled, rolling up his crime scene suit.

"No. From memory no wine rack. Fridge had one tin of Guinness," she said.

Macpherson nodded, satisfied with the answer. He tossed the suit at his DC.

"Thanks Diane," said Reilly, catching Macpherson's balled up overall and lifting out the box of blue overshoes and nitrile gloves.

"Try to keep him out of trouble."

Reilly acknowledged she would, and Pearson searched in her pocket for keys and blipped open the forensic vehicle. She took a seat and a sip from a bottle of cola stowed in the door bin. She waved as the detectives moved off.

Reilly handed Macpherson his gloves and booties on the front steps of the cottage. A dream-catcher hung in the window next to a pair of small wellington boots, and a child's anorak was hooked by the hood on a brass hanger screwed to the side of a larger coat stand.

"Let's see if the boffins missed anything then," said

Macpherson, leading the way.

The porch opened into a large, brightly lit reception hallway, with up-lighters and a large glass chandelier in full flame. The stairs to the first floor were on the right, with the entrance to a family living room and the kitchen on the left. A PC masked, gloved and shod in overshoes stood sentry as they entered. Macpherson confirmed that they had signed the scene log and explained that they would be doing a search of the first floor. The PC waved them on. Voices and the sounds of Pearson's team packing up equipment in the kitchen drifted through. There was a short peal of laughter as they went about their work.

Macpherson let Reilly take the lead up the staircase. The carpet looked newly laid, the pile angled from the brush of a handheld vacuum.

The landing was wide. Clean. Decorated in soft colours and furnishings. A radiator cover held a vase and pictures of the family. The master bedroom was at the end, with two other rooms between it and the top of the stairs. One was decorated in bright blues and greens, with dinosaurs on the walls and picture books on the floor. The other was a dressing room. It had floor-to-ceiling wardrobes, a dressing table and a set of drawers. The main bath was next to it.

"You check in there. I'll nosey in the master," said Reilly.

It didn't take long to find what they were after.

"Nothing in the bathroom," said Macpherson.

"Found these." Reilly held up several small packets of medication, the label of a local pharmacy on the front stating dosage and a warning.

"Sertraline. In Jimmy's name. Full packet, but the issue date was a fortnight ago."

"If he was off his meds and it's true she'd dropped the bombshell she was leaving, it adds to the hypothesis that he snapped."

Reilly dropped the packet and the pills into a clear ziplock evidence bag.

"Right. Outhouse then?"

Chapter 18

REILLY COLLECTED A torch from the boot-kit of the Vauxhall and they walked in file across the luxuriant grasses from the gravelled turning circle to the two-storey building in a similar whitewash to the cottage. An automatic floodlight illuminated an arc out to thirty feet. The mammoth shadows of the moths and daddy-long-legs fluttering around the heat danced across the field. The long stems of meadow cats-tails lashed at their legs and the rainbow heads of larkspur, blanket flower and English marigold which were a sea of swaying colour in the daylight, were dark in their wake.

"Age before beauty," said Reilly, unlatching the old door and nudging it open with her toe.

Macpherson took the offered torch and stepped across the threshold.

He cast the beam around the door frame and thumbed an old bakelite switch. The dull click-clonk of fluorescent overheads warming up echoed in the dark, and then there was a low hum as they flickered to life and illuminated the space.

Aside from the single door through which they had entered, there was a set of doubles, lashed closed with a chain and padlock. A decrepit Nissan under a dust sheet nosed against the doors. Its hubs were rusted and it was up on a trolley jack.

The rest of the main floor comprised a lawnmower, a

couple of ride-a-long cars, a rocking horse with the name Ruby hanging from its straggly mane, a few push-bikes with flat tyres and stacks of wooden packing crates. Stairs led up to an old hayloft, with several of the planks that formed the steps and at least three spindles missing.

Along the rear wall was a counter-top with cupboards above and below that once had been an old kitchen but had been retrofitted to form a workshop. Oily engine parts, the flywheel from a strimmer and a selection of tools scattered the surface or were hung on nails tapped into a wooden backboard. Shapes were stencilled around with a thick-tipped marker.

The whole place smelled of damp, cut grass and fuel.

"Over there," said Reilly, indicating a spot cleared in the far corner with a small table, a work-lamp and an armchair that looked older than herself.

"That's quite the collection," she said as Macpherson eased up beside her.

A large wicker basket held the remains of at least thirty bottles of spirits. Reilly picked out a few branded vodkas and gins, but most of the others had names she didn't recognise and labels screaming out budget paint-stripper. Beside the work lamp was an ashtray of crushed butts and a double-edged Wilkinson Sword razor blade.

"That's a serious stash to get through," said Macpherson, his knees cracking as he squatted to lift out a bottle. He held it to the light to better read the back.

A piece of bright material was wedged down the seat cushion. Reilly pulled it out. The centre was stained and crusted with what could only be dried blood.

"Bag that," said Macpherson.

Reilly did as directed. Macpherson reached down to pull an old trunk from a space under the bench.

"Erin?"

"What is it?"

"Get Diane."

Reilly peered over his shoulder. In a bed of rags was a broken wine bottle. The serrated edges were black, and her guess as to what it could be was confirmed as Macpherson played the light of the torch along the bottle to where the slim neck was strangled by five bloody fingerprints.

Chapter 19

HENRY SCOTT'S WORDS shrivelled on his lips as Taylor entered Interview Room 3. Her expression carried a storm of impatience and her face was set in stone. Carrie Cook followed. She eased the door closed. The engagement of the lock seemed much louder in the tense atmosphere.

"Interview continues 11:47 P.M. Same persons present." Taylor set down her notebook and placed her phone and pen on top of it.

"Jimmy, I'm tired. You look shattered, so cards on the table. I'm not pissing around anymore. What happened at White Cottage this afternoon?"

"Inspector, can I object? Your tone is..."

"Mr Scott. You're not in court now so why don't you keep your objections for someone who's willing to listen to them?"

Cook felt a flutter of anxiety in the pit of her stomach at the confrontation. She jammed her pen between her teeth to suppress the need to grin, a ridiculous side effect she had borne since childhood that had done her no favours at home or in class.

"Jimmy. Good news. Julie has come through her surgery. She will, with a bit of grace, be fit for interview once the medical team gives us the OK. So, this whole fabricated story of an accident is going to get an entirely new perspective once the sun comes up."

Harding paled and brightened all at once.

"She's OK?" He put his hands on the table and leaned in, eyes wide.

"No. She's not OK," snapped Taylor. "She's had life-saving surgery for a gun-shot wound that rightfully should have killed her." Harding took his hands away, ghostly palm prints evaporating.

"And then when she does come round, someone is going to have to tell her that her dear wee boy is dead!"

Harding opened his mouth to speak.

"Shut up, Jimmy," said Taylor. A glare at Scott was enough for him to heed.

"You've been lying to me all day, and to be frank I'm a bit pissed off."

"I didn't…" Harding crossed his arms, resting his big hands on his own shoulders. His cuffs rode up.

"You didn't what? Shoot them?"

"No…"

"You didn't shoot them now?"

"It was an accident."

"Was beating Julie an accident too?" said Taylor. "Sam."

The wall monitor blinked to life. The PSNI logo disappeared, to be replaced by a vivid jpeg image in glorious gory high definition.

"Image Bravo, zero one. Looks nasty. Do you want to state what it shows?" Harding lowered his head.

"Julie Cosgrove. Moderate bruising to the face and subconjunctival haemorrhage to the eye. I've got the doctor's notes. Walked into a cupboard door."

Taylor looked across the table. Harding was staring at his hands, now folded in his lap. Scott looked to the screen, noting the injuries and date stamp.

"Next," said Taylor. The image changed. "Two weeks later. Patient returned presenting sudden onset of pain to upper left arm. Lost footing. Treated for muscle strain and received X-ray to right hand. Significant internal bruising to proximal phalanx of thumb and metacarpal. Painkillers prescribed. You don't have to write all this down, Mr Scott. We'll be here a while. I'll have DC Cook prepare you the reports afterwards. Do you remember what's next, Jimmy?"

Harding mumbled. He shook his head. When he looked up there were tears in his eyes.

"A bit louder please."

"A cracked rib," he said, defeated.

"Three. Cracked. Ribs," said Taylor. "What happened this time?"

"She slipped on the stairs."

"She slipped on the stairs. Have you any idea how pathetic that sounds? She fell twice? Inside a week? There's more incidents after these. Can you remember them all?"

Harding opened his mouth to speak, then closed it. He looked to the ceiling and wiped his tears. Taylor tapped the file under her hands.

"This is just a case of systematic spousal abuse. Was it the drinking, Jimmy? Did it get out of hand? Arguments ended up getting physical? You weren't drinking today, so we won't be using that as an excuse to mitigate what you've done."

"It was an accident," Harding shouted. The silence after the abrupt outburst was deafening.

"It must be the most accident-prone house in bloody Belfast," said Taylor.

Bzzzt. Bzzzt. Buzzt.

Taylor's silenced mobile hummed. The dull resonance was amplified by the desk. She picked it up and glanced at the screen. Macpherson. The call cut off before she could silence it.

"I was almost sympathetic to you earlier," she said. "You've lost your son. Your wife is hanging on by a thread. Now…" She pointed at the livid red ridges on Julie Cosgrove's torso. The deformity of the cracked bones was visible below the skin, stark against the white cotton of her bra.

"Now it looks like you're a man with an anger problem. One you took out on Freddie Moore. One you take out regularly on your wife. What happened today? Why did you turn that gun on your family?"

The hiss of static preceded the flat tone of the room-to-room intercom.

"DI Taylor. Can you break a moment?"

Taylor looked into the camera and nodded. She collected her phone, her pen and the folder. Cook followed suit.

"I wonder what else we have." Taylor stood, looking down at the now pitiful shell of Harding. His eyes were raw. He was unable to look her in the face.

Scott ran a finger around his collar. He at least, understood the weight of the growing evidence against his client and how it could tip the scales when it came before a jury.

"I suggest you two have a final brief. When I come back in here I expect it to be with the final nail, and after that I'll be recommending the PPS throw everything including the kitchen sink at you."

Harding placed his hands on the table, a foot apart,

ready for the shackles. His chin was on his chest. The inevitable conclusion had been reached.

"Interview suspended. 12:08 A.M."

Chapter 20

MACPHERSON LEANED BACK against the formica worktop. He glanced to his left to make sure he wasn't about to bang his head on the old kitchen units.

"Are you sure? Do you not need more light in here or something?"

"I'm sure," Pearson nodded. "I'm going to have them sent for testing, but I'm telling you, ninety-five percent. These are Julie Cosgrove's prints. I've lifted enough in the kitchen to tell the difference. Look." She held an index finger up to the fan of prints around the neck of the broken bottle. "Similar. She has delicate wee hands like me."

"But you're sure?"

"Pretty sure." Pearson arched a brow. "I can't be a hundred percent until we do a proper match against the control sample, but I'm as sure as I can be standing here. Do you want the rest of these dusted?" A sudden scowl clouded her face as she calculated the number of stashed bottles.

"Won't do any harm," said Macpherson.

"What about the edge? Is it blood?" asked Reilly.

Pearson half nodded.

"I'd say it's likely. We'll run it too."

"Thanks, Diane. Sorry," said Macpherson. "It's been a long day. I didn't expect to drop more on you."

"I'll get the crew over. We'll have these done in an hour or so."

"Keep me in the loop, won't you?"

"No worries. Tell your boss I'll have reports on the kitchen out by tomorrow afternoon."

The two detectives expressed their gratitude and left the outhouse as Pearson called her team from the van where they had packed up and were waiting to leave. Two gloomy faces passed them in the wildflower meadow.

"All about the OT lads," said Macpherson.

"Not much use to me tonight. I had a table booked with the missus at eight."

"Just think about all the ways the double time can buy her affections back."

"It'll be six weeks before I see it, and I'll be hearing about the job being more important than her the whole time."

Macpherson chuckled as the grumbles turned to distant mumbles. Pearson's business voice greeted them as the men entered the pool of light spilling from the outhouse door.

"Is that us then?" said Reilly.

"I think so. I'll just give Ronnie a call and give her the…" He cut short, thumbing the end button on the call. Reilly's head appeared from behind the boot lid.

"What is it?"

Macpherson pulled a fresh glove from his pocket and knelt down. The gravel scrunched under his weight. He twisted and put a hand on the column of the pedestrian gate wrapped in luxuriant green hedgerow.

"Torch?" he said. Reilly passed it across. He clicked the beam on and swept it across the ground beside the rear wheel of the Vauxhall.

"Shit, did I hit the…" Reilly lowered the boot lid. She

stopped, her hand running over the intact rear lamps of the car. The ground under the rear wheel sparkled with shards of toughened coloured glass. Macpherson played the beam up the gate post to a broad white streak of paint.

"The SOCOs are going to frigging string us up," said Reilly as Macpherson stood to face her.

Chapter 21

"WHAT IS IT, Sam?"

"Harding's GP reports just came through," said Simpson.

"And?"

"Your wish is my command." Simpson pushed his chair across to the conference table where he had already spread the paperwork out.

"Now these all coincide with the timeline we have for Julie's injuries. You'll see that up to this date," Simpson double tapped a letterhead with a fingernail, "there are several sports injuries and one incident he reported as an accident at work." Simpson turned in his seat and clicked his mouse.

"That injury should have been reported to the Health and Safety Executive. He was off for over three days. Harding, or rather his boss, Harry Derek, didn't follow it through."

"He probably didn't want the inconvenience of having the place shut down. It shouldn't but it happens all the time. What was the injury?"

"They thought it was a broken wrist, but it was a severe sprain. He was put in a splint and on pain relief, which stopped him operating machinery."

"I'll get Doc to speak with Derek in the morning. What else have we got?"

"He had two bouts of concussion and a visit for eighteen stitches. Football injury. Elbow to the face." Simpson mimed jumping for a header.

"I think he played rugby," said Cook.

"It was rugby," said Taylor.

"Anything consistent with his wife fighting off a beating?"

"He had ointment prescribed for deep scratches to his arms and shins. The GP report backs up his own statement that it was in the course of his work."

Taylor nodded, skimming ahead. Then she slowly ran her eye back across the documentation.

"When did the anti-depressants start?"

Cook helped scan the paperwork, with Simpson giving a few clicks of the keyboard and mouse.

"Eight months ago," they replied in unison.

"Give or take around the time he took up with Connie Moore."

"Maybe she did get him to seek help."

Taylor sucked her teeth.

"What's this one?"

"Glazing the outhouse. Slipped on the ladder. Twenty-five stitches to meat of his right forearm," said Simpson. He scooted back to the table and looked at the page Taylor was reading.

"These two need locking up in a padded room where they can't hurt themselves," he said. Taylor shook her head in disbelief as she read another entry.

"We have two adults here. Parents. Regularly seeking treatment for injuries sustained at home and they have a young child. Are there any independent reports from the health visitor or passed on to social services from the GP? The last one I read had given them the OK," said Taylor.

"No," said Simpson, distracted as the laptop pinged a tone.

Taylor picked up a psychiatric evaluation from Harding's GP. He was under pressure at home and at work. He'd been sleepless, restless and agitated. Was he stressed? Most likely. Depressed? Probably. Had he thought about injuring himself? Sometimes. Had he thought about doing worse? Not seriously. He wished he could just stop the world, but he wouldn't leave his boy fatherless.

"Here's the report from Sergeant Harris. The incidents when uniform attended." The DC shifted his seat so Taylor and Cook could look over his shoulder at the monitor.

Taylor read down the mail. The calls had been placed by Julie Cosgrove. When Echo One Two had attended the scene, her husband was profuse with apologies for wasting their time. Julie Cosgrove likewise.

She could read the frustration between the lines in the report. Domestic incident. Evidence of alcohol. Both parties apportioning blame to themselves. Matter resolved.

"Nothing on things looking out of hand?" asked Taylor.

"That's it. Heat of the moment. Sorry, officer. Won't happen again," said Simpson. Taylor turned away just as the laptop dinged again.

"Oh. Hold your horses."

"The sarge has added an amendment. He spoke to both PCs after he'd pulled the report. Meadows from section four said she remembered the two incidents she had attended. It wasn't the first time, she'd been called out to have a word in the past over violent conduct. Says it was quite a few years ago, but she was certain she recognised the householder, although it was with a different spouse."

"She'd been out to Jimmy Harding for a previous domestic years ago? Why do we not have that on his file?"

Simpson clicked the attachments. He blew out a slow whistle as they downloaded.

"Get everything we can on this. Now." Taylor dropped Harding's psychiatric evaluation on to the table and pulled out her phone.

Chapter 22

REILLY HAD GUIDED the Vauxhall down the winding bends of Craigantlet into the suburbs of the sleeping city. The midnight glow cast a dome over the valley from the rich farmland on one side to the desolate Black Mountain and the bleak silhouette of Cavehill across Belfast Lough. A Norwegian gas tanker was making steady progress in the thread of black water that lay between blinking anti-collision lights.

The A55 was dead, which was to be expected until the rush hour kicked in after seven o'clock the next morning. The Sydenham by-pass was the same. The neon fronting of George Best City Airport was still ablaze, but the last flight had landed hours earlier to beat the noise curfew and the first commuter flight to the UK wasn't due to lift off until after six. A single taxi was parked in the lay-by below the airport footbridge, the driver catching a doze behind the wheel.

The carriageways turned into arterial suburban roads lined with shuttered shops and the occasional flare of a takeaway that was still open.

Reilly pulled into a cul-de-sac of narrow, manicured hedgerows. The pavement was tree-lined, the terrace houses dark. The single sentinel of a streetlight cast a pool about halfway down. On the turning circle at the end, four larger semi-detached properties stood equidistant from each other, bordered by low redbrick walls and wrought-iron railings. Light seeped between a crack in the curtains of number twenty-three.

"Still awake then," said Macpherson.

Reilly ratcheted the handbrake and killed the ignition. The engine block ticked as it cooled.

"You sure about this?" she said.

"We're here now…"

The front door of the house opened and Colin Cosgrove exited, barefoot and wearing pyjama bottoms and a grey hoody. He was carrying a stack of pizza boxes and an empty milk carton. As he dumped them in the recycling bin, his head jerked up, startled at the noise of the car door opening.

"Jesus. You scared me there."

"Guilty conscience?" said Macpherson, a disarming smile as he approached.

"Has something happened?"

"Colin? Have you left the door open?" Louise Cosgrove's voice drifted from the hallway. The porch carriage light blinked on and illuminated a small front garden with perennials in bloom. A Toyota Avensis was nosed into the narrow drive and a Peugeot was reversed into a smaller paved spot under the front eaves

"Mind if we come in?" said Macpherson.

"Daddy?" Debbie Wright appeared in the light, her face rosy from a scrub. Her hair was piled on top of her head and the fleece collar of her dressing gown was pulled up.

"Is it Julie?"

"Can we come in?"

"Yes. I suppose. We aren't long back from the hospital." Cosgrove offered them entry. Debbie turned and headed for the kitchen, calling her mother.

Macpherson walked into the broadside as he passed the bottom of the stairs and waited for Cosgrove to close the front door.

"What do you want?" Louise Cosgrove was similarly dressed to her daughter, wrapped in a long peach robe. She had a glass of wine in hand. "Has something happened to Julie?"

"Lou, give them a minute. Through there, Sergeant," said Cosgrove, gesturing to the front room. A television flickered in the bay window. A news channel was dissecting the day's headlines from Westminster and around the world. Cosgrove muted the volume and sat on an armchair. The Belfast Telegraph was folded in the seat's seam and two remote controls were lined up on the arm. He picked up a mug from the floor and took a sip of tea.

"Have a seat."

"Never mind a seat. What's going on?" said Louise.

Reilly took a perch on the edge of the three-seater nearest the television and furthest from the door, where Louise Cosgrove brandished an angry glare. Macpherson stood at parade ease. He edged the vertical blinds aside and peered into the drive.

"Your wee car, Debbie?"

"The Peugeot. Yes. Why?"

"Was with your dad when he spotted a nick out of it," said Macpherson, letting the blind fall closed.

"Is this about the bloody tail-light?" said Colin Cosgrove, swallowing another sip of tea. His elbow caught the remote and knocked it to the floor.

"It is," said Macpherson.

"Sergeant, if you've come to my house in the middle of the night to tell me you've found who crashed into Debbie's car…" Cosgrove groaned as he bent to retrieve the control.

"Is that it? You're rapping my door for that when you haven't put that animal Harding behind bars yet? The bastard that took our wee boy and you're worried about a stupid hit and run?" Louise Cosgrove's voice rose, the hand with the glass wavering. "Get out of my house and don't come back unless it's to tell us you've charged that piece of filth. I've a mind to ring Chief Superintendent Law now and tell him where his subordinates' priorities lie."

"Debbie, were you up at White Cottage today?" said Macpherson.

"Me? No." Debbie shook her head.

"You didn't see Julie at all today?"

"I was working."

"All day?"

"Yes."

"Why are you questioning my daughter?" Louise Cosgrove commanded the centre of the lounge.

"Debbie, tell them nothing. What is this, Sergeant?" She set the glass of wine on the mantelpiece and put her hands on her hips. "How dare you come in here at this time of night with this carry on?"

"Mrs Cosgrove, I'm sorry. I understand this is the worst of times, but I've questions I need answered."

"You do. Like, why was he allowed to walk the streets and kill my grandson?"

"When was the last time you spoke to Julie?" Macpherson turned back to Debbie. She shifted, her hands in her dressing gown pockets.

"Two days ago."

"She came for lunch," said Louise. "We had a bit of a catch up. He was making her miserable again. Back running after that tart."

"She wasn't happy," Debbie agreed. She sat on the opposite end of the couch to Reilly. "We told her to just leave him."

"And was she going to?"

"She said she'd think about it. She had Tommy to think of."

"Where did that get either of them? He didn't deserve that wee boy. I hope he bloody rots." Louise snatched up her wine and sank it.

"I think she was going to this time. I do. I really do," said Debbie.

"Are you done? Can this car thing wait until another time?" Colin Cosgrove stood and placed an arm around his wife.

"Not really," said Macpherson.

"For God's sake, I don't need to claim on the insurance or want to press charges. Whoever hit it, let them alone. Concentrate on putting Jimmy Harding away."

"Did Julie take a drink?"

Louise Cosgrove sucked in a breath. Her husband broke in before the fury.

"What's that got to do with anything?"

"Might be something. Might be nothing."

"Get out," Louise snarled. Macpherson let the tension wash over him. Debbie stared at her slippers.

"Debbie?" said Reilly.

"She…"

"Out!" Louise Cosgrove hurled her glass across the room to shatter above Reilly's head.

"Jesus. What's all the bloody noise?" A bleary Daniel Wright entered, wearing a washed out tee and shorts and rubbing his eyes.

"What's going on?" He looked from face to face.

"Nothing. They're going," said Colin Cosgrove.

Reilly stood, flicking shards from her hair and a few large pieces of glass from her jacket.

"I'm afraid we can't," said Macpherson. "Debbie, why were you at your sister's this afternoon? You reversed the car into the gate. There's paint on the post and glass on the drive. The forensic team won't be long in matching it."

"I haven't seen Julie since Wednesday," Debbie Wright protested.

"You were at work all day? Someone can corroborate that?"

"Yes."

"Can you explain what happened to your car?" said Macpherson.

Debbie Wright didn't answer the question. Colin and Louise Cosgrove looked at the DS as though he had sprouted two heads.

"I had the car," said Daniel Wright. He picked up the broken stem of Louise Cosgrove's glass and sat beside his wife. He looked to his in-laws and then at her, his eyes imploring forgiveness. The face of a traitor.

"I had the car. I know why you're here."

Chapter 23

VERONICA TAYLOR SHOOK her head and rubbed her eyes.

"Yes. I'm looking at it now. He's going to go on record?" She moved the phone to her other ear and tapped Simpson on the shoulder. A gesture to hold what he was doing.

"That's something, I suppose. Are you two heading back?"

Taylor moved to the conference table and took an edge. She listened to Macpherson as she looked down at the doctor's evaluations and medical reports.

"No, don't bother. The two of you get home and get some sleep. We'll wrap up here and do the handover in the morning. The DPP needs his two breakfasts before he's firing on all cylinders. Cheers, Doc. Good job. Tell Erin I appreciate her putting up with you." Taylor gave a low chuckle and moved the phone from her ear to avoid the worst of the retort. She stood and moved nearer to her two DCs.

"You don't mean that. See you in the morning. Night."

She killed the call and peered past Cook at the report on Simpson's screen.

"Stabbed?" Cook edged her chair aside to give her inspector better access.

"Stabbed. Scalded. Burned and beaten." Simpson scrolled down the page. "Jesus, this makes grim reading."

Veronica Taylor looked at the wall-mounted screen.

Jimmy Harding hadn't moved, apart from to cross his wrists. His head hung low. His eyes remained focused on a spot on the table and Henry Scott seemed to have given up trying to engage him in conversation, preferring to scroll through his phone. He already had his jacket on, ready to sweep up the formalities to follow.

"How long does this go back?" she asked.

"Three years. Although the complaints weren't raised until the end of the relationship."

Simpson dragged and dropped the data. He added it to the print queue along with the preliminary reports Taylor had just requested from the Forensic team at Seapark.

"That doesn't explain why it didn't go anywhere. This level of abuse? Someone should have caught it." Cook looked from the screen to Taylor. "This is criminal."

"It is, Carrie." Taylor took a deep breath and straightened her jacket.

"Let's go and put an end to it. I want to make sure that little Tommy Cosgrove is the final innocent victim of this."

Chapter 24

HALF A DOZEN electronic chirps. The dull clunk of the lock release and then click clack as it re-engaged.

Veronica Taylor took her seat, placing the evidence folder between herself and Carrie Cook. Cook, sitting sideways on her chair, teased her skirt hem down and then started the recording equipment.

"Interview resumes 1:47 A.M. Same persons present."

"Thanks, Carrie," said Taylor. She sat back and sighed.

"It's been a long day, Jimmy. Mr Scott here looks just about beat." She smiled. Henry Scott huffed a breath and checked the oversized dial of his wristwatch.

"I got it wrong," she said, leaning forward to rest her elbows on the table. "I'm not afraid to admit it. You had me more than once and nearly got away with it too. What I don't understand, Jimmy, is why you would do it?"

Jimmy Harding looked a beaten man. The first and second fingers of both hands had the nails bitten to the quick. His hair was dishevelled and Taylor could smell the fug of anxiety and stress.

He rubbed his forehead.

"Why? Why what? I keep telling you it was an accident."

"I see. OK. We'll do this my way then. Sam?" said Taylor.

Once again the PSNI logo dissolved to be replaced by two scenes of holiday relaxation and a further two snapped on a boozy night out. The last showed a cozy picture of domestic bliss, partners wrapped in a blanket before a blazing log fire.

"Do you recognise the woman on the right, Jimmy?"

"What is this, Inspector?" Scott looked at the images then to his client with an expression of surprise.

"Well, do you recognise the woman?"

"Jeannette Burrows," said Harding.

"Jeannette Burrows. Pretty girl. I'd have given my right arm for those cheekbones when I was her age."

The girl's hair was similar to Taylor's in colour, although shorter, with the luminous sheen of a fresh horse chestnut. She was tanned, with dark eyes and a wide innocent smile. The only flaw was a series of angry scabs on the left arm which held up the camera for the selfie.

"Next image."

Scott flinched, a natural reaction when faced with the horrific contrast between the woman who had been and the woman who now was. Jeannette Burrow's hair, lacking the previous lustre, was scraped back from a pale, frightened face. Her dark eyes were haunted and ringed with angry bruising. Stitches marred the beauty, physical scars that would never heal and were a constant reminder of the psychological damage that she would never get over.

The brutal cuts severed the top lip and gouged a path upwards, slicing through the edge of the left nostril and leaving the apple of her cheek hanging in a loose flap of flesh.

"Brutal, isn't it?" said Taylor.

"Inspector, if you are pursuing this as an additional charge, I suggest you get the formalities out of the way first." Scott turned a few degrees in his seat to better avoid the image in his eye line.

"Are you going to tell him or am I?" Taylor sniffed, folding her hands on the table and searching the top of Harding's head, which faced her.

"Jimmy? I'll ask again. Look at that face up there and tell me why?"

Harding looked up. His face was twisted in pain and grief.

"She didn't mean it."

Taylor slid the folder to the centre of the table and flipped the cover.

"It goes back five years. When I read this and your records side by side I couldn't tell the difference. Did you ever meet Jeannette?"

A tear rolled down Harding's cheek.

"Once." His voice broke. "In town. I didn't know it was her at first. She'd a hood up. Had lost stones in weight. When she saw us I've never seen anyone so scared."

"Do you blame her?"

"Julie said…"

"What did Julie say to explain that?" Taylor snapped.

Harding put his hands over his eyes and shook his head.

"We didn't make the connection at first because she was going by her middle name when we investigated the initial complaints. Ruby, isn't it? I can see why. Suits her in that picture."

They all looked at the image of two young women lounging on a beach, one with glossy chestnut hair and the other with deep red curls. Arms and legs entwined. The look of adolescent love on the faces.

"Started innocuously enough. Trips and falls, minor accidents, and then it got more hot and heavy until Julie,

Ruby, did that."

"Julie didn't mean it. She's ill…" Jimmy Harding paused. The narrowing of Taylor's eyes dared him to follow through with an excuse for the barbarity.

"Is that why you put up with it? Because she has a sickness? Depression? Aggression? Psychopathy?"

"No."

"Sam?"

The images changed to a set of bottles and a slide of finger-print analysis.

"These are on the fly, but we'll have them ironclad for the jury."

"What's this?" asked the solicitor.

"Twenty-one spirit bottles recovered in Mr Harding's outhouse," said Cook.

"Julie is an alcoholic and a violent abuser, isn't she, Jimmy?"

"No."

"Image Charlie, zero one. A shattered wine bottle. The prints around the neck are those of Julie Cosgrove. The blood on the pointy end is Jimmy's," said Taylor. Scott's surprise reached his hairline.

"No!" Harding swept the file off the table, tears of frustration and shame flowing.

"Jimmy, we have a witness."

"No."

"Daniel Wright was at your house today. He saw what happened."

"No." Jimmy Harding pushed back from the table.

"These are the preliminary forensic findings on the weapon discharge. Your prints are on the weapon. Your clothes are covered in gunshot residue and blood. Sam?"

The image on the screen changed to Harding's shotgun in the lab, with arrows, diamonds and text boxes transposed on top.

"You grabbed the barrel. You were trying to disarm her. That's what happened. She had been drinking. She lost control again, but this time hitting you a slap or coming at you with a bottle wouldn't be good enough."

Jimmy Harding leapt to his feet. His breath heaving in panic.

"Freddie Moore had been winding her up, telling her you and Connie were carrying on behind her back again. She took the bait."

"She didn't…"

"Sit down, Jimmy."

Harding paced the room, fists balled.

"Jimmy. It's not your fault. You don't need to keep it hidden any more," said Taylor.

"Jimmy. Is this true?" Scott stood, hands up to pacify his cornered and defeated client.

"It was an accident," Harding screamed.

"Jimmy, come on. Sit down. Tell me. You don't have to be afraid any more. Do it for Tommy. Tell the truth for him." Taylor's voice was calm.

Harding swayed. He put his hands against the wall to steady himself. The colour drained from his face.

Taylor stood. Cook reached for the panic button.

"I'm OK," he mumbled.

"Sit down. It's all right." Taylor took him by the arm and eased him back into the seat. Cook removed her fingers from the button. Scott shifted his seat a little closer.

"I'm sorry," Harding said, the anguish cracking his voice. His eyes were raw, his mouth twisted in grief and pain.

"You don't need to be sorry, Jimmy. It's over. She can't hurt you now."

Epilogue

"I STILL CAN'T believe it." Sam Simpson stared at the holiday image of Julie Cosgrove. A large glass with straw and customary umbrella. A carefree smile. Wind in her hair.

"You never know what goes on behind closed doors, Sam," said Taylor.

Simpson blew out a breath, gave a half shake, half nod of his head and pointed at the monitor.

"What will happen to him?"

"Hopefully he'll get the help he deserves. Family liaison will take over. Now the abuse is out in the open, if he keeps talking his GP will refer him to the proper bodies for help. It's tragic, right enough," said Taylor.

"What about her?"

"She's going nowhere. Her mother will kick up a storm, but as long as the son-in-law stands by his statement, it's cut and dry. He was at the house at the behest of his wife to pick up some bags Julie had promised to her earlier in the week. Heard the argument and saw her brandishing the shotgun. To let Harding take the wrap for it was probably more for the sake of his wife and mother-in-law than any affinity he had to Julie. I'll speak with the DPP in the morning and see how he wants to pursue the formal charge against Julie. Then we wait for Diane Pearson's final evidence reports from the scene."

"To shoot your own kid, though."

"She needs help as much as Jimmy Harding. Has to if

she was going down the road of murder-suicide." Taylor looked at the two young women in the picture. A glimpse at what might have been.

"Maybe her family didn't approve of the relationship with Jeannette. Julie vented her frustrations on her. Eventually she bowed to family pressure and took up with the first fella that came along."

The age-old tale of hurting the ones you love. Burying the truth. Denial and repression building to aggression and a point of explosive release.

"When she fell pregnant and then moved out to the cottage, her mother started again. Julie might have been using the drink to cope with the guilt or because she's turned her back on a different life to please her family and now they still weren't happy. Behind that smiling face, Julie Cosgrove is a very sad and very angry woman. She's ill, Sam."

The image of the happy family lay amid the chaos of the observation room conference table. The gap-toothed smile of a little boy was a harrowing reminder of the tragedy that had struck a picture-postcard cottage in the windswept fields overlooking the sleeping city.

On the monitor, Cook led Harding and Scott from the interview room to appear on the landing lobby camera, where a uniform PC waited. She shook hands with both and spoke a few words to Harding. Sympathies and best wishes. Taylor watched the broken man give a solemn nod. Scott led the way as solicitor and client followed the officer down the stairs, each in their own thoughts as they took the short walk down a few floors to the rear parking bay.

"You did good today, Sam."

"Thanks Guv," said Simpson. He spun his chair round. "I appreciate it." He bowed his head. "Lesson learned. First instincts can be wrong. I'm sorry about that." He gave a grateful smile.

"They can be right, too. We just can't let ourselves be blinded to other possibilities. You did good."

The door access code chirped and Cook entered. The scattered evidence was restored to order under her arm. She kicked a small wooden wedge into place, holding the door open for the room to air and for ease of wheeling the requisitioned files back down to central records.

"You too, Carrie. Thanks. It's been a long day. I appreciate the effort. Take a few extra hours in the morning. I'll get the paperwork vetted for the DPP on Julie Cosgrove."

Both DCs expressed their thanks.

"If you ever want to escape the dark side, Sam, I could use you."

"Leave Inspector MacDonald?"

Taylor laughed.

"You hoping he'll bring you back a set of maracas?"

"No. I appreciate it, but I thought you had a new start coming on?"

"I don't know what you're encouraging them for. They're only doing their bloody job." A gruff voice caught them unawares. Taylor turned to the door with a smile for the red face that entered.

"They need to get that flaming lift fixed." Doc Macpherson bustled into the room with a six pack of cola under one arm and a carrier bag hanging in his big fist. "What? Did you think us two have been running round the countryside all day for you lot to steal the bloody glory from under us?"

"Can you transfer me instead?" said Erin Reilly, another fat carrier bag clutched in her hand.

"Aye. Ronnie, I need to have a word with you about this one. Insults. Insolence. Insubordination…" Macpherson dropped the bag onto the table.

"If I go to HR with a complaint from you they'll laugh me out of the station."

"What's all this?" Cook sidled over. She rustled a finger in the carrier bag. "Indian? Doc, I don't care what they say about you. They have you all wrong. Is that pakora?" She nudged her DS.

"The Maharaja was open so we… I say we, but it was my idea." He winked at Taylor.

"For God's sake." Reilly rolled her eyes and ripped open the carrier. "Never listen to him. Help yourselves. There's enough here to feed the station. Slick, what do you fancy?"

Taylor watched the group huddle around the cartons and debate what looked best. She felt famished but had no appetite. She was wrung out after the day and her mind was still occupied with Jimmy Harding and the days, weeks and months he was about to face. Hopefully, with whatever friendship he had with Connie Moore and the support of the Dereks, he would come through the ordeal. She scooped up the family picture. A last look at the smiling face of a little boy whose life was cut far too short. The next time she would see him he would be on Professor Thompson's slab.

Reilly was dishing out. Cook had a palm full of tandoori pakora and was laughing from behind her free hand as

Macpherson protested against Reilly's refusal to heap another spoonful of biryani chicken onto his naan. The playful banter of the team washed over her. Macpherson smiled and held up a tin of cola.

Taylor closed the file.

"I swear I don't know where you put it. You haven't rested your jaws all day," said Reilly.

Taylor accepted the can from Macpherson's big hand. His eyes wrinkled in mirth. As he opened his mouth to speak she cut across to answer for him.

"You know you can't fatten a thoroughbred, Erin."

INTO THIN AIR

A DETECTIVE INSPECTOR TAYLOR CASE-FILE

PHILLIP JORDAN

FIVE FOUR PUBLISHING

Chapter 1

"AIDO, IT'S ME. Where are you? Ring me back when you get this."

Aoife Quinn stabbed the call-end icon in frustration and gunned the Porsche Cayenne across traffic, the manoeuvre earning a blaring toot of ire and rapid flash of headlights from a beat-up box van driver forced to jab his brakes to avoid a collision.

"When's Daddy coming home?"

"Daddy's at work, Sophie. He'll be back later," said Aoife.

"Why do you keep ringing him if he's at work?"

Aoife adjusted the rear-view mirror and looked at her daughter in the back seat. Sophie batted a plush toy giraffe off the passenger headrest while her twin brothers, at last, dozed quietly.

The SUV juddered as she hit a traffic calming ramp at speed, the twins' eyes snapping open with the jolt. Their mouths and plaintive wails filled the cabin of the car a second later.

Aoife's phone trilled.

"Aido…"

"No, it's me…"

"I told you I'd sort it. Stop torturing me," she snapped.

The twin cries rose to a crescendo as she pulled up outside her house, searching in the central console for the gate release fob. She shushed the crying babies to no avail, as the voice over the hands-free continued to speak, persistently talking over Aoife's attempts to interject. She sighed, impatiently tapping the steering wheel as the gates swung open.

"Look, I'm running late. I've just got in and his car's not here. He told me he would speak to you today himself," she said, pulling up outside a double garage, the electronic handbrake whining as it engaged.

"What do you mean you haven't seen him?" She paused as the caller answered.

Aoife pulled the phone from its holder and got out, thumping the door closed and dampening the sound of the cries inside. External carriage lights illuminated as she paced away from the car, the handset to her ear and tossing her hair out of her eyes as the wind kicked up across the dark expanse of manicured lawn, mature cedars and yew trees creaking as they swayed in the strong breeze.

The house was in darkness and she felt a tight knot of anxiety creep into her tummy as the Porsche's internal light bloomed on and Sophie shouldered the rear passenger door open and climbed out.

Aoife turned as a car passed the closing gates, the twins' cries were growing more agitated from the rear seat. She shifted the phone to her other ear.

"Look, I'll have to call you back."

Chapter 2

"How the other half live, eh?"

Detective Sergeant Robert 'Doc' Macpherson ratcheted up the Volvo's handbrake before the car had quite stopped, kicking up a spray of pink pebbles in the process and drawing the attention of a uniformed constable standing at the entrance porch.

"Is she never away back to her school yet?" he said, clicking back the seat and swinging his legs out.

"Here, take your sweets and try not to antagonise anybody else today, okay?" Detective Inspector Veronica Taylor rustled half a dozen brandy balls from a packet and shoved them into her sergeant's huge hand, the paw at odds with the rest of his stature which had earned him the moniker of one of Snow White's famous friends.

"Sure, I just told him the truth…"

"But how many times have I to tell you? If you can't say anything nice, say nothing at all." Taylor pushed her car door closed as Macpherson popped one of the boiled sweets in his mouth and surveyed the lush lawn.

"Whatever happened to free speech?"

"Come on, will you." Taylor moved off, crunching across the pebbled driveway towards the police constable as Macpherson continued to admire the landscaped grounds.

"Do you think they have one of those ride-on lawnmowers for that?"

"Hi, Leigh-Anne," said Taylor in greeting.

"Ma'am. Sarge." PC Leigh-Anne Arnold nodded in reply as Macpherson trundled across the driveway towards them. Arnold's hands were shoved into the front of her body armour, and her neck warmer, which she had tucked in tight, warded off the early morning chill.

"Have they still not clocked your birth certificate?" said Macpherson, offering out a brandy ball. "Here, one of these will put hairs on your chest." He hawed out a breathy steam, the plume scented with the heat of the boiled candy.

"My mummy told me never to take sweets off strange men," said Arnold, a twinkle of blue eyes set in a baby face.

Before he could reply, the PC's TETRA radio warbled on her lapel. She lowered her mouth and responded.

"Sierra-Seven, received. They're here now."

Arnold jerked her chin towards the front door. Taylor nodded.

"Any developments?"

Arnold shook her head.

"None. Mrs Quinn is inside."

"She on her own?" said Macpherson.

Arnold nodded.

"And she still hasn't heard from her husband?" said Taylor.

"He went for a run yesterday morning before work. She found out later in the day he hadn't made it to the office, and when he didn't return her calls or come home last night, she called it in."

Taylor looked out across the immaculate gardens her eyes eventually settling on the mud splashed Porsche Cayenne parked askew in front of the garage doors. A steady stream of school run and commuter traffic thrummed on the road outside the gates.

"Lead the way, Leigh-Anne. Let's see if we can find a simple explanation of where Mr Quinn has disappeared to."

Chapter 3

"MRS QUINN? I'M Detective Inspector Taylor. I hoped I could ask a few questions about your husband."

Taylor offered a sympathetic smile as she entered the kitchen. Aoife Quinn was rifling through a stack of letters and junk mail, sifting, it seemed, every other page onto a growing pile to one side. In between scanning the sheets, she flicked through a Filofax.

"Mrs Quinn?"

"Sorry." Aoife looked up, her eyes red rimmed through lack of sleep and her voice on the edge of tears. "I'm sorry, I'm just trying to find something. Anything. A note, an appointment I forgot about…"

A phone trilled. Aoife snatched up the untethered landline handset, glanced at the display, and stabbed the end button.

"Bloody nuisance numbers…"

"It's okay. Come and have a seat. This is Detective Sergeant Macpherson. We're here to see if we can help." Taylor laid a hand on Aoife's elbow and steered her away from her fruitless task to a barstool at the wide, marble-topped island.

The Quinn house was a large, detached property on the fringes of Stranmillis. The affluent Malone Road threaded a short distance to the west, while beyond the kitchen's floor-to-ceiling bi-fold doors, the River Lagan meandered toward Belfast Lough under the shade of tall pines. On the other side of the water lay the lush grassland and swaying wildflowers of the Lagan Meadows Nature Reserve.

"You've your hands full there I'm sure," said Macpherson, moving to stand by the large Aga range. He nodded at a sideboard full of photographs. Aoife Quinn followed his gaze, and the dam of tears broke.

"I'm sorry. I didn't mean to…" Macpherson raised his palms as the woman buried her face in hers.

"Stick the kettle on," said Taylor, pulling a wad of kitchen roll from a holder beside the microwave oven. "It's okay, Mrs Quinn, cases like this usually resolve themselves. Come on, why don't we sit over there and you can tell me what's been happening?"

Aoife choked back a sob with a nod and rose, pointing over Macpherson's shoulder.

"There's coffee brewed. Cups are under there," she said with a sniff.

Macpherson clapped his hands. "I don't suppose you've any biscuits to go with it?"

Taylor's lips drew into a tight line, and Aoife Quinn gave a small, exhausted chuckle.

"Top right cupboard," she said, leading the way to a plush cream sofa and glass coffee table arranged to enjoy the view of the river and wild meadows at the bottom of the garden.

"I'm sorry. State of me." Aoife dabbed the tissue to her eyes and dragged in a ragged breath.

"Don't be. It's just stress. Where are the children?" said Taylor.

"My mummy's. She came over and took them for me last night. Sophie was upset, and I was climbing the walls."

"Sophie, your wee girl? She's the spit of you," said Macpherson, handing her a mug of coffee. "I didn't know how you took it so…"

Taylor watched as the woman wrapped her hands around the mug, seeking its comforting warmth. Her gaze drifted out across the lawn as Taylor's took in the surroundings.

The sitting area was well appointed, the sofa complemented by free-standing chrome lamps and contemporary chalk-painted sideboards, the shelves of which, along with the walls adjacent, held snapshots of treasured family memories.

Predominantly the photographs featured the children; the blonde Sophie in days before the arrival of the twins, in parks, on beaches and posing with her proud parents beside a swimming pool, a certificate and ribbon clutched in her hand. Dotted between those were pictures of her two little brothers, their squashed faces captured in the rictus of joy or placid peace as they journeyed from identical Babygros through a range of matching outfits, balanced on the knees of parents and sibling. Their hair was much darker than their sister's, and they very much had the look of their father.

Sophie Quinn was the picture of her mother. She had the same heart-shaped face and long blonde tresses although she did have her father's eyes. Pictures of Aoife and Adrian Quinn's wedding, holidays, and social events showed a handsome, happy couple, and that contentment seemed to deepen in those photographs of them with their children.

Macpherson clunked a plate of Fortnum and Mason shortbread and a sleeve of Godiva Chocolatier biscuits on the table, taking a seat to Taylor's left and raising his mug in gratitude.

"When did you last see your husband?" said Taylor. Quinn nursed her cup, yet to take a sip.

"Yesterday." She glanced at the clock. "About this time yesterday. He was heading out for a run before he went to the office. I was fixing the kids their breakfast."

"You weren't here when he came back?"

"He wouldn't normally come back. He'd head straight on to work and shower and change there."

"This is routine then?" said Taylor

"Yes. He goes running most mornings. Says it chases the cobwebs away and sets him up for the day."

"Fair play to him. If it wasn't for my bladder chasing me out of bed, I'd struggle to get up," said Macpherson, whipping a second chocolate biscuit off the plate.

"You reported he didn't make it to work yesterday, though?"

The warble of a mobile phone cut off Aoife's answer. She plucked the phone from her pocket and once again ended the call, placing the phone atop an iPad that lay on the sofa. She shrugged an apology and Taylor gave a half shake of the head to dismiss the need.

Aoife then took a sip of her coffee, quickly following with a second longer gulp and another shrug.

"I didn't know until late. Sophie was in a state by the time I found out. Adrian always takes her to swimming because by that time of the day I'm putting the boys down. She missed it last night." Aoife put her coffee down beside the biscuits. "I'd been trying to reach him and when I realised the time and he still didn't answer, I called Jackie."

"Jackie?"

"Jackie Mahood. He's Adrian's business partner. I thought they had got caught up in something. Adrian is pushing for an expansion of the firm's business and they've had the odd late one with investors."

"What is it your husband does for a living?"

"He's in renewable technologies."

As she said it, Taylor noted the touchscreen panels that had replaced switches and then the integrated sensors that were dotted about discreetly to control light and heat as needed rather than the conventional technologies that could be found in most homes. The iPad that lay on the sofa beside Quinn was no doubt another device that controlled further aspects of her smart home. She considered it for a moment.

"So it was Mr Mahood who confirmed he hadn't made it in?"

Aoife nodded.

"Was that out of the ordinary?"

Aoife shrugged.

"If it was, Jackie never said. They were supposed to have a meeting yesterday, but Jackie said he never showed up."

"What about work? You said he was in the middle of an expansion. Was he stressed with it? Any problems he talked to you about?"

"Not really. I don't think Jackie and he saw eye to eye on some of the specifics but they both understood it would raise the company to the next level."

"Could you give us the address? I'd like to ask Mr Mahood if he has any inkling as to why your husband might skip their meeting."

"I'm his wife. I think I'd have more of a notion if something was going on with Aido than Jackie Mahood." Her tone grew sharp and a scowl crept across her fine features. Taylor offered a sympathetic smile; the woman looked ragged.

"It's just routine, Mrs Quinn. You'd be surprised at what we can sometimes find with just a different perspective. If this expansion deal did have an element of stress or caused worry, Mr Quinn may have kept it quiet so as not to burden you," said Macpherson.

Aoife nodded, her hand brushing the iPad for non-existent crumbs.

"Has anything like this ever happened before?" said Taylor.

"No," said Aoife.

"And aside from work, nothing else you are aware of that might explain the absence?"

"None."

"You've checked his diary, emails?" Taylor pointed at the iPad. "Can you track his phone location from that?"

"It wasn't set up and I've checked his diary and personal mails. Maybe there was something on his work calendars but I can't access those."

Taylor nodded.

"Okay, I know it doesn't feel like it, but, it hasn't been too long and there's probably a reasonable explanation. We'll make some enquiries and arrange an appointment with Mr Mahood. If your husband does get in touch or you think of anything, any small detail at all, let me know." Taylor pulled a contact card from inside her jacket and laid it on the coffee table.

Aoife picked it up, running a fingertip across Taylor's printed name.

"It's just not like him. He's dependable. He's our rock." Her tears bloomed again, and she sobbed, her throat constricted with emotion as she spoke. "Oh God, what if something terrible has happened? What am I supposed to tell the kids?"

Chapter 4

"That's a sin."

DC Chris Walker stooped to closer inspect the deep gouge in the paintwork of the gunmetal grey BMW i8 Coupe. The scar cut a path from the driver's door handle to the rear quarter panel and couldn't be argued away as an accident.

"I wouldn't leave a shopping trolley around here, never mind a hundred grand motor. If you want my opinion, he was asking for it," said Detective Constable Erin Reilly, who stood at the front end, taking a snapshot of the registration and then a wider angle shot of the vehicle in situ with her mobile phone. The car sat alone in a chevroned bay of the Drumkeen Forest Park car park.

Above and around the two police officers, bird song trilled and the keening of wind rustled through mature woodland. The dense canopy and thickets of the forest park insulated them from the rumble of traffic on the main A55 ring road less than five hundred metres away and offered a sense of peace and calm serenity, albeit the park was caught in the noose of the main arterial road, a commercial shopping park and a nearby housing estate.

"He's lucky the wee buggers over there haven't stripped it for parts or raked it to within an inch of its life," added Reilly, offering a nod to the wall of greenery on the other side of which stood the Drumkeen Housing Estate.

Walker stood back to admire the car's unblemished side, tucking in his shirt tail which perpetually worked its way loose, and calming his hair with the palm of his hand, the wind assaulting a long sandy fringe that was deftly cut but failing to hide a rapidly receding hairline.

"Still, it'll cost a fortune to fix that," he said, wincing.

Reilly walked a circuit of the car, examining the vehicle for any other signs of vandalism or disturbance, but finding none.

"We'll need to find him first to tell him the bad news," she said.

She stooped by the rear driver's side tyre where a handful of cigarette butts were crushed on the tarmac, and a sliver of wrapping and a squashed packet lay half buried eighteen inches into a pocket of long grass.

"Hello?"

Reilly stood, catching sight of a woman walking briskly across the car park. Behind her, the facade of the RSPB's (Royal Society for the Protection of Birds) northern headquarters blended into the undergrowth. The old stone walls were gripped in the thick arms of climbers and wrapped in broad vines of Irish and Boston ivy. The building, which had been repurposed by the wildlife charity, was formerly the stables of the Hill family estate.

"Hello, can I help you?" The woman was in her thirties. Dark shoulder-length hair swept around her head as she walked, and she brushed it out of her face, plucking a strand from recently applied pale pink lipstick. She stopped as she reached them, pushing her hands into the pockets of her gilet. Underneath she wore a thick Aran sweater, prepared for both the unpredictable weather and the muddy paths that wound through the woods, with her black jeans tucked into wellington boots.

"Detective Constable Reilly. This is DC Walker. We had a report about an abandoned car?"

"That was me," said the woman. She half turned, leaning toward the old stables that suddenly looked ominous as clouds rolled across the sun, plunging the path to the entrance door and the forest tracks into twilight. "You'll want to come away in, it looks like it's about to bucket." The woman beckoned, then turned on her heels and walked away.

Reilly glanced across to Walker who was looking to the sky as the first fat droplets of rain hit the BMW's windscreen.

Chapter 5

MACPHERSON'S WORDS OF goodbye caught in his throat as the gates to the Quinn home eased open on hydraulic rams and a dark green Land Rover Discovery gunned across the threshold, churning up pebbles as it traversed the short distance to pull in behind the detectives' car.

"Is this the fella?" he said.

The Discovery's door swung open violently, cracking against its hinges, and a stocky figure stepped out.

"Not him," said Taylor as the man stamped across the drive. She held up her phone. "Erin and Chris have found the car though."

Macpherson gave a harrumph of approval and eased to intercept the scowling figure.

"Can I help you, sir?"

"I wouldn't bloody think so. Is she in?" As he angled to step around the detective sergeant, Macpherson snapped out a hand, the shovel-sized palm stopping the man in his tracks.

Taylor stepped up and reached inside her coat for her warrant card.

"DI Taylor. Have you business with Mrs Quinn?"

"Too damn right I do? Where is she, and more importantly where's that reprobate of a husband?"

The man was half a head taller than Taylor. What hair he did have was ginger and shaved to a fine fuzz. The sideburns and beard were much longer and failing to hide the reddening of his cheeks. A tuft of similar hair sprouted from the open collar of a plain white shirt worn beneath a charcoal pinstripe suit.

"Jackie?"

Aoife Quinn stood on the porch, her expression strained as she rubbed the knuckles of one hand with the palm of the other.

"Where is he?"

"I don't…"

"Mr Mahood is it?" said Taylor.

Jackie Mahood jerked the lapels of his suit jacket and cocked his head.

"It is, aye. So have you lifted him or what?"

Aoife Quinn had taken the steps from her porch and was approaching, while Leigh-Anne Arnold had cracked open the door of the liveried police Škoda and was climbing out.

"Let's just all calm down here, shall we? Mr Mahood, we haven't lifted anyone. Mr Quinn is missing and—"

"Done a bunk more like," said Mahood, cutting over Taylor with a scowl and running a hand across his scalp.

"Have you any insights into where Mr Quinn might have gone or why?" continued Taylor patiently.

Mahood opened his mouth to speak, but Aoife got in first.

"He didn't come home, Jackie. He's not here. I don't know where he is." Her voice was husky with emotion.

"Do you think I do?" he snapped.

"Well do you, sir?" said Macpherson. "Because Mr Quinn's diary says he was meeting with you yesterday and this lady only has your word to say he never showed up!"

"Are you serious?" Mahood looked down at Macpherson's gruff expression.

"If there's anything you can help us with, Mr Mahood, it would be appreciated," said Taylor.

Mahood threw his hands in the air and did a one eighty. When he spun back, he was pointing a finger.

"If I knew where he was I'd carry the bloody head off him," snarled Mahood. He peered over Taylor's shoulder, addressing Aoife. "The investors pulled out last night. Aido shafted the expansion deal because he couldn't keep his trap shut. You want to know where he is? Well, I'll hazard a guess he must be pissed up somewhere working out how to tell you he's just ruined the best chance he was ever going to have of making himself a millionaire, and over what?" Mahood made to say more but cut himself off with an angry shake of his head. "If he shows up tell him to call me."

"Mr Mahood, if you have a minute…" said Taylor.

Jackie Mahood hauled open the Discovery's door in a fit of temper.

"I've not the time or inclination. Phone my PA and she'll set something up. I've a business and a reputation to try to save right now."

Before any more could be said, Mahood slammed the door closed and gunned the engine, the big Land Rover kicking up another storm of pebbles as it roared off down the drive.

Chapter 6

THE OVERGROWN BRANCHES and thickets of luxurious ivy leaf had been clipped back around the red double entrance door of the RSPB visitors centre to afford access, and Reilly, followed by Walker, entered a short hallway of stone tile floor and whitewashed walls. The hallway ended in another door, wedged open to reveal the room beyond, where, fussing with paperwork at an antique desk was the woman from the car park.

"Just as well I spotted you or you'd have been drowned. I'm Laura Roberts." She beckoned them towards her with a wave and a warm smile, moving away from the desk to flip an antiquated Bakelite switch on the wall, the action illuminating the space and the wall to wall displays of natural wonders and curiosities.

The rain hammered off two plate glass skylights and streamed down the four windows that stretched along the gable wall facing the car park.

"Are these all real?" said Walker, an air of wonder in his tone.

"Yes. Well, they were at one stage. Wonderful aren't they?"

Walker nodded his head, jaw slack as he traversed the aisles, slowly moving between cases of taxidermy and woodland scenes set on raised and roped off platforms. Dotted between the displays were photographs of the forest, tall information boards and a plethora of drawings and paintings by visiting school children.

Reilly paused beside a small thicket, depicting a red fox pawing the corpse of a fat moorhen. The animal's muzzle was bloody from the kill, its ears pricked back and tail set in rigid alertness, as beady yellow eyes studied the intruder.

Reilly was absorbed by it, her eyes drinking in the details, the matted down of the bird, the raised red fur along the fox's neck and her paw prints in the soft earth.

A series of short staccato barks sent her heart into her mouth.

"Jesus…"

Chris Walker backed up into a tall display of leaflets and postcards, the carousel racing away on its five wheels to collide with a case of roosting songbirds.

"Olly! No." Laura Roberts clicked her fingers as a small Jack Russell terrier continued to grumble, half in, half out of his bed underneath a display cabinet of red and grey squirrels.

"Flip. My heart's doing a dinger here," gasped Walker.

"Sorry, shush you," cooed Roberts to the dog. "Here. Good boy, into bed." She tossed a baked dog biscuit in beside the terrier and he hopped back into his basket, albeit with a rumble of discontent at having been disturbed. Roberts smiled reassuringly at the two startled detectives.

"His bark's worse than his bite."

"We've a sergeant a bit the same," said Reilly, returning the grin. Her eyes drifted back to the fox which watched her warily. "So, the car, Mrs Roberts?"

"Please, call me Laura."

"You said it's been abandoned?" continued Reilly.

"It's been there since yesterday morning. Hasn't moved an inch. Please." Roberts indicated the two seats parked opposite her own on the other side of the desk.

As Reilly sat, she pulled across a pamphlet resting on the edge of Roberts' desk, the cover showing a murmuration of starlings in flight against the sunset backdrop of the Queen Elizabeth Bridge.

"Stunning isn't it?" said Roberts.

"It sure is. You can see this from our canteen window in Musgrave Street. Is this true?" said Reilly, holding up the leaflet. Its stark title proclaimed the gregarious songbirds' numbers were in free fall, the rapid rate of decline enough to prompt action by environmental and protection groups in a bid to stave off potential extinction.

"Tragically, yes. We are estimating a fifty per cent dip in flock numbers over just the last few years which is astonishing. I've never seen anything like it, and although our research is in the early stages and we are looking at the climate change impact on food supply, there is almost certainly a chain of causation linked to the scale of building development and redeployment of our land use." Laura Roberts sighed. "You'll have seen it for yourself driving over, the city limits have stretched far beyond where they were when we were children."

"Makes you glad for pockets like this," said Walker.

"Islands of tranquillity amid the madness, definitely." Roberts smiled again, the corners of her eyes wrinkling. Her skin was tan from a life spent outdoors, and a band of freckles running from cheek to cheek gave her a youthful look. Walker blushed under the glare of her grin.

"Who's responsible for seeing to the gate, Laura?" said

Reilly. Roberts puffed out her cheeks.

"Could be me or one of the groundsmen. I opened up yesterday and today. That's when I noticed the car was still here," she said.

"And it's unusual for vehicles to be left overnight?" said Walker.

"We try to discourage it." Roberts nodded to a small polite warning notice by the entrance door. "We're close to the estate and while the gates stop cars and motorbikes, you can't stop the kids from climbing over and getting up to mischief."

"But it's still an occasional occurrence?"

"Yes."

Reilly looked at the woman, her face puzzled.

"So why report this one?"

"Well, that's the thing. I've seen the owner of the car several times over the last few months. He arrives and heads out the red track on a run, he's usually back within the hour and then leaves."

"Do you know him?"

Roberts pulled a face, eyes narrowed and mouth twisted noncommittally.

"I know him to see, and you can't exactly miss the car."

"No, she's a beauty," said Walker with an appreciative nod which Roberts returned.

"Spoke to him?" said Reilly, pencil poised above notebook, confident that Roberts would get to her point, eventually. She gave the same expression.

"Hello. Nice day." She shrugged and raised her eyebrows. "I was in here yesterday morning getting sorted for a meeting when I heard a car speed in. You just knew they were flying by the revs, then skidding to a stop. I went out to set the record straight with the driver and there was a jeep, just abandoned, you know? Behind the car, blocking it in." She motioned in the general direction of the BMW.

"Okay," said Reilly, giving a dip of her head. "Can you describe the driver?"

"Yes, I think I can, but that's not the thing…"

"Go on?" said Reilly.

"When I went out, he had confronted the owner of the BMW who was just at the edge of the woods. Neither of them looked happy to see the other, and if I'm being honest, I'd say the two of them looked to be arguing."

Chapter 7

MUSGRAVE STREET STATION was a modern glass and steel structure surrounded by the city's glorious past. The Police Service of Northern Ireland station was wedged between the red brick and sandstone Victorian edifice of Belfast Coroner's Court to the rear and the recently restored chromatic facade of a former ironmongery warehouse to the right. To the left lay the entrance to Victoria Square Shopping Centre and the Jaffe Fountain, the centre's glass viewing dome offering a bird's-eye view across the warren of teeming streets and entries that made up the rest of Belfast City Centre.

While it may have been a modern affair, Musgrave Street station, by the nature of its business, relied upon the remnants of a recent past for protection. The main building was surrounded by a six-foot-high double thickness concrete blast wall and above that, another twelve feet of corrugated steel enclosure was festooned with CCTV cameras to cover all routes past and provide electronic eyes for the manned security sanger on Ann Street.

Royal Irish Constabulary constables who would have stabled their horses and worked out of the old barracks a hundred years before would no doubt marvel at the metamorphosis; so too might they be amazed at how much of the old city and the old tensions remained. The unresolved political and social pressures that plagued the northeast of the isle at times still violently erupted across a city where the distinguished past remained very much in its own battle against the onslaught of modernity.

"Well, isn't that just a weeker?" said Macpherson, leaning back his chair and rolling his eyes. "Your man's vanished into thin air and while I'm out chasing shadows to the point my stomach thinks my throat's been cut, you two are twitching."

"Have you seen this though?" said Walker, pointing an RSPB sponsorship form at his sergeant. Reilly chuckled into her tea, unsure if her partner's enthusiasm for his recent excursion into the city nature reserve was genuine or had been heavily influenced by the willowy Laura Roberts.

"I don't need to go to Drumkeen Forest to see a couple of tits, son," grumbled Macpherson, dropping the front legs of the chair to the floor as Veronica Taylor entered conference room 4.12 to join her team. The inspector paused briefly, holding the door and receiving a comment of thanks from DC Carrie Cook who trailed behind.

"What's the craic with you?" said Cook, setting her laptop on the long table and proceeding to hook it up via a long USB cable to the large-screen monitor that dominated the wall.

"Peter Pecker here is channelling his inner Attenborough," said Macpherson.

Cook smiled as her fingers rattled across the keyboard. Room 4.12 was one of the dedicated meeting rooms set aside for team briefings and, on occasion, for informal interviews. The floor-to-ceiling windows looked out over Ann Street and east towards the Queen Elizabeth Bridge, the Lagan Weir and beyond that, the famous Belfast shipyard and its twin cranes, Samson and Goliath.

"I'm ready, Guv," said Cook. Taylor nodded her thanks and flicked back a few pages in her notes.

"Right, let's see what we're looking at. Do you want to kick off Carrie?" said Taylor.

"Adrian Quinn. Age thirty-four. Bladon Manor, Malone. Call received through triple nine this morning at seven forty-eight am, made by his wife, Aoife Quinn. Mrs Quinn reports her husband is incommunicado. He didn't make it to his place of work and hasn't been seen nor spoken to in twenty-four hours."

Taylor nodded her thanks.

"Doc and I visited Mrs Quinn this morning. As to be expected, she's climbing the walls. The couple have three young children and Mr Quinn going off the radar is completely out of character. Professional man, well liked and stable home life. Carrie?"

Cook dragged the mirror image of her laptop screen to the wall monitor. Taylor flipped through her notes as the DC continued.

"Adrian Quinn. Managing partner of Helios Sustainable," The screen showed the company website and a picture of the man himself, standing with an earnest expression and wearing a hi-vis jacket in a field of solar panels. The banner across the top extolled the Helios mission to empower communities with its safe and affordable renewable energy products while committing itself to engaging in the fight against climate change through innovation and technology.

"Are we sure he was on a run and wasn't down there hugging trees and done himself a mischief?" Macpherson rustled through his jacket pockets, came up empty handed, and scowled at the screen.

"Did you get out the wrong side of the bed again?" said Cook, drawing a smirk from Reilly, as she added another window to the screen to show the younger detective's snapshots of Adrian Quinn's abandoned car.

"I'm only after saying. I could eat the decorations off a hearse. You know we missed our tea rushing back here."

"And the sooner we're all on the same page, the sooner you can get to Butler's and work on your heart attack," said Taylor. Macpherson put up his hands in surrender, and Taylor continued. "We met Mr Quinn's business partner this morning. He confirms Quinn didn't arrive at work, and he's as surprised as anyone regarding the disappearance."

"I'd go as far as to say if we hadn't been called to look for him, we'd have been called to scrape him off his drive. Your man Mahood was raging, whatever the craic is," added Macpherson.

"Mr Mahood's grievance seems to stem from trouble with investors. Helios, according to Aoife Quinn, were in the process of an expansion deal. She mentioned some tension between Quinn and Mahood on the specifics of the negotiations but what I gleaned from Mahood's rant was that the deal has hit the scuppers and something Adrian Quinn has said is behind the derailment." Taylor paused, taking a sip of water. "Mahood wasn't for elaborating this morning but Doc and I have an appointment with the general manager of Helios Sustainable this afternoon to glean a bit more background."

"If the deal has broken down irrevocably, then it might be a reason for Quinn to go to ground," said Cook.

"Aye, and it might be a reason to put him there. Mahood

was talking millions so cocking up might have consequences," said Macpherson.

"Chris, Erin?" Taylor pointed at the image of Quinn's car.

"Guv," Reilly shifted forward in her seat. "BMW i8, registered to Mr Quinn and reported abandoned in Drumkeen Forest Park. There was no sign of forced entry but the damage to the driver's side looks malicious."

Cook homed in on the long ragged scar.

"Ms Laura Roberts confirms Quinn as a regular visitor to the park and that she could place him there yesterday morning but she didn't see him leave."

"What time was this?" said Taylor.

"Approximately eight am."

"Which lines up with what the missus is saying," agreed Macpherson.

"Laura reported another vehicle on scene. A jeep. It blockaded Quinn's car and then he and the driver had an altercation," blurted Walker.

"Laura, now is it?" said Macpherson with a sly wink. Walker flushed.

"Ms Roberts, sarge. Sorry, Guv… I…"

"Pay him no heed, Chris. What kind of altercation?" said Taylor, with a look and a half shake of the head at her grinning sergeant.

"Initially she said it was verbal, and reading between the lines as she described it, I'd hazard a guess the two men knew each other." Reilly jerked her chin to Cook, who selected another file from the database.

"This is CCTV from the RSPB building. It's not very good but you can see Quinn arriving, then shortly afterwards, a second vehicle. Looks like a dark Range

Rover, but the quality isn't good enough to get a plate and the camera covering the parking bay and the path beyond was useless."

Cook had hit the play icon and the grainy black-and-white image of Quinn's distinctive coupe, followed shortly by the other vehicle, played in jittery time-lapse.

"Ms Roberts said the verbal turned into a scuffle. She went inside to get one of the groundsmen for assistance, but when they returned the unidentified male was back in his car and reversing off. She reports seeing Quinn resume his run," said Reilly.

"Did she get a description?" Macpherson peered at the image as Cook spun back frame by frame.

"IC One male, mid to late thirties, shaven head. Not much more."

"Could be Mahood. He has a buzz cut, and he drives a Land Rover," said Macpherson.

"I'm not sure if that's the same model, and you can't tell the colour," said Taylor. "Play it through again for us, Carrie."

Cook hit play, and the five watched first Quinn's and then the mystery car roll down the single tarmac track overshadowed by tall trees and pass across a cattle grid before disappearing from view.

"Carrie, let's assume Quinn came from his home along Malone and then onto the A55 ring. Can you access traffic cameras between Drumkeen Drive and the Minnowburn Road junction and see if ANPR caught him?" said Taylor, her mind tracing the most direct route from Quinn's home at Bladon Manor and the forest park.

"Let me try. Say between seven thirty and eight am?"

Taylor nodded and Cook began a short process of logging remotely into the traffic incident control centre. A few minutes later she had isolated the appropriate gantry cameras covering the dual carriageway that encircled the south of the city. "Call me out the reg, Chris," said Cook. Walker obliged and a minute later she had an image of the coupe travelling north toward the Drumkeen Estate. A few seconds after that she caught the 4x4.

"He's flagging him down," murmured Walker. The team watched the footage as the coupe was trailed by the bigger vehicle, its lights flashing as it aggressively drove through the morning traffic to latch onto the tail of Quinn's BMW.

"Bingo," said Cook, freezing the frame as the second of the two cars turned left into the estate and towards the entrance of the park. She switched tasks to run a vehicle PNC check on the registration now caught on screen, and waited patiently for a result. "Dark blue Ford Everest. No markings. Vehicle comes back to a Raymond Kilburn. Flat 3C Drumkeen Walk."

Macpherson hissed out a breath. Cook raised her eyes from the keyboard to look at Taylor. The inspector had a crease between her eyebrows as she studied the image on screen, searching the blur of the windshield for the face behind the wheel.

"Raymie Kilburn is known to us. He's got form for theft, minor assault and extortion, and he's on the fringes of the local paramilitary gang that operates out of the Drumkeen Estate. We suspect he's involved in loan sharking for them. Chasing up debts, meting out punishments for non-payments, all that good stuff."

"Why would he be chasing Adrian Quinn into the forest

for a barney though?" said Walker, the question as much to himself as anybody else. Macpherson harrumphed.

"That's what you're going to have to ask him, son." He pointed at the image of Kilburn that Cook had dragged up from his e-record. "But keep your wits about you while you're doing it because that bugger would steal the eye out of your head."

Chapter 8

FOR A FUTURE-facing company engaged in fast-paced technological advancements and innovation, the premises of Helios Sustainable was, when viewed down the narrow approach road on the Forest Hill Industrial Estate, distinctly underwhelming.

The warehouse and industrial unit was sprawling, taking up the entire southern end of the small industrial park with office and production facilities comprising drab grey brickwork topped by lime green cladding. The entire compound was surrounded by a galvanised anti-climb perimeter fence and dotted with CCTV cameras.

There was no gatehouse so Taylor drove the Vauxhall straight through the open gate, following a sign which pointed to a dozen free visitor spots.

"Looks like Mr Personality is here right enough," said Macpherson, crunching down on a cinnamon lozenge and pointing to Jackie Mahood's Discovery. The vacant spot beside it was marked by a brushed stainless steel sign bearing the name of Mr A. Quinn, Director.

"It's a bit more dilapidated than I thought it would be," said Taylor, cutting the ignition and unfastening her seatbelt.

"It's what's on the inside that counts, Ronnie. Have I taught you nothing," said Macpherson with a wink, pocketing the remainder of his sweets and stepping out into the forecourt.

Helios' double entrance doors were framed by two large potted conifers and beyond the glass, they could see a more modern reception area than the outside gave credit for. Macpherson had paused a few metres ahead of the car and as Taylor turned to blip the locks, both turned their heads to raised voices as the front doors opened.

"You tell that to your solicitor, Jackie. I'll see you in court."

"You're damn right, you will. I'll have you for every penny, you two-faced bitch," snapped Jackie Mahood. He held the door open and glared after the retreating woman, tie loosened and shirt sleeves rolled up. Both antagonists had faces like smacked backsides and sensing the presence of others the woman bit back a further retort and hefted the box she carried higher in her arms, angling off to the right towards a silver Mercedes.

Mahood watched her go with a sour look of contempt on his face.

"You better not be here to torture me. I told you this morning to make an appointment," he said, shifting slightly to bar the police officers entrance while keeping an eye on the Mercedes which gunned to life and roared out the gate, a spray of gravel and trail of exhaust in its wake.

"Anybody would think you're avoiding us, sir?" said Taylor with a smile.

"I'm up to my bloody eyes so I am."

"So your PA said. We're here to see Richard Seawright." Taylor waited patiently to see if Mahood would relinquish the threshold. He grunted.

"Any sign of that other waste of space?"

"If you mean Mr Quinn, then no. Not yet, sir," said

Taylor.

"Jackie? Margaret's just told me you sent Kate home…" Behind Mahood, another man was badging through the reception turnstile. He caught himself as he saw the visitors.

"They're all yours, Dicky," said Mahood, letting the door go. Macpherson caught the brushed steel handle in a big fist. "And Kate won't be coming back. I'll be in my office."

Richard Seawright looked from the faces of the two police officers to his boss's retreating back, swallowing a few times to take in the sudden pronouncement.

"Mr Seawright, Detective Inspector Taylor. This is DS Macpherson." Her voice seemed to break the spell and Seawright nodded, bidding their entry into the reception proper.

"Sorry about that. He's under some serious pressure."

Taylor watched as Mahood graced the top step of a wide floating stairway, glancing back over the balustrade towards her for a moment before breaking the look and striding on. There was a nip of stress to his features certainly, and that could be expected given the weight of responsibility for the business having been thrust solely upon him, but there remained a brash and bullish bravado that had been apparent earlier that day; it was one of the tells that piqued her senses. Her job was to investigate crime, uncover its perpetrators and bring them to book and Taylor did that ninety per cent of the time by following the evidence, which was unequivocal, and by reading people. She had arrested and charged enough individuals portraying the same demeanour over the course of her career to know Jackie Mahood was hiding something. A front of arrogance or incredulity always came first, more often than not giving way to anger and then to quiet resignation as the truth was pulled thread by thread from the chaotic tapestry of an investigation until finally, like the denouement of a magician's trick, all was revealed and then in quiet resignation the suspect would lay out mitigation for their crime while their solicitor started bargaining.

How long any of that took varied, but Taylor knew she would get there in the end. If Seawright was correct and Mahood was under pressure, then he would make mistakes and she would be there to pick them apart and confront him, but for the moment, she couldn't be sure whether those would lead to the location of Adrian Quinn or something else entirely.

❖❖❖

"I told you not to judge a book by its cover," Macpherson wrapped his big hands around the two-inch galvanised steel tubing that formed a safety railing at the edge of the gantry where they stood overlooking the Helios production area. He gave a quiet whistle of admiration and to his left Richard Seawright smiled, his chest inflated with pride at the stunned expressions of the two detectives.

"What exactly are we looking at?" said Taylor, nodding appreciatively at the hustle of gowned and masked employees fervently beavering away at their workstations, the gleaming area below reminding her more of a sterile hospital environment than a manufacturing facility.

"This is a final testing area. Once we have established the cells perform as expected and comply with industry standards they move into the final phase of cleaning and defect inspection beyond those curtains." Seawright pointed a finger towards a set of heavy rubber crash barriers that segregated the test bay from the area beyond.

Taylor skim read the framed promotional material set at strategic intervals along the walkway. The info dumps were a means to showcase the impressive set-up Helios had established, and to educate and inform those who took the factory tour be they school children, paying customers, or canny investors.

"Hard to believe it's just sand," said Taylor, turning again to look down on the army of testers.

"Essentially." Seawright laughed. "Silicone really, which is the main component of beach sand. Given seventy per cent of the earth is covered in water it makes it the second most abundant resource on the planet."

"You must have some squad down on Portstewart stand with their buckets and spades, Mr Seawright," said Macpherson, shaking his head.

The plant manager chuckled again, relishing the opportunity to regale someone else with his passion.

"Each of the photovoltaic panels is crafted precisely and soldered together in our manufacturing area. The cells are then integrated into our patented matrix frame, which we offer to market. Our most common being the sixty-cell but we are seeing an uptake in our forty-eight-cell residential frame as well as the larger seventy-two-cell. You have to be looking for it but if you're travelling up the M2 towards Antrim you can see one of our first solar farm installations. The site was formerly twenty acres of arable farmland, and the land and the installation cost five million pounds but when you consider it will generate the owners half a million a year in energy surplus, you can see the investment potential, and that's before subsidies."

"Daylight robbery," said Macpherson, stony faced and taking the offered chair next to Taylor.

"We're making money while the sun shines, sergeant, of that there is no doubt," said Seawright with a grin. He had ensconced himself behind a utilitarian desk. The walls of his office were decorated with technical drawings of the Helios PV system and hi-res promotional photographs of deployed equipment along with a few of himself, Jackie Mahood, and Adrian Quinn at a business awards event. The centrepiece of the wall behind Seawright was a prestigious looking scroll proclaiming Helios Sustainable as winner of the Renewable Energy Innovation Design Award. A matching laser cut glass trophy sat on the desk.

"Who's that?" said Taylor, pointing out a photograph of the three men and two women.

Seawright's grin died.

"You mean the lady on the left? That's Katherine Clark."

"That's who we just saw leave, yes?" said Taylor, returning her gaze to Seawright. Never one to miss and hit the wall, she had decided on broaching the uncomfortable subject as soon as the opportunity arose.

"It is," Seawright winced. "It's unfortunate, and I expect temporary. I'm sure Jackie will calm down given time."

"Calm down? That man? If you don't mind me saying, he looks like he's fit for a stroke," said Macpherson.

"Who is she?" said Taylor. Seawright glanced at the picture, evidently taken during happier times.

"Kate is Adrian's PA. The other woman is Margaret Dawes, Jackie's. That was the night we won highly commended at the Irish Energy Awards."

"Has she been dismissed?" said Taylor, frowning.

"It's complicated."

"Mr Seawright, you've just spent half an hour explaining irradiance, power output and temperature tolerances." Taylor raised a brow and sat a bit straighter. Seawright let out a breath. "Is it to do with Mr Quinn's disappearance?" she asked, offering a route into the conversation.

Seawright nodded, then abruptly stood and strode to the window, cracking it open a few inches before returning to his seat. His cheeks were flushed.

"We are working on a fairly aggressive expansion. We have plans to triple our production capacity with the building of another plant and we've also secured locations to establish a further four solar farms, which had been granted approval by the office of regional development and would have allowed us to operate carbon neutral as well as generate a significant return of spare capacity to the grid."

"Would have?" said Taylor. Seawright nodded slowly.

"There was a meeting scheduled to finalise the plans with the department of regional development, the planning service NI and our investors but unfortunately it was hijacked."

"Sorry, you've lost me now?"

"An environmental protest group got wind of our expansion plans and set up a picket outside. The meeting was deferred and subsequently, a formal notice of complaint has been lodged with the minister of infrastructure and a planning breach submitted to the council."

"I thought the tree huggers would be lining up to hang garlands around your necks?" said Macpherson, his face creased in confusion. Taylor gave the leg of his chair a kick. Seawright shook his head sadly.

"We are committed to ensuring Northern Ireland is at the forefront of the renewable revolution and confident that our products and innovations can reduce carbon emissions and pave the way for a cleaner greener future…"

"But?" said Taylor.

"But you can't make an omelette without breaking a few eggs," said Seawright. "There is some concern, setting aside the positives of clean energy, the employment, and the reduced impact of fossil fuels, that repurposing the land will be detrimental from a conservation standpoint. Given that it's arable land, the objection is that habitat will be destroyed, the ecology of the area will suffer and that's setting to one side the impact of a two-year construction plan."

Taylor nodded slowly, beginning to understand.

"Mr Mahood thinks Katherine Clark blew the whistle."

Seawright nodded.

"Better than that, he had IT check her hard drive, and he found an email."

"But surely she understood the benefits?" said Macpherson.

"You would think so, sergeant."

"What did Mr Quinn say?" asked Taylor.

"Defended Kate to the hilt, as could be expected," said Seawright, the last uttered in an undertone.

"What do you mean by that?"

"Adrian argued she was entitled to hold an opinion and was confident that the issues could be argued away when judged against the merit of the project. He claimed it was healthy to encourage debate and find ways around those initial detrimental impacts."

"But Mr Mahood wanted her gone?"

"He did. He was very vocal about it."

"Mr Quinn won out?"

"Kate has worked *closely* with Adrian since day one," said Seawright. The emphasis wasn't lost on either detective. "Jackie bought into the firm a few years ago. Adrian had grown the firm from his shed to what you see today, but we wouldn't be looking at the future we are without Jackie. Off the record, he thinks Kate clouds Adrian's judgement and gets away with it because she has been beside him for the whole journey and gets more of a say than her position should allow."

"When did all this come to light, Mr Seawright," said Taylor.

"The planning approval meeting was to take place three days ago. Myself, Adrian and Jackie, and the Health, Safety, Quality and Environment team were to meet yesterday to formalise a response to the objections, but Adrian was a no-show and then Jackie's investment backing pulled out. I suppose I have to say at the minute, it all looks quite bleak."

Taylor sat back and turned her attention to the photograph of the smiling faces. She couldn't help but agree. It did look bleak, for the company's grand plan, Katherine Clark's immediate employment future and most of all for the missing Adrian Quinn.

Chapter 9

"UH-HUH?"

Raymond Kilburn stood framed in the opening of his front door. He was as described and fitted the caricature of the hard man to a T.

A receding hairline was clipped back to the scalp, leaving a fine suede of dark five o'clock shadow, and his face told the tale of too many scraps. His nose was flattened and a heavy bovine brow overhung puffy brown eyes, with evidence of a more recent incident glaringly obvious by the plaster over his right eyebrow and a blooming black eye beneath.

A tattoo of a pair of red lips kissed the right-hand side of his thick neck, which rolled into broad muscled shoulders and a barrel chest squeezed into a regulation two sizes too small black tee shirt. From inside the flat came the snarling bark of at least two dogs.

"Raymond Kilburn?" said Walker, forcing his voice an octave lower and pulling back his shoulders.

"You knocked the door, who were you looking for?" Kilburn nonchalantly leaned against the frame, crossing one ankle behind the other.

"DC Reilly. DC Walker. Do you have five minutes for a chat?" Reilly held out her warrant card, looking over Kilburn's shoulder to the hallway beyond.

"I didn't know you lot were doing social calls? You'll be wanting tea and custard creams next?"

"Do you mind if we come inside?" said Reilly.

"Do you not need a warrant for that?" Kilburn smiled, the movement doing little to soften his features.

"Do we need one?"

Kilburn chuckled and rolled his eyes. "Hang on a minute."

Before either of the detectives could speak, Kilburn slammed the door closed, the black knocker rattling hard against the PVC and setting off another series of loud barks from inside. Walker quickly stepped back down the steps towards a path that led around the side of the flats.

"Where are you going?" Reilly spun around as Walker dug in his jacket for his TETRA radio. The look on his face said he wasn't taking the chance their lead was flying the coop.

The front door opened again. Kilburn, taken aback at only seeing Reilly, moved to peer past her to a stuttering Walker.

"Did you think I was doing a runner or something? You lot have no faith in people. Come on in."

The hallway was gloomy but clean and a plug-in air fresher was winning the battle with the whiff of damp dog. The offender, barks having died to a low grumble, was peering over a child safety gate fastened across the kitchen door. Kilburn turned right into the lounge, flopping down on an armchair.

"I should thank you really," he said, gesturing to the television. "You've saved me from listening to that lot drone a load of shite." The TV was tuned to an afternoon magazine show, the panel discussing the day's current affairs, celebrity gossip and showbiz news. He muted the cackling presenters and gestured to the sofa. The lounge was bright and overlooked the main road where the dark blue Ford Explorer was parked. Beyond, a wall of trees could be seen on the other side of four flat football pitches bisected by the driveway into Drumkeen Forest Park.

The arm of Kilburn's chair and the laminate floor had lost the battle to the dog, scratches and teeth marks having been gouged from the edges of each.

"Did you think you were going to find the place stacked with gear?" said Kilburn clocking Walker's observations. The DC blushed.

"So, to what do I owe the pleasure?" said Kilburn.

Erin Reilly pulled out her notebook and shuffled forward on her seat.

"Is that your car down there, Mr Kilburn?"

"You're the detective, love."

"We're investigating an incident over at the forest yesterday," said Reilly. Kilburn sniffed, a hand unconsciously going to the plaster over his eye then dropping back to the arm of the chair.

"Oh aye, what's it to do with me?"

"Do you recognise this man?" Walker held up his mobile phone, the screen displaying a picture of Adrian Quinn in a business suit.

Kilburn's lips twisted, but he didn't reply.

"He's missing," said Reilly.

"Again, what's that got to do with me." Kilburn shrugged. He had retrieved the remote control for the TV and bounced it off the fabric of his chair.

"ANPR cameras on the carriageway show your car flashing its lights and driving aggressively to intercept another vehicle." Reilly jerked her head in the direction of the A55. "Cameras from the forest park drive show you tailed the vehicle to the parking area and an eye witness places a man fitting your description and this man in an argument."

"Couldn't be much of an eye witness," mumbled Kilburn with a shake of the head, an expression of annoyance flashing across his face.

"For the record, are you saying they're mistaken?" said Reilly.

"I'm saying their eyes must be painted on."

Reilly could see agitation beginning to rise in Kilburn. The gentle tapping of the remote had turned into a slightly more aggressive stabbing motion.

"You're not denying anything then?"

"I'm not admitting to anything either," snapped Kilburn.

"I'm not asking you to admit anything, Mr Kilburn. We're trying to find a missing person and regardless of the circumstances, you may have been one of the last people to have seen him."

Kilburn paused the abuse of the remote control and looked at Reilly, his eyes narrowing.

"Do you think I'm daft? If this boy turns up dead or injured, you'll be looking at the last person to have seen him as the culprit."

"If you know that, then you know that's the likelihood," said Reilly with a shrug. "Victims either know their attacker or it's the last person to be seen in their company. Give us a reason to rub you off the list."

"I don't know him," said Kilburn.

"But?" said Walker, sensing the hesitation in the

statement.

"I did have a barney with him."

"Yesterday?"

"Aye, yesterday."

"Can you tell us what it was about?"

"Oh aye, the arrogant bastard nearly killed my dog."

Reilly shared a look with Walker.

"Mr Kilburn, you chased this man along the ring road, blocked his car in and had an altercation in front of a witness. There was no mention of a dog present?" said Walker.

"That's because she's in there recovering." Kilburn stabbed a thumb towards the kitchen. "I see your man in his fancy car most days heading into the park for a run. I'm normally on my way back out with Duchess. Anyway, start of the week we were the other way about, the frigging car's electric and you don't hear it until it's on top of you. The wee dog stepped out, and he clipped her. Bastard just drove on."

"You didn't report it?" said Walker. Kilburn laughed and looked at Reilly.

"Is he new to this?" Reilly waited on him to elaborate further. "Of course I didn't report it, sunshine. I knew the dickhead would be back and there was more chance I'd get through to him than you lot."

"Mr Kilburn, I have to warn you, taking matters into your own hands isn't a sensible option," said Reilly, marking a note in the book to review Kilburn's history in relation to section 39 assaults.

"You're telling me," said Kilburn with a huff of breath. Silence hung in the air for a beat until he shifted forward in his seat and waggled a finger at Reilly's notebook. "I hope you do find the bastard and do you know what? You're right."

Walker raised an eyebrow, shaking his head as Kilburn shifted his gaze between the two police officers.

"I want to report a hit and run and I want to report an assault."

"Mr Kilburn—" said Reilly, but Kilburn cut her off.

"You want to show me that I should keep my nose out of it and you're worth your salt, then you stick it to the bastard that did this." Kilburn jabbed two thumbs in the direction of his face.

Reilly focused on the split skin under the broad plaster and the glorious purple haze around his eye.

"Your missing man smashed me in the face with a bloody big log. I know you've been sitting there thinking I'm the one with the history of violence but have you even took the time to look past his fancy car and bloody three-piece suit?"

When neither detective responded, Kilburn sighed and slumped back in his chair.

"I didn't think so, but I tell you this for nothing. If he had the balls to do this to me and think nothing of the consequences, then who else has he been stupid enough to get on the wrong side of?"

Chapter 10

"I SUPPOSE IT'S five o'clock somewhere," said Macpherson.

Katherine Clark shook her head wearily and set her glass beside an uncorked bottle of Dönnhoff Riesling. Taylor, entering the open-plan lounge behind her detective sergeant, noted by the remaining contents that it wasn't her first tipple of the day.

"Obviously, I'd offer you some but you're on duty," said Clark.

"By the look of things you've been released from your work responsibilities for the moment." Taylor jutted her chin to where the box of personal effects from her workspace at Helios sat on a stool pulled out from the breakfast bar.

Katherine Clark had piled her hair up on top of her head and divested herself of the smart check, navy two-piece suit and camel overcoat she had worn earlier in the day, to wear a pair of black skinny jeans and check shirt over a white vest top.

Double doors to a Juliette balcony at the front of the apartment were open and the hum of steady traffic threading along the main arterial route of the Lisburn Road droned in the background, competing with the melodic rhythm of pop music stemming from an Alexa device on the kitchen worktop.

Clark's apartment overlooked a block of thriving

shopping outlets. Directly opposite her balcony, a queue had formed outside a Caffe Nero, and the shops, boutiques, wine bars and restaurants alongside seemed to be enjoying an equally brisk trade. The windows at the other end of the open-plan living space offered a view out over an M&S food hall and across the roofs of terraced streets to the Boucher Road and the imposing smudge of Divis and the Black Mountain beyond.

"A temporary blip," said Clark.

"You expect Adrian Quinn to be back then?" said Taylor. Clark fussed with her hair and shrugged.

"Even if he's not, Jackie Mahood will be on the phone before the week's out when he realises he hasn't a clue about anything other than his way around a profit and loss account."

"You've no idea where Adrian could be?"

"No." Clark shook her head.

"Is Adrian the type of man who keeps secrets?"

"He's the more introverted of the two but I wouldn't say secretive, no."

"Richard Seawright tells us you've been there from the start, that you worked closely with Adrian. Are you sure he never mentioned anything, gave away any hints something may be bothering him, or share any concerns?" said Taylor, taking the offered armchair as Clark moved away from the small kitchen island and sat on the sofa opposite, curling her legs underneath her.

"I bet you that's not all he bloody told you."

"Would you like to tell us your side of it?"

Clark sighed and rubbed a hand over her eyes.

"Where do you want me to start?"

"Beginning's as good as anywhere," said Macpherson, nudging down beside Taylor and offering across his packet of brandy balls which Clark declined.

"Adrian and I used to work together at an electrical contracting firm. He spotted a gap in the market for photovoltaic panels when they first came on the scene way back. He's wild for wanting to know how things work so over a few years he had pulled what was on the market apart enough times to understand there was a more efficient way of building them while improving the aesthetic and the output. He started a cottage industry out at the house and then when he moved out of the shed up to the unit he brought me across as an administration manager."

"Smart buck then, is he?" said Macpherson, crunching down on a sweet.

"More brains than he knows what to do with," agreed Clark.

"And you'd agree he's not the type to drop off the radar?"

Clark shifted as she addressed Taylor, dropping one foot to the floor.

"It's not like him, but then things had got quite heated over the last while."

"With the issues surrounding the expansion project?" said Taylor.

"Not just that. I suppose you have to understand the relationship between him and Jackie."

"They're business partners," said Macpherson, giving a stiff nod. "In cahoots to make a ton of money and from what we saw at the factory they're doing that alright."

"We *were* on track," said Clark, pursing her lips and giving a reciprocal nod.

"You were?" said Taylor.

"I mean until all this."

"And the relationship between the two partners?"

"Not what it used to be," said Clark with a shake of the head.

"Any specific reason other than the leak of the expansion plan to the environmental group?" said Taylor. Clark's lips set in a tight line and she pressed herself back into the sofa, drawing her foot from the floor again.

"It wasn't a leak."

"I don't think that's how your boss is choosing to see it," said Macpherson.

"The thing you have to understand about Jackie is he wants the last word. It's his way or no way and Adrian was getting fed up with it." Clark abruptly stood. She moved to the kitchen island and retrieved and recharged her glass of wine, aiming it at the two detectives as she returned to her seat. "Adrian and I built that company from the ground up, there would be no business if it wasn't for him, but Jackie thinks because he bankrolled some investment that he can have the final say and he's not shy in casting up how he could take his investment and move on."

"You're saying he was strong-arming Quinn for control?" said Taylor.

"Do you not call it blackmail or something?" said Clark, taking a long sip of the Riesling.

"Blackmail only works when you have something that compromises the injured party and you're willing to leverage it for gain," said Macpherson.

"And I'm saying Jackie was threatening to reconsider his investment if Adrian didn't agree to his scope for the expansion." Clark's hand, not occupied by the glass, gesticulated to emphasise her point.

"Well, one thing's for sure the expansion and any big payday is off the table now the cat's out of the bag and you've more objections coming in than beaten dockets after the Grand National." Macpherson gave Clark a stiff nod and sat back in his seat.

"What specifically were Jackie's demands, Katherine?" said Taylor.

"He'd highlighted half a dozen sites for solar farms. Typical Jackie had beat the owners over the head with his cheque book and acquired four straight off the bat. Adrian was aware there might be cause for objection on a couple of them and wanted to thrash out a conservation plan before word got out. Jackie wanted the train to be too far out of the station to turn back. One of the sites Adrian point-blank vetoed." Clark took a sip of her wine.

"Do you know his reasons for the veto?"

"He said the land wasn't suitable, something to do with subsidence or substrate. For whatever reason Jackie wanted that tract and was willing to use the threat of pulling his shares out of the business if he couldn't have it."

"Would you be able to tell us where these sites are?" said Taylor. Clark nodded.

"It will be public record now. Three were on a crescent of agricultural land between Drumbeg and Carryduff with another inside the city limits on a patch of council-owned ground marked for redevelopment."

"Thanks, I'll take a look at them." Taylor scratched a note

to research the sites and their significance, if any. She closed her notebook and set it on the arm of the sofa, appraising Clark, whose cheeks had developed a tint of rose either from the wine or her frustrations at the actions of Jackie Mahood and her sudden unemployment. "Katherine, you don't have to answer this, but did you leak the information on those proposed developments knowing it would halt progress and spite Jackie?"

Clark gave a single, silent nod.

"Publicity is a double-edged sword," said Taylor.

"One I've just fallen on." Clark gave a weak smile.

"Did Adrian Quinn ask you to release that email?"

Clark didn't nod straight away, but she did and then followed it up with a half shake that wobbled the hair piled up on her head.

"Adrian built the business and our reputation through relationships, not by steamrolling people or tying objections up in red tape. He was confident that dialogue would see the proposed production facility given the green light, and the protests assuaged by ensuring all the environmental responsibilities of the build were met and any impact offset by creating a biodiverse parkland around the factory."

"And Jackie?"

"Crunched the numbers and said an injunction would cost less in time and material."

Taylor took a breath and pondered what she had learned from the woman. Her gut told her Katherine Clark was, so far as she herself knew, telling the truth. That truth may be skewed somewhat in her loyalty to Adrian Quinn, but given what she had seen of Jackie Mahood, she couldn't argue with the label of hard-nosed businessman and bean counter. Clark interrupted her thoughts, setting the empty glass on the floor and leaning forward, eyes searching each of the detectives.

"You need to understand that's the man Aido is," said Clark. "He stands up for what he believes in. We've taken a financial hit lately but he still put people and protection of the environment above pure profit. We've had ups and downs in shifting the retail focus from fossil to renewables and this year alone we've had two suppliers tank and we'll never see our money come back. Adrian knew Helios needed this expansion to climb out of the hole, but he wasn't going to compromise on his beliefs. He hasn't made one redundancy in the lifetime of Helios and he re-mortgaged to make sure he didn't have to this time either."

"He must have been confident the gamble would pay off?" said Taylor, taking up her notebook and writing a bullet point to check Quinn's bank records.

"It wasn't a gamble to him. He knew by putting the word out and going about addressing objections in the right way, it would pay dividends in the end."

"But he couldn't be seen to do it himself," said Taylor.

"He didn't need to do it himself. He had me, and I'd do anything he asked." Clark's tone was assured and unapologetic. Taylor snapped her notebook closed and returned it to her inside jacket pocket, setting her gaze on the woman opposite.

"Katherine, was your relationship with Adrian purely professional?"

Clark opened her mouth to deny it and then shook her head instead.

"What has that got to do with—"

"Adrian Quinn is missing, and it's my job to ensure he returns to his life safely. The reasons why he has disappeared are likely to stem from personal or professional challenges he has been facing so I'd appreciate it if you were straight with me."

"Aido wasn't just my boss, he was my best friend," said Clark, her eyes welling up as Taylor's words hit home. During the moment it took for Clark to compose herself, Taylor reassessed what she had seen of the apartment and gleaned from the woman's body language.

"Did you ever cross the line with him?"

"Was I sleeping with him?"

The two detectives waited in silence for her to answer her own question.

"Once. We slept together once, before the boys came along."

"And that was it?"

"That was it. It wasn't a mistake, it just wasn't meant to be," said Clark, her voice thickened with emotion.

"You love him, don't you?" said Taylor.

The dam of the day's emotions broke and Clark tipped her head forward to hide the tears, but they dripped like raindrops onto her jeans.

Taylor sensed the pain of emptiness and loss radiate from the woman to saturate the fabric of the apartment which, like the owner, was delicately feminine and perhaps a bit clinical, but most apparent of all was missing the heart that would make it a home.

She opened two more mental files to sit beside the one containing financial motivations for Adrian Quinn's disappearance; the jilted lover and the scorned wife.

Chapter 11

THE DOOR TO the RSPB headquarters was closed and there were no lights on inside or any sign of Laura Roberts. The overgrowing ivy seemed to have made more progress in wrapping the old stable block in its tendrils just as the area around Adrian Quinn's car and the path to the forest park's walking trail was now festooned in red and white police tape.

"We'll start with a grid around the vehicle and then work our way out."

Erin Reilly nodded, following the fingertip of the search team leader as it crossed the planned search area on an ordinance survey map spread out on the bonnet of his van.

"Great. Can I have you traverse the path to where the altercation was reported and, depending on what we find, adjust the plan from there?"

Constable Brian Butler gave his agreement with a murmured affirmative and a thumbs up, accepting Reilly's gratitude with a smile as he turned to open the back door of the Ford Transit Connect and ready his partner for action. Reilly paused as the cage was opened and as Butler readied the dog's yellow working harness. She took a moment to ruffle the floppy ears of the chocolate Labrador and accept the excited kisses as the dog waited to be put to work.

"Erin, where do you want him?"

Chris Walker stood thirty feet away from the cordoned-off BMW and gestured down the lane at an approaching vehicle recovery truck.

"Send him over there until Diane's folks have finished up." Reilly directed Walker to a gravel area of overflow parking to the far right of the car park, and as he trotted across to intercept the driver she made her way to the cordon surrounding Quinn's car.

"Don't suppose he left us a note, Di?"

Diane Pearson peered through the open passenger door from her position on haunches at the open driver's side. She gave a shake of her head as she stood, losing a strand of her ash blonde hair from the hood of her forensic Tyvek over suit; the forensic science service senior crime scene investigator tucked it back in before removing her nitrile gloves and making her way to Reilly.

"Diddley squat, Erin." Pearson removed her facemask and turned to follow Reilly's look towards the other two SOCOs who were carefully going through the rear seats, footwells, and the open boot of the BMW. "The spare key you gave us did the job of getting in. Locks and alarm were still engaged. No sign of attempted forced entry or evidence of anything other than he pulled up and got out. Suit bag was hung in the rear with a pair of brogues, and a towel and cereal bars on the front passenger seat, bin bag on the floor, probably for his mucky guddies. So, it's looking as reported. Your guy went for a run and hasn't come back."

"The damage to the side?"

Pearson shrugged.

"Broad flat object, single point of contact and I see one ridge so if you're asking me to take a punt somebody keyed it. Sorry, I've nothing more definitive but then maybe that's a good thing?"

"Yeah maybe," agreed Reilly. The suspicion that they would open the boot to find Quinn's body had never really left her until Pearson had given the word there was no sign of violence beyond that against the polished bodywork.

"Cheers, Di, give me a shout when you're done and we'll get the lads to lift the car."

Pearson smiled and retrieved a new set of gloves from her kitbag set on the outside of the cordon.

"How's my old mate Doc doing?" she said.

"Still losing friends and alienating people," said Reilly, as Pearson's broad grin and chuckle disappeared behind her mask. "I'll give you a shout if we turn anything up, okay?"

"When we're finished here, we'll be in the van," said Pearson, turning with a wave.

Reilly met Walker halfway back to the row of police vehicles and the dog handler's van. A dozen uniforms, kitted out in rifle green waterproofs and PSNI logoed caps, stood in a loose semi-circle waiting for the off; each held a long pole to aid balance and pace the step-by-step search of the undergrowth and woodland that would be led by Brian Butler and Flynn the Lab.

"We good to go, Brian?" asked Reilly, as Butler patted the dog's neck and secreted her tennis ball in his waterproof overcoat.

"Ready when you are, Erin."

"Okay, ladies and gents. You've seen the brief. Adrian Quinn, missing, and last seen heading into the woods more than twenty-four hours ago. We've initially four search areas as per briefing pack. Alpha through Delta extending from the path intersection over there where it's reported Mr

Quinn engaged in a scuffle with a man subsequently identified as Raymond Kilburn." There were a few raised eyebrows and a low murmur of recognition at the name. "Flynn will run the ground to the location and we'll be led by her and Brian. All good?"

A chorus of curt affirmatives and nods returned, and Reilly gave Butler a thumbs up. Walker, carrying a plastic evidence bag, passed it across to the dog handler who presented the contents to his partner, a white undershirt belonging to Adrian Quinn and donated by his wife for the purpose of the search. Flynn's tail whipped back and forth, her tongue lolling from a happy mouth and her paws tapping the ground in eager anticipation.

"Go find," said Butler, his voice charged with excitement and encouragement.

Flynn set off at a trot, disappearing into the knee-high grass that bordered the car park and the pathways, her tail wagging as she picked up pace, sweeping ten by ten-metre squares through the undergrowth; an occasional pause and glance back to her master who encouraged her on.

The search team spread into a long line and began the trek across the open ground towards the tree line, the bounding dog cutting a swathe ahead. Reilly and Walker followed Brian Butler in the centre of the phalanx, taking the meandering path that Quinn would have followed. Reilly caught Butler stiffen a second before she caught a change in Flynn's body language. The dog's tail had flattened and her nose had dropped. She looked up for direction.

"Good girl, Flynn. She has something," said Butler veering off the path to where his dog had ceased her methodical sweeps through the grass and was nose down in the undergrowth.

"Good girl." Butler's voice was effusive in praise, and he reached inside his coat to reward the dog with her ball. Flynn panted happily, her tail whumping against her handler's leg.

"What is it?" said Reilly, stepping forward.

"Branch."

Walker carefully eased the grass aside to reveal the arm-length stump of deadfall; on one end a darkened smear that looked like blood.

"Mark it and leave a man here. We'll give Diane the nod to collect it."

"Could be the weapon Kilburn told us about?" said Walker.

"Yep, and it will lend credence to his side of the story if it's his blood and not Quinn's." Reilly jumped at an excited bark from Flynn.

"Something else?"

"Good girl, go find," said Butler, nodding. "We're getting the wind onside, it's blowing across from the west right onto her nose."

Flynn dropped her ball and soared off like a sleek brown missile. Any methodical back-and-forth sonar sweep lost to the laser focus of a scent now caught on the breeze. She bounded through the tree line, a series of sharp barks in her wake as Butler, with Reilly and Walker in tow hurried after her.

The dog's yellow vest flitted between trees, Reilly catching sight of her scramble down a bank of heather and broadleaf ferns.

"Flynn, easy," Butler's voice was measured, his concern the dog might turn a leg on the uneven ground and jutting root systems in contrast to his partner's excited headlong charge.

The police officers scrambled down the bank, Reilly clutching at the mossy bark of broad oaks and elms to ease her descent as Walker slip-slided gracelessly away to her right. They crashed into a small clearing at the bottom of the slope at the same time. The ripple of water and the quack of wildfowl signified their proximity to the meandering River Lagan a little further ahead through the trees.

Flynn was frozen stock still on the boundary of the clearing, her eyes darting to her handler, but her nose pointed to a patch of overgrown shrubbery in the understory of the forest canopy.

"Good girl, Flynn. Great job." Butler gave his dog her ball, and Reilly patted the excited animal as she got close.

Shoved in amongst the leaves and the deadfall was a stuffed black bin liner. At some point in the bag's journey down the slope it had split and, on impact, some of its contents had spilled out, amongst them a single muddied ASICS running shoe and an orange Under Armour vest.

"Call it in, Chris," said Reilly, ruffling the dog's ears. "You've some nose on you, girl."

Flynn's big brown eyes looked between Reilly and a red-faced but chuffed Brian Butler. She dropped her ball at Reilly's feet and woofed her impatience for another game of go find Adrian Quinn.

Chapter 12

"IT'S JUST HIT me you know, I'm some mentor." Macpherson pulled the Volvo up kerbside, puffed with pride and in absent-minded satisfaction he tried to rip off the handbrake.

"Self-praise is no recommendation, Doc," said Taylor with a chuckle as she unfastened her seat belt.

"Aye, credit where credit is due you've some eyes on you, but I'm telling you, you must have fair soaked up some expertise from me over the years."

"You should put in for the training college. Think of all those recruits you could mould into wee carbon copies." Taylor exited the car as a horrified look broke on her sergeant's face at the thought. "But let me know when you take the notion to the chief super. I want to be there to see his face at the thought of that."

Across the entranceway of the Quinn property, Leigh-Anne Arnold's Škoda patrol car remained parked.

"Ma'am." Arnold lowered the driver's window as Taylor and Doc approached.

"Leigh-Anne, all quiet?" said Taylor, leaning down with a hand on the roof.

"Mrs Quinn hasn't gone out. Her mother came back with the kids about an hour ago. No other visitors."

"No press or anything hanging about?" Arnold shook her head.

Taylor pursed her lips and gave the constable a nod. The

reports had gone out to the radio and television networks appealing for witnesses in and around Drumkeen Forest Park alongside a description of Adrian Quinn and his suspected route the morning of his disappearance. So far nothing had come from it but if the investigation did segue down a darker path Arnold and her colleagues would have a job of it keeping the vultures from the Quinns' gate.

"We've a few things to run past Mrs Quinn. Sign us into the log there, will you?"

"Will do, ma'am."

Walking to the high automatic gate, Macpherson thumbed the intercom as Taylor took in the expanse of the property and that of its neighbours. Bladon Manor was a desirable address in a leafy upmarket suburb and if Helios had been clipped by a few suppliers going belly up and the expansion deal going sour, cash flow was going to be a problem and there was nothing like the notion of losing your fancy home to twist the thumbscrews on marital bliss.

There was a brief crackled exchange and then the gates began to hum open. The two police officers entered, taking the narrow brick path up towards the house.

"Final demands?" said Macpherson, shaking his head. "I could barely read the date on the milk."

"I didn't think much of it at the time and she said she was looking for a note from Adrian. I noticed two piles of paperwork, the bigger stack was all bank and insurance related. I clocked at least two demand notices," said Taylor, thinking back to their previous visit.

Aside from the Porsche which hadn't moved, there was a Mercedes E-Class estate nudged up on the turning circle near the edge of the lawn. So far no one had come to the entrance porch to welcome the visitors. "Based on what Katherine Clark said about re-mortgaging to shore up the factory I'm wondering why Aoife Quinn didn't come clean and tell us they had money problems."

"You wouldn't think it to look at this place," said Macpherson, again running an appreciative eye across the landscaped gardens.

"You hardly ever do." Taylor had just reached the porch steps when Aoife Quinn opened the door.

"Inspector? Have you…" Her question died on her lips, wanting to ask but not really wanting to know the answer.

"No, Mrs Quinn, we have no news yet. I just wanted to follow up with a few more questions."

"Okay, come in. Excuse the mess, the kids are back and they go through the place like a whirlwind."

There was no mess that Taylor could lay her eye on, but somewhere upstairs she heard the tinkle of childish laughter and thud of small feet.

"It's the police, Mum. This is my mum Caroline."

Aoife's mother had shared her fine bone structure with her daughter, and although she offered a warm smile, the tension around her eyes didn't lift.

"Any news?"

"Sorry, ma'am. We are recovering Adrian's car now and have a few leads to follow up but nothing concrete," said Taylor. Then turning to Aoife. "No word here? No calls?" Quinn had backed up against the worktop. The telephone handset was in its cradle to the right of her elbow, blinking alerts to missed calls. Aoife shook her head. She looked ready for tears.

"Would you mind if we sat down?" said Taylor.

"Tea?" said Caroline Quinn.

Taylor shook her head, Macpherson following her lead and for once declining a second polite query when asked were they sure.

"I'll go and make sure the kids don't interrupt you."

"Thanks, Mum. Please." Quinn offered them the same seats as before. The only difference was a few of the morning tabloids had been skimmed through and left open on the coffee table. A pen lay on the open page of the classifieds section.

"Did you speak to Jackie?" said Quinn. She sat on the edge of her chair, knees together, feet apart and palms clamped between her thighs.

"We spoke to a manager at Helios, Richard Seawright. We'll be going back to speak with Mr Mahood after this."

Quinn's eyes dropped away, a look akin to relief crossing her face.

"We also had a conversation with Katherine Clark," said Taylor softly.

"Oh." Mention of the name prickled across Quinn's expression, hardening it, and the single syllable came out through clenched teeth.

"Mr Seawright told us she's a fixture at Helios and a long term colleague of your husband?"

"Why don't you just spit it out, Inspector." Quinn's eyes narrowed and she sat back with crossed arms. "Did I know about my husband's affair with her? Yes, I did. He told me and I forgave him. Anything she thinks she knows about what's going on with Aido you can take with a pinch of salt." As she spoke, the tremble of emotion built in her words.

"She didn't have any information that might lead us to where Adrian is but she did mention some recent financial impacts suffered by Helios."

Quinn gave a half shrug.

"When does a business ever run smoothly? It's not like the administrators are at the door, is it? With Jackie's investment and getting the expansion deal back on track, it will be a storm in a teacup. Katherine Clark likes people to think she's more important to the running of the company than she really is."

Taylor took out her notebook and made a show of reviewing a few points. She was sure Quinn's explanation was one that Adrian had drummed into his wife when she had asked similar questions.

"You looking to get rid of a few things?" Taylor jutted her chin at the classified ads and Quinn blushed.

"Some of Sophie's stuff; prams, trampoline, the things she never uses anymore. You know anybody?"

"She's a bit big for a pram and the bouncing would kill my old knees," said Macpherson with a sympathetic smile and a nod to Taylor.

"Mrs Quinn, are you having trouble financially?" said Taylor.

"No," said Quinn. "Not really."

"I couldn't help but notice the statements—" Taylor was cut off by the phone ringing. Quinn sprang to her feet and grabbed the handset.

"Aido?"

"Hello? For God's sake!"

Taylor stood as Quinn jabbed the call end button and tossed the handset onto the counter.

"Mrs Quinn?"

"It's nothing. Stupid kids or something."

"How long have you been getting them?"

Quinn beckoned Taylor to sit and flopped back down in her armchair.

"A while. Adrian said to ignore them."

"Did he give any indication if he knew who it might be?"

"No. Well, he said it might be people with a grudge against the new work. You heard about the environmental protestors?"

"Do they ever speak?" said Taylor, nodding to indicate that they had been informed of the complaint and protest.

Quinn shook her head. She was hunched over and tense and began to bite the thumbnail of her right hand. "No, not a word."

"We'll look into it, okay?" said Taylor. Quinn didn't respond.

"The bank statements, and maybe these calls? Did Adrian borrow money?"

"No." The words were out before Taylor had finished.

"I'm going to run a credit report and find out, Aoife. It'd be easier if you gave me a heads-up on what I'll find?"

Quinn put her head in her hands.

"Okay. Okay. Yes, we're up to our necks in it all thanks to my wonderful husband."

Taylor nodded and waited for her to carry on.

"Saint Aido. Never let anyone down in his life. He'll go without, so everyone else gets what they're due. It's a pity he never thought what that would mean for his bloody children."

"How bad is it?"

"It's worse now I don't know where Aido is and Jackie is telling me this expansion project that was to put everything back on track is ruined."

"You must have a few quid in the bank though?" said Macpherson. Quinn snorted.

"Aido had to plough everything he could into Helios. His pride couldn't see him upstaged by Jackie, even though he was the firm. There wouldn't be a business without his drive and technical ability or the loyalty of the staff to him."

"When did he tell you he had re-mortgaged the house?"

"He didn't; I found out by accident."

"Do you think he might have had reason to borrow elsewhere as well?"

"No… I don't know." Quinn threw up an exasperated hand. "All I know is he's missing and I want him home. I don't care about the bloody house or the stupid money, I want the kids to have their daddy back."

Taylor heard a genuine plea in Quinn's voice and felt a stab of sympathy for the woman. She had aged a few years in the time since they had met and clearly hadn't slept or found time for a minute's peace. She seemed adrift amid the mod-cons of the lavish house and its expansive gardens. As their eyes met, she felt sympathy rise to pity and had the same overwhelming sensation that she had felt in Katherine Clark's apartment, that feeling of a house missing the joy and beating heart that made it a home.

❖❖❖

"What are you thinking?"

"I'm thinking she's in the dark as much as us and I'm thinking Aido Quinn might be in bigger bother than we thought?" said Taylor.

Macpherson gunned the Volvo across the Newforge Lane junction, habitually glancing to his left down the tree-lined road that led to the PSNI Sports and Social Club and memories of many a heady night and a heavy head.

"Dodgy loans?"

"Raymie Kilburn. He's the last person to be seen with Quinn and we know he's a shark for the hoods in Drumkeen Estate," said Taylor, nodding.

Macpherson weaved into the left lane and took an inside racing line around the House of Sport roundabout heading south on the A55 back towards Drumkeen Forest and the Forest Hill Industrial Estate.

"You bringing him in?"

Taylor shook her head and reached for her mobile, thumbing open the home screen and placing a call.

"Carrie? It's me… yeah, not so bad. Do me a favour, we've just come from the Quinn house and they've been receiving nuisance phone calls. Have a check through the telecoms company and see if we can find the source."

Taylor waited as Carrie Cook replied.

"Approximately half an hour ago while we were there, and probably over the last few weeks. Do the needful on a credit check for Quinn too. It looks like he's in a bit of bother… Yeah, we were just talking about Kilburn…" Cook's query was identical to Macpherson's.

"No, not until we see the extent of the debts or unless Erin and Chris get something. We're going to Helios to see Jackie Mahood here, so I've one last thing. I'm going to text you a few addresses linked to the Helios expansion deal. Run them down and see if there's anything out of the ordinary about them. Cheers, Carrie, we'll see you in a bit."

Taylor closed the call just as Macpherson hit the first traffic calming measure on the road up to Helios Sustainable. As their progress slowed to negotiate the humps and the building loomed ahead she could see the car park had emptied as was to be expected for the time of day. Thankfully, the big green Discovery was still parked where it had been earlier.

❖❖❖

"Who let you in?"

"You're a man after my own heart," said Macpherson, pointing at the thick-bottomed tumbler containing an inch of whiskey that sat beside a glass decanter.

"Not a bad time, is it?" said Taylor, receiving the expected scowl from Jackie Mahood.

"Sit yourselves down and make it quick if you can."

Mahood swivelled his high-backed chair and slid out from behind his desk, picking up the tumbler and taking a swig. Swirling the liquid around in his mouth before he swallowed, he took a satisfied breath.

"Hope you're not planning on driving home?" said Macpherson, taking the seat to Taylor's right.

"I'll be lucky to be out of here tonight," grunted Mahood. "That wee shite's left some mess behind him."

"Do you want to elaborate?" said Taylor, easing into the plush visitor's chair and crossing her legs.

"Fuck sake, are you serious. Do you want me to tell you about how he squandered a couple of hundred grand of my money on a new inverter I told him would never work or how that other bitch shafted me to the green gang?"

"I thought it was the business's money?"

Mahood hissed a tut and turned to look out of the floor-to-ceiling window behind him. On the other side of the glass, the factory was dark, bathed in pools of low light from LED bulkheads and overhead spot, the workforce having trickled out a few hours earlier.

"Aye, well. It is. It was. But it was only there to spend because of me." He thumbed over his shoulder towards the rows of darkened workstations. "Where do you think that came from? The fairies sure as hell didn't bring it."

"Was there a bit of a power struggle going on, Mr Mahood?" said Taylor.

"Tug of war more like."

"I see…"

"No, you don't." Mahood turned back and collected his glass. "You think I'm an overbearing arrogant prick and you'd be right. That how I ended up with the cash to fund Aido's passion project."

"You must have seen some worth to stump up?" said Macpherson.

"I'm not daft, renewable is the future." Mahood aimed the glass at the two officers. "Now, I'm not on my save the planet high horse here, it's just good business to get in on the ground floor, and to be fair to him, Aido knew what he was about."

"So, what's with the tug of war?" said Taylor. "Did you not want the same thing in the end?"

"I thought we did. To get stinking rich and make a bit of a difference while we're at it. It made a change to the cut and thrust I was used to."

"Which was?"

"The City. Investment banking. It didn't matter two hoots about what we bought or sold, or the impact those trades had out on the ground or in the long term, as long as the stock dividends went up. This was different. Aido was on to a winner and, played right, Helios could be a market leader."

Taylor tapped her foot as she considered Mahood, his candour and his nod to having a continued belief Helios could move him past whatever grievances the two directors were having at present.

"What do you think's going on with Adrian's disappearance?" she said. Mahood took another sip of his drink and held the liquid in his mouth as he pondered. He swallowed.

"Look, you're coppers, not entrepreneurs but you're not stupid. Aido's been throwing good money after bad and I had to stop him before he sent ten years of his own hard work and a few million of my money down the drain."

"And how did you go about that, sir?" Macpherson slid forward on his chair and gave Mahood a steely glare.

"Like any responsible parent. I gave him a stern word and threatened to take his bloody bank card off him." Mahood sat. "Look, what we need as a company is to stick to what we know. What we are good at. The manufacture and installation of PV panels. The product is sound, affordable, tried and tested. Aido was trying to get the next generation off the ground before the bloody market had embraced the first. It was suicide."

"That's an interesting interpretation," said Taylor, noticing Macpherson stiffen at the mention of the word.

"You know what I mean. Look, I don't know where Aido is. If he's topped himself then he's a bloody coward for one and a fool for two. He's a cracker of a wife and three great wee kids." Mahood turned to look out across the factory.

"Do you think he's just thrown the toys out of the pram?" said Macpherson.

"Come here, look at this." Mahood moved back to his desk and half turned his monitor so the two detectives could see. Tapping in login details he then launched a selection of spreadsheets across two monitors.

"Mr Mahood, I don't know my arse from my elbow when it comes to those so you'll have to tell me what I'm supposed to be looking at." Macpherson had rifled a set of reading glasses from his inside pocket and peered at the screen. Taylor leaned in, suppressing a smile at the expression she had heard a hundred times before. The old dog wasn't daft but he couldn't stand the long way round or pretentious explanations, something Diane Pearson refrained from when delivering her forensic reports and which Professor Derek Thompson now watered down when he was wrist deep in a cadaver explaining the intricacies of cause of death.

Mahood smiled at the detective sergeant.

"Now you're a man after my own heart. I'll cut to the chase. We've two sets of transactions here, this one…" Mahood highlighted a column of cells, each colour coded and representing a financial transaction. "Shows payment made to a number of tender suppliers for R&D on a new inverter coil. Here, about three months ago, I told Aido to stop. After that, you can see at least another dozen transactions."

"He was co-director, and you admitted he's the more technical of the two of you. What's the issue?"

"The issue is I told him to stop because I had his theory

independently reviewed and a paper presented on why it was too early to work. There were other developments needed, advancement in other parts of the design we aren't even close to engineering. You can't just drop a Ferrari engine in a bloody Nissan Micra, can you? And anyway, this inverter, it made no sense. There was a flaw with the design that I can't get my head around."

Macpherson harrumphed a nod at the analogy as Taylor looked down the column and mentally totted up. If Mahood was right, Quinn had been blowing the company's budget at a rate of knots for what would be no apparent return.

"I told him if we refocused on the plant expansion," Mahood held up a hand and counted off fingers. "One, more volume; more volume equals more sales and more profit. Two, investment in solar farms gives us a passive income. By the time the engineering problems had been worked around to suit the new invertors we would have already made the money back to explode out of the gate."

"When you asked him to stop pursuing this, do you think he continued? Somehow found an alternative means of funding?"

"He might have done but those two companies there, and a third, went to the wall over the last couple of months." Mahood shrugged. "As I said, what they proposed isn't the issue. It's that nobody is going to be able to use it."

Taylor considered the timetable and the actions of the man who from the germ of an idea and a deal of foresight had grown a shed project to something like Helios. Across the corridor outside Mahood's open door, Adrian Quinn's office lay dark. Nobody so far had said he was reckless, nor a gambler. If anything, Katherine Clark's revelation and his wife's corroboration that he put employee welfare before his family made the situation all the harder to fathom.

"There's no one else offering the same solution he might have tried?" said Taylor, noting down the company names.

"There's a reason all three of them are dead in the water."

"What's that other list?" said Macpherson. Mahood shook his head, a tick of frustration in the grind of his jaw.

"These are the company expense accounts."

He dragged the second spreadsheet over the top of the first on his main monitor screen.

"Who has access to that information?" said Taylor, skim reading the figures, pausing at some of the more eye-watering amounts.

"Me and Aido. My PA, Margaret East and Katherine Clark."

"So?" Macpherson thumbed his glasses back up his nose, the light of the monitor reflecting off the lenses.

"So unless I'm very much mistaken Bulgari, Louis Vuitton and a dozen treatments at a health clinic have fuck all to do with my business, and that's before all those cash withdrawals."

Taylor followed his finger as he highlighted the long list of spurious transactions.

"And it's not for client gifts or hospitality?" she said. Mahood scowled and shook his head.

"Did you talk to Adrian? Had he signed them off for Kath…" Macpherson's voice trailed off as Mahood continued to shake his head.

Taylor's phone began to ring as Mahood replied, she glanced down at the screen to see it was Erin Reilly.

"It wasn't Katherine," he said. "It was Aoife."

Chapter 13

A SECOND CORDON of red and white tape now fluttered in the breeze around the thirty-foot-wide depression at the bottom of the slope. In the centre, Diane Pearson and another member of her team carefully collected the contents of the bin liner, transferring each item and then the carrier bag itself into sealed plastic evidence bags.

"They confirmed blood on the branch and have it secured. Diane says she could be another half hour down here. What do you think?" said Walker.

Erin Reilly scanned the rutted undergrowth on which they stood, her eyes trailing back up the slope to where it was likely the bag had been flung, and then to her left where a significant stretch of vegetation showed signs of distress and damage to the thin, reedy branches of the trees and the supple ferns and bracken that nested at their feet. Working their way back up the hill, a section of the search team picked under loose leaves and slowly caressed the bank in a fingertip search to ensure no other items, either from what looked like Quinn's possessions or from anyone else had inadvertently been snagged.

"What do you think, Brian?" she said.

Brian Butler looked down at Flynn, who was prone on the forest floor happily chewing at her favourite tennis ball.

"Not a bother." He reached down to take the dog's ear and knead the velvety soft fur. "You ready again, girl?" Flynn dropped the ball and lay looking up with her deep brown eyes, her tongue flapping as she panted.

"This area here looks like someone trekked through," said Reilly, indicating the broken undergrowth. "Maybe whoever tossed the bag down saw it split and had to retrieve something, then, rather than scramble back up went through there. I can hear the river so there must be a towpath beyond this thicket?"

"Certainly looks like egress from this clearing." Brian Butler reached down to pluck up Flynn's toy, giving a nod of agreement.

"Go find, girl."

The dog let out an excited yelp and leapt to her feet, taking Butler's gestured command to follow the path leading out. Reilly called to the nearest searcher.

"Sarge, I need four of your lads to follow us, and then can I have the rest of the team conclude the search of the bank and then push out from this clearing on two vectors to intersect again with the running trail along the edge of Alpha?" She received a nod of understanding as the sergeant called out four names and directed them onto Reilly's heels. She strode briskly to catch up with Flynn, Butler and Walker.

"Did you see how happy she was to get that ball? Amazing isn't it," said Walker as she caught up, then as an afterthought. "Do you think we could get Doc one to bring him back down when he's off on one?" Reilly chuckled.

"If you hand Doc a tennis ball when he's up the high doh you may get to know a good surgeon."

Flynn was twenty feet ahead, steadily padding through a narrow track between the trees, her nose brushing from side to side and occasionally rooting through the longer grasses that edged what was opening up into a broader and more well-used track.

"She's got something, but she's sweeping," said Butler. "If there was transference or material taken from the clearing she'd go until she finds it or loses the scent. I'm watching for a snap of her head." He made a dog-head shape with his hand, touching two middle fingers to thumb, extending index and pinkie as ears and flicked his wrist. "If she catches a positive scent that will be the first indication."

Flynn continued to weave along the trampled path which rose up a short grassy bank before circling east toward the main trails. As the trees began to thin out and the sound of wild birds scattering in the trees sounded, Butler got the signal he was looking for. The dog's head cracked to the left and then dipped, her tail flattened, and she bounded off the track and into the undergrowth.

"Go on, after her," said Reilly with an excited lift in her voice as she ducked under a branch and heaved another bough of deadfall from her path.

The three moved as quickly and as carefully over the terrain as they could, the thumping steps of the four-man search squad following. She caught a shout from up ahead, pushing through vegetation to find Butler approaching his dog, cooing praise. Flynn wasn't paying any attention to the ball. She had flattened herself on the ground, laying across a patch of earth, scattered leaves and clumps of thick bracken.

"Hang on," Reilly raised a hand to the searchers. "The dog's got something. Usual protocol; work in from the outside, watch your step and keep your eyes peeled for secondary evidence."

Following her own advice and holding aside a branch for Walker, she stepped closer to Butler and the dog. The police constable's face had pinched, his expression one of concern.

"What's she got?" said Reilly.

"Nothing good," said Butler.

"Then what's she doing?" said Walker, coming to stand at Reilly's shoulder beside the handler and his dog.

"It the way she's laying. She'll only signal like that if she scents a cadaver."

"Shit," said Walker.

Reilly studied the dog; usually exuberant and ready to receive her reward she now instead lay prone, her chin to the ground between paws and her doleful brown eyes gazing up at Butler and the two detectives.

Reilly pulled out her phone.

Chapter 14

THE SPLUTTER AND rattle of petrol generators hummed in the distance as the cavalcade of police support vehicles taking over the Drumkeen Forest car park grew with each passing hour. Reilly had pulled the search team and, around the copse where Flynn had pinpointed the potential for a dead body, erected a cordon, the centre of which was now occupied by a four by four pop-up forensic tent and illuminated by half a dozen high-powered floodlights.

Inside, Diane Pearson and her initial team were supported by another crew from the forensic science lab at Seapark. Reilly herself was still clad in a Tyvek over suit from her initial walkthrough with the investigators before pulling back to let them take over the grim task of confirming Flynn's find.

"Did you not have any boots in the car, sarge?" said Chris Walker, standing a foot or so away from Reilly.

Macpherson glared up from looking down at his sodden shoes. Pressing the ball of his foot against a jutting rock sent the water seeping from the stitching of the well-worn leather.

"When you get to my age, we'll see how often you can be arsed to be bending down and changing your shoes, son," grumbled Macpherson, pulling the collar of his suit jacket up to ward off the whip of wind that had kicked up as dusk had dropped.

"I was a boy scout myself. Be prepared," said Walker,

snapping off a salute and a grin.

"In my day we'd to go out to work from when we were ten years old. We'd no time for bloody dib dob or wiggle woggle. What's the craic with you, anyway? Is it fancy dress or what?"

Walker's grin slipped as he looked down at his attire. The DC had the look of the first day of term about him, although rather than a blazer and spit-shined shoes he wore a bright orange and blue GORE-TEX jacket, the hood now pulled up and drawstring tied in a neat bow under his chin, and a pair of matching waterproof over-trousers pulled over Barbour wellington boots.

"What's wrong with it?" said Walker, the dent in his pride peeking through in his question. Macpherson looked him up and down and gave a small smile.

"We'll not lose you in the dark, that's for sure."

"Leave him alone will you," said Erin Reilly, nudging the DS with an elbow. "I wish I'd thought of bringing something warmer."

"Yous are too bloody soft." Macpherson shook his head, straightening and jerking the lapels of his suit jacket, then, as a gust blew across the ridge, he batted away his fluttering tie. "I remember in my day—"

"Oh Christ, Chris. Where's the tennis ball?" said Reilly with a chuckle.

"Tennis ball?" Macpherson's face screwed up in confusion.

"I got it new," protested Walker. "I was thinking of doing a bit of trail walking, maybe seeing if I could volunteer a bit with the—"

"Aha!" Macpherson clapped his hands, his face cracked

in mirth as he suddenly understood. "You're dolled up for your girlfriend, the bird lady."

"I am not…"

"You don't need to explain it to me, son," said Macpherson. "Fair play to you. I'm glad to see you finally putting yourself out there. Just maybe hold off asking her out until we've squared away the investigation." He gave the younger man a wink and Walker's face bloomed brighter than the patches on his coat as he turned away, grateful to see the tent's flap open and Diane Pearson peek out. She searched the commotion outside her forensic bubble, finally settling on a spot ten feet away from the trio where Taylor was in conversation with a uniformed inspector who had arrived to commandeer responsibility for the increased search team presence. Alongside them was one of Pearson's colleagues.

"Once the dog identified possible remains, we set the teams on a double back on the other deposition sites and concentrated on the routes from the car park to each. So far we've established a possible access route and two potential egress points from this clearing. I've stalled the search until first light and closed the park and established an outer cordon." Taylor nodded as the inspector concluded the update.

"What about people already on site?"

"I've officers in the car park making enquiries of anyone returning to their vehicle and two cyclists doing a route of the trails to round up anybody still here. There's a lot of ground to cover and it's as leaky as a sieve."

Taylor knew the task was unenviable. The forest park covered an extensive area and could not only be accessed from the main entrance but a host of other points around the perimeter from residential gardens and towpath walks along from the Lagan Meadow and Shaw's Bridge to other conservation and picnic spots like the one sited at the Lockkeeper's Cottage.

"We've only released the details to the press this morning. Do your best to maintain the integrity of the sites. If this is bad news, I'd rather get a chance to tell Aoife Quinn to her face before there are pictures of a burial site on the tabloid websites."

The inspector nodded his understanding but also gave a shrug. Taylor returned the gesture. She knew he would try to, and she wouldn't hang him if somebody did sneak through and out the discovery before the press team could do it.

"Mal?" Taylor gave Pearson's deputy a jerk of her chin.

"We've confirmed the presence of blood on a branch collected near the entrance to the trails and the clothing collected from site two matches the description you supplied of Adrian Quinn's gear. There was a matching Under Armour soft-shell jacket in the car. The branch, the clothing and the bag that contained them have been sent back to Seapark for further tests."

"Smashing. What about in there?" said Taylor, turning to see Pearson duck under the cordon, and drop her mask and hood.

"Hiya," said Pearson in greeting, reaching down to her kitbag to remove a bottle of diet cola. It opened with a long hiss, and she took a swig.

"Di, what's the craic? Anything for me inside?" said Taylor.

Pearson slowly recapped the cola and shook out her ash blonde hair into the breeze.

"Initial search by K9 identified possible remains. I'd say, by what I've seen so far, what we're looking at in the tent is potentially a deposition site. Six by six-foot-square of recently disturbed earth with a rudimentary attempt to disguise the excavation after the fact with deadfall and uprooted flora and fauna. Could be a forensic goldmine for fibres, hair, possibly DNA once we can properly access the burial, but first things first, we're about to start taking off the first layer of soil."

"Anything else we can do?" said Taylor. Pearson shook her head.

"For the sake of three wee kiddies, cross your fingers it's not what we're all thinking." Pearson gave a resigned half shake of her head. "You ready, Mal?"

The deputy forensic officer gave an assured nod and ducked under the tape, holding it up for his boss, who followed, raising her hood and re-securing her mask.

"Not good news then?" said Macpherson as Taylor approached her team.

"Di says it's odds on they'll find a body."

"Jesus," mumbled Macpherson, suddenly feeling the evening chill and wrapping his arms around his chest.

"Guv." Erin Reilly appeared from behind the two, absent the Tyvek over suit and wearing a police baseball cap. A scarf wrapped around her neck was tucked into an oversized police fleece jacket. She offered an identical garment to Macpherson.

"Had a few going spare," she said, nodding back to the car park. Macpherson looked at her outstretched hand,

Reilly briefly thinking he might refuse, until he nodded gratefully and shrugged his arms into the fleece and pulled the zipper right up to his chin.

Taylor looked down at the forensic tent. Already illuminated from within by portable battery lights, the brighter flare of a camera flash lit the sides. Pearson, she knew, would document every skim of soil that was scraped from the surface and her eye for detail and complete dedication to her art would sift the material for any singular piece of matter that in some way did not belong until she revealed the body.

The trees swayed in the gathering breeze and the callous caws of roosting rooks seemed to mock the DI as she cast her eyes in thought up to the bony branches and considered where the day had brought them. Her overriding thoughts lingered on how whatever was about to be revealed may close the initial phase of the case and kick it into a much higher gear; while one question would sadly be answered it left a list of others and while separate, each felt as tangled with the next as the overcooked spaghetti in one of Macpherson's Bolognese dishes.

Another flash lit the fabric of the tent and she plotted a mental map of the forest; from Quinn's car to the alleged altercation with Kilburn, the dump of clothing, and here, a quarter mile further to what might be a final resting place. Whatever was going on with his business life in Helios, was it enough to end a life? Mahood was certainly a force of nature. But a murderer? And as complex as the relationship was between the two men, Quinn's personal ties to Katherine Clark, the veiled undercurrent of marital disharmony and financial irregularity added an unwelcome and intangible layer of suspicion on the women.

Taylor pondered the possibility of any one of those two quietly dispatching Quinn and manhandling him to this remote spot unseen with scepticism. But when she considered Jackie Mahood or indeed Raymie Kilburn, there was not so much doubt. Not unless there was a combination of factors and actors. She started as the door flaps to the tent opened and Diane Pearson stepped out.

Her thoughts along with the muted conversation on the outside of the tape faded to absolute silence as the senior forensic investigator approached. Pearson shook her head sadly.

"It's a grave alright," she said.

"Quinn?" said Taylor, the cordon tape fluttering against her thighs.

Pearson shook her head again.

"No. Somebody's buried a dozen dead puppies."

Chapter 15

"You're quiet this morning? You didn't hit the Maharaja on the way home last night, did you?"

Macpherson gave a weary smile and a small shake of his head, lowering the driver's window to allow in a stream of cool, refreshing air as he turned the Volvo into Bladon Manor.

"Didn't sleep too well."

Taylor looked across at her friend and surrogate father figure. The man who had practically raised her following the death of her parents, and guided her through her formative years as a student and police officer, had three moods. A grim dourness he reserved for his work, a deep loving warmth for the family he embraced in his huge bear hugs and a melancholy that appeared from time to time. The first she knew was an act, for the man's heart was as big as his hands and while he was direct and sometimes abrupt he only had an interest in developing his colleagues and subordinates to be the best investigators they could be, and to be embraced by the second was to know the love and loyalty of a man who would unquestioningly move heaven and earth for a friend. The third was more complex and one that touched most of her colleagues at some point; it could at times roll in and disperse as quickly as a summer storm, or it could build slowly and darken the edges of the mind like angry black clouds settling upon the craggy peak of the Cavehill.

It wasn't entirely unexpected that spending hours, days, weeks and months engaged in a profession that saw them deal with the worst humanity could offer, seeing firsthand the personal toll it took on victims, their families and wider communities would eventually tip the scales and produce either an outburst of emotion as thoughts and feelings were processed or a closing down as the cork was wedged in further to bottle up those personal opinions that might threaten impartiality and duty.

Taylor laid her hand on his forearm as he changed down a gear, approaching the Quinn household, knowing that while Macpherson held no aversion to man's inhumanity to man, when those callous and vindictive crimes crossed species to affect innocent and defenceless animals he struggled to maintain his professional equilibrium.

"Couldn't get the thought of them wee dogs out of my head," he said glancing at her, then back out the windscreen. "We see some shite day-to-day but every now and again there's one wee thing just gets under your skin."

"I know." Taylor gave him an empathetic smile.

"God love them," said Macpherson. His jaw pulsed as he gritted his teeth and pulled up outside the house.

God love them indeed, thought Taylor, thinking not only of the tiny sleek bodies of the Staffordshire bull terrier pups but also the three Quinn children and what they might soon be going through.

❖❖❖

"I need to get this one to school," said Aoife Quinn. She had one hand on the door and in the other held the hand of her daughter, Sophie. The little girl peered round from behind her mother to look up at the two detectives. Somewhere deeper in the house a plaintive wail rose from another sibling to be echoed a moment later by the other.

"It won't take long."

"Has something happened?"

"Might be better if we came inside," said Macpherson, and whether it was due to his look or the hangover of melancholy in his tone, Quinn eased the door aside and ushered them in.

"Sophie, go and get your bag and break," said Quinn. The little girl complied without question and danced off into the kitchen. Quinn opened a panelled door and let the two officers enter a bright day room before following.

The room was carpeted in a thick fawn wool blend, the vacuum marks still apparent on the surface, and one wall was papered in gold floral wallpaper, the colour adding to the warm ambience of the room. A white marbled fireplace with a brass insert and two, red, three-seater sofas were illuminated by a large bay window and a dozen downlighters set in a corniced bulkhead and an elegant central ceiling light.

"What's happened?" said Quinn, partially closing the door but not shutting it.

"We've discovered some of Adrian's clothing near where his car was parked."

"I don't understand? What do you mean by some of his clothing, like his jacket or something?"

Taylor shared a brief look with her DS.

"Take a seat, Mrs Quinn."

"No. Tell me what you mean."

"We found your husband's running gear discarded in

woodland near the trail on which he was last seen."

"But how? I… I'm sorry, you're not making any sense."

"No, I'm sure we're not," agreed Taylor. "Clothing items matching the descriptions you supplied to us were found in a bin bag amongst the undergrowth. We've recovered them for analysis."

Quinn finally sat, although Taylor wondered how much of it was a conscious decision and how much was her legs going out from under her.

"Was there any sign of…" Quinn cut herself off and once again Taylor knew she was avoiding tempting fate.

"No, our search led to several other areas but so far no sign of your husband."

"Is that all you've come to tell me?" A hint of anguished aggression sprang up in Quinn's voice, at once elated they weren't there with bad news but tempered by the fact there was no further progress.

"Actually we spent some time at Helios last night and have a few questions you might be able to help us with."

"About Helios? There'd be better-placed people to help you with that, Inspector."

"It's about your husband's expense account."

"And?"

"And there's a list of transactions we need some clarity on."

Quinn narrowed her eyes. She had propped an elbow on the arm of the chair and angled her closed knees away from the two officers who now sat ninety degrees to her left on a matching sofa.

"What kind of transactions?"

Macpherson removed the printed list of expenses

Mahood had furnished them with the evening before.

"Do you have access to your husband's company credit card?"

"No."

"Mrs Quinn, I'm not interested in whether you've broken Helios policy or not by using company credit for personal purchases. I just want to know what the cash withdrawals were for?"

"What are you talking about?"

Macpherson brandished the list, stood and took a step towards her, handing it over.

"Mr Mahood singled these out as transactions outside the scope of normal expenditure. You'll see reading down. Somebody went on quite the spree. Jewellery, high-end fashion outlets—"

"This wasn't me…"

"Mrs Quinn, Jackie Mahood spotted this a while ago but chose to keep an eye on it rather than raise it as an issue with your husband. He suggests his enquires with the stores identified you as the client in the transactions."

"Right, okay, so what if I bought a few things? It was my husband's company." Quinn seemed non-plussed now she had been rumbled, thought Taylor, maybe even a little hostile, as though this was the first opportunity she'd had to vent her frustrations. Perhaps she had supposed she would be caught in the act by her husband; an excuse for confrontation over money and matrimonial obligations.

"As I said, Mrs Quinn, I don't care about shoes and handbags. I'm more concerned over the thousands of pounds of cash withdrawals."

"That wasn't me."

"Mrs Quinn, we can request ATM and bank CCTV. Our investigations are leaning towards your husband being in financial difficulty, which was exacerbated as his access to regular company credit was under scrutiny. Did he have you access this cash for a reason? Did he tell you he needed it to further research or pay suppliers? Maybe even pay off a loan shark."

"A loan shark?"

"It's an avenue we are considering."

Quinn shook her head vehemently. "No."

"Mrs Quinn, it might help us uncover what's happened to Adrian if we understand to what extent he was in trouble?"

"I'm telling you it wasn't me." Quinn had scanned the list and pointed triumphantly at a line item. She thrust the list back at Macpherson, storming out to return a second later. In her hand, she brandished a hospital appointment card.

"There you go. Take that away and check. I was at hospital with the twins when I was supposed to be lifting five grand from the bank." She waved the appointment card and when neither detective reached for it she put it on the sofa between them. "Go on. Go and check."

"Mrs Quinn…" said Taylor.

Aoife Quinn opened the day room door wide.

"I want you to go. I need to take my daughter to school."

Chapter 16

"Thanks, Carrie, you're a lifesaver." Macpherson accepted the two paracetamol and cup of black coffee from Carrie Cook.

The team were sitting around the same table in briefing room 4.12 as they had been the previous day, although this time they had significantly more information but also an equal number of questions that needed answers.

"You look like you need a day off," said Cook, sitting opposite.

"Bad night that's all." Macpherson averted his eyes, avoiding any further engagement in conversation as to why he wasn't his usual gruff self, and Walker for once seemed to read the tension and refrained from making any digs with his sparring partner.

The monitor at the head of the table displayed a rifle green background and the Police Service of Northern Ireland crest.

Taylor waited until her DS had necked the pills and taken a swig of the coffee, accepting his stiff nod as his signal he was ready to get on with proceedings. Cook had rigged up the long HDMI cable and connected the screen to her laptop and was busy logging in.

Erin Reilly had her own laptop in front of her and was busy organising the various emails and updates that had come in overnight from the forensic science laboratory at

Seapark while Walker pondered the ordinance survey map that was laid out, carefully folded to show the southeast of the city and the area and roadways around the Drumkeen Estate and forest park.

There was a knock on the door which opened to admit Detective Chief Inspector Gillian Reed. She waved them to ease and took up a position at the head of the table to Taylor's left.

"Morning, I won't keep you from the coal face but I've to appraise the chief super in five, and the press office has been in contact with queries from a few of the local print and TV outlets regarding our operation at Drumkeen Forest Park. I've seen from the initial reports that we had mixed results, so, have we had any developments overnight from the items recovered?"

Gillian Reed exuded a calm and measured demeanour, and while those colleagues and crooks who were not in the know often mistook her for a bean counter or the duty brief, the DCI was a seasoned detective, forged in the fires of division and sectarian conflict, albeit in designer heels and looking like she had stepped out of a shop window.

"It's a bit early, ma'am. The items recovered matched those described as belonging to Adrian Quinn but forensics are yet to return any confirmation of positive trace on them or the log recovered." Taylor glanced at Reilly as she spoke, receiving a nod of confirmation.

"And the deposition site?"

"Negative. No traces of Quinn."

"That's something I suppose," said Reed, using a pair of horn-rimmed spectacles to better review the information Carrie Cook had launched onto the monitor.

"The site contained the bodies of twelve young staffies." Taylor took a quick look at Macpherson who had half turned in his chair and by the bulge in his jaw was gritting his teeth. "We know there is an element within the estate who use the forest for dog fighting and badger baiting, so I expect these were just unwanted pups. Callous but…" Taylor shrugged.

"I take it we ticked all the boxes, Veronica?"

Taylor nodded, knowing the DCI hadn't come up the Lagan in a bubble.

"Forensics removed the animals and carried out an extensive dig and investigation to ensure they weren't decoys for other remains."

Taylor raised a finger to Cook, who pulled up the site photos of Pearson's excavation. The soil had been carefully removed, and each layer photographed; an occasional glare of Tyvek over suit or a gloved hand was caught in the camera's flash as the slideshow detailed the dig to expose the dogs and then a deeper dig to ensure nothing was buried underneath, the tactic of a decoy often used by organised criminal gangs as a means of subterfuge in the disposal of something else.

"Okay, anything else at the minute?"

"We've established Quinn hasn't used his mobile phone since the morning of his disappearance, Chris?"

"That's right, Mr Quinn made two calls on the morning before he went missing. One to the switchboard at Helios and a second to an unregistered mobile. On that, we've no further hits, no calls, no triggers on masts or GPS. It's likely it ran out of battery or was turned off," said Walker.

"And the car?"

"Other than superficial damage, forensically clean aside from Quinn, his wife and his daughter. We're checking the onboard GPS."

Reed nodded and, satisfied for the moment, stood.

"What's the direction this morning?"

"We're about to review the Quinns' financial position to see if it may be relevant to his disappearance and some follow-up on Helios."

"Let me know if Seapark returns anything." Taylor nodded, the sentence ambiguous but the meaning behind implicit. Was there blood on the clothes and is this a murder investigation.

"Ma'am."

Reed exited, closing the door behind her. Taylor waited a beat.

"Erin, keep one eye on those reports from Diane. Give us the nod when they land. Carrie, do you want to kick off?"

"All set, so, I followed up on your requests. First off, the Quinns' nuisance calls. We've a few." Cook dragged and dropped a spreadsheet of call histories and expanded the window for ease of view.

"Two specifically; this one ending in seven, one, zero by far the more persistent and the other four, four, eight coming at more irregular intervals."

"Did you manage to identify which called when we were there?" said Macpherson.

"I did, and narrowing down to those specifics it was seven, one, zero and I've a match. Katherine Clark."

"The PA?"

Cook nodded. Taylor considered what it meant. Clark and Aoife were known to each other, and although the relationship was likely strained because of Quinn's infidelity, why did Clark not speak, even to ask if there was any news. She came to a conclusion at the same time as Macpherson.

"Aoife Quinn knew who was calling and didn't engage."

Taylor nodded.

"Passive-aggressive punishment? My husband might be missing, but it's nothing to do with you?" suggested Cook.

"Maybe, was there a history prior to…" Cook was nodding as Taylor drifted off.

"Absolutely. Loads of calls over the last weeks and months. A few lasted several seconds, some up to half an hour."

"Which suggests Quinn himself was taking those," said Taylor. "Okay, we'll have another word with Clark. What about the other number?"

"Similar pattern. Numerous calls over the last few months. No discernible pattern and no call time to suggest conversation, although there's one significant finding."

"It's the same number that Quinn called the day of his disappearance," said Walker.

"We've nothing else?" said Taylor

"Not a thing." Both Cook and Walker shook their heads.

"Okay, Carrie, prioritise this number and pass it on to intel. If it pings or comes up against anything else, we need to know."

"Guv."

"How did the finances look?" Cook closed the call histories and brought up the financial records.

"There are a few different accounts, personal banking, savings and credit. Payment history shows he's avoided defaults as far back as recorded. You'll see the savings accounts which were riding high eighteen months ago have taken a battering when the funds were transferred into these two cash accounts. There's also a hefty re-mortgage."

The team followed Cook's cursor as she highlighted the rows and columns of transactions.

"That puts him well over his credit utilisation, which places him now in the risk bracket for most lenders. Card payments have run up over the same period and there's been quite a few cash advances. The regular end of month clearance has also changed to minimum payment."

"His company card needed stitches too, the battering it was getting." Macpherson pointed at the screen. "Are those ATM withdrawals?"

"Yes. Sometimes two or three a day."

"Did you get through the report from Jackie Mahood?" said Taylor. Cook nodded.

"Not all of it, but most of the cash withdrawals correspond with these personal withdrawals."

"Like he was pulling out cash on both cards at the same time?" said Walker.

Cook nodded again. "We're looking at a few cards linked to the company. I confirmed his wife's hospital appointment which corroborates Aoife Quinn didn't make a cash withdrawal, at least in that one instance. We're still open to her being able to access one of the cards for other spend though."

"And those transactions?"

"Mainly high-end boutiques and jewellers. Dropped a few grand on clothing in Victoria Square and at a diamond merchant off Ann Street, ah…" Cook skimmed a few pages of the itemised transactions and her follow-ups. "A few of the shop owners knew Quinn by name, several confirmed a customer matching her description. Callan's of Castle Lane confirmed a transaction of three grand for a twenty-four-carat white gold chain with a curled-u pendant? No idea what that means."

"She was fairly getting payback for his trip behind the bike sheds with Clark," said Macpherson. He had leaned forward and was scanning each of the eye-watering amounts on the list. Walker smirked as Reilly tapped on the keys of her laptop. Taylor was glad to see Macpherson's morose mood had been lifted with the advent of more work.

"It's a bird," said Reilly, spinning her laptop around.

"Ah, a curlew?" said Walker, nodding appreciatively at the website listing for the chain and pendant. "You can tell by the bill."

"Three grand is some bill, David Attenborough," murmured Macpherson, toying with the rim of his plastic coffee cup.

"The bill." Walker tapped the screen. "They're one of Europe's largest wading birds. Amazing, isn't it? They spend the winter along the coast, on the mudflats and estuaries before moving inland to breed. Places like Lagan Meadows or the marshes and arable fields, you know, like the ones bordering Drumkeen Forest Park." Walker had a grin from ear to ear as he regaled the room with his knowledge.

"Tell you what, your girlfriend's going to be beside herself if you keep up that talk," said Macpherson, brightening. Walker's face turned sombre.

"They're on the red list, a high risk of extinction." He shook his head sadly.

"Bit of advice, son, you were doing well up to extinction. Death talk's a passion killer."

As Walker rolled his eyes, the rest of the team gave a relaxed chuckle. Taylor seeing the mirth returned to Macpherson's eyes gave him a nod which he reciprocated. An unspoken gesture that he was fine.

"Pay him no heed, Chris," said Taylor. "We all need a hobby and there's worse you could be doing, like hustling half the Law Society at poker."

Macpherson shook his head, an expression of innocence on his face.

"For supposedly intelligent professionals, I can't for the life of me work out how they don't know when to fold."

It was Cook who drew the conversation back to the task at hand.

"Speaking of extinction, based on what I can see here, Quinn was heading towards having his own lights put out if he continued at this level of spending."

"Which brings us to his rescue plan, the ill-fated expansion deal," said Taylor.

"And coincidently breeding grounds." Cook killed the financial spreadsheets and drew up a collection of Google maps and images of farmland. "These are the three sites acquired for the expansion project. Each had achieved planning status for a PV installation over three acres per location. The concern raised by the environmental groups is that these areas border protected habitat for migratory birds and the impact of construction would be detrimental to that habitat and the wildlife's survival."

"Shocking." Walker shook his head. Cook flicked up another screen.

"This is the contentious one Katherine Clark highlighted. It was initially for sale with approved planning permission for two hundred homes. It looks like Helios made a bid for that and also managed to acquire the area behind it which was dead ground and council owned. The paperwork designates it as the location for a new Helios production facility, although there's a question mark over this as Helios also have an acquisition a few miles away for that."

Taylor looked at the shaded plan view of an area that cut across from the southern end of the Annadale Embankment, hemmed in on one side by the river and the other by the A24, and nestled near Drumkeen Park Golf club and the edge of the forest.

"Any idea why Adrian Quinn would veto it?" she said.

"You mentioned substrate, but it passed all the regulatory controls and was on sale for residential build. Bar objections similar to the ones Helios are battling, nothing leaps out."

"Clark said he wanted an area with enough land around to create a parkland," said Macpherson. "An olive branch to the other side?"

"And given that location, he couldn't do that." Taylor nodded.

"Why is Mahood so adamant to get his hands on it?" said Reilly.

"Probably only one reason. He knows if he owns that land, the price is going in one direction. Look what's around him, everything is protected and no one can ever build on it. With the rate that building expansion is moving towards the outskirts, in a few years, he could offload that site for a fortune." Taylor could see now why Mahood was eager to seal the deal for the land but not why Quinn didn't buy into what seemed like a shrewd deal. As she sought an angle, there was a knock on the door and Leigh-Anne Arnold peeked in.

"Ma'am?"

"Leigh-Anne?"

"I thought you'd want to see this." Arnold handed over her mobile.

A Facebook live stream was underway and showing an altercation between a group of individuals and an angry mob. The camerawork was poor and the images jumpy, but she still identified the logo and the galvanised fence around Helios. The crowd seemed to be outside and pressed up against the gates.

"Is this another protest?"

Arnold shook her head.

"That's the workforce. They're saying on here Helios has shut up shop. For good."

Chapter 17

"….at the renewable technology company's headquarters in south Belfast. It's reported Helios has ceased all production, with one worker at the factory which produces photovoltaic panels telling this programme the news was delivered this morning out of the blue by a factory manager. This devastating blow for the company and the workforce comes amid the ongoing search for their founder and company director, Adrian Quinn, who was last seen…"

Macpherson pulled the Volvo to a stop a hundred yards from the gate as there was no way to get any closer. The narrow road was choked with Helios staff, some still in their protective coveralls or hi-vis vests, milling about on the road in front of the closed iron gates.

A police patrol car had managed to negotiate the human barrier and was now parked across the entrance, two constables just about holding back the tide of discontent and shock that minute by minute was building through the masses.

"What's the craic?" Macpherson jerked his head toward the factory, where a group of women stood on the periphery of the crowd, marked out as office administration by their navy attire and Helios branded pale blue blouses.

"Told us they had to close…"

"Aye, first thing." A second woman nodded, dragging on a cigarette. She blew a cloud of smoke into the air.

"Gathered everybody up and said with Mr Quinn missing and losses over the past year they couldn't sustain the business."

"Load of shite…" muttered a third.

"Who delivered the news?" said Taylor.

"Seawright."

"Where's Mr Mahood?"

"Didn't see him, the yellow bastard, but his car's in there."

"Thanks."

"Can they do this?"

"Is this not against our worker's rights?"

"My personal stuff's still in there…"

Taylor and Macpherson moved toward the gate. Neither had an answer to the questions that erupted behind them.

The antagonism and fervent anger in the crowd grew as they approached the gate and with the absence of company bosses to take the flack, it was beginning to fall on the two constables as the comments continued.

"Joke. It's a frigging joke…"

"We're the ones in the right here…"

"What are you protecting them thieves for? What about my pension?"

"Ma'am, sarge." One of the constables gave a nod as the two detectives eased through the bodies, Taylor brandishing her warrant card and Macpherson with an expression that would sour milk when any of the protesting employees made to challenge their progress.

"What happened?"

"Got a call to attend when the printing unit across the road reported that this was kicking off."

"Anything serious?"

The constable turned down his mouth. "Not really, catcalling and a bit of grandstanding by shop steward types."

The constable glanced over her shoulder at what was slowly descending into a mob, a few rabble rousers now taking up chants against Helios, Jackie Mahood, and the police protection. He gave Taylor a half shake of the head, which she returned in understanding, the thin blue line once again tasked with keeping apart the disaffected masses from the object of their discontent. It was a shared experience they had both endured and which thankfully at the moment didn't involve petrol bombs and slabs of broken up pavement.

"Can you let us in?"

"Aye, come on." He gave a stern look at the front lines as he pulled up the locking bolt and then slid the gate latch, granting eighteen inches of space to squeeze through before he slammed the locks home again behind them.

The noise seemed weirdly louder this side of the fence, thought Taylor, unable to strike the images of an old black-and-white Hammer horror movie from her mind, the looming shadow of Helios Sustainable cast as the bastion of the beast and all that was missing from the mob outside was their torch and pitchforks.

"Is Mr Seawright about?" said Taylor

There was one young girl still at reception and their arrival had caught her unawares. The switchboard under her gaze was lit up like the city on the eleventh night, and the piles of filing and paperwork around her ankles were stacked as precariously as the bonfires themselves.

"How did you get past—"

"We're with the police." Taylor saw a fleeting expression cross her face and saw a family resemblance. "Is he your daddy?"

The girl nodded.

"We know the way, pet," said Macpherson, giving her a sympathetic smile. There was a fear on her face, one that said the affection of her peers was now very much absent.

As they ascended the stairs, Taylor noted the lights in Adrian Quinn's office were on but no one was in the room. A few filing cabinets had drawers open as did his desk and it was the same for Mahood's, except his office looked much less ransacked than the former. Entering Seawright's they found him also absent, although as they returned to the head of the stairs his voice could be heard from a room at the end of the landing.

"Mr Seawright?"

"Hello? Oh…"

"I'd normally ask if it was a bad time but I'd say that's a given."

Richard Seawright looked frayed to the edges. He was sitting in the centre of a long conference table with a spider phone pulled towards him and a legal pad filled with scribbles under his hands.

"You can't imagine."

"What's going on?" said Macpherson, easing around to the left and leaning against the wall under the company name which was fixed in brushed steel letters.

"We're handing over to the administrators and I'm trying to collate all the pertinent records associated with the last financial quarter and collate a list of debtors and creditors."

"Is the boss about?" said Taylor, nodding out the window behind Seawright to the large green Discovery.

"Jackie?" Seawright's voice broke, and he gave a nervous cough.

"Unless Adrian Quinn's turned up?" said Macpherson.

"I don't think that's going to happen?"

"Is that right? You know a bit more than us then, so you do." The DS pushed off the wall to walk over to the window.

"I just mean… Jackie's not here, alright."

"So is that scotch mist down there?" said Macpherson, pulling apart the slats of the blinds. The movement sent a roar of noise up from the crowd at the gate.

"His car? His car's here but he's not." Seawright was beginning to stammer.

"Mr Seawright, what happened? What's driven this since our last conversation" Taylor drew out a chair and sat; Seawright closed his eyes and rubbed the bridge of his nose.

"I took a call from Jackie this morning. He said he had no joy with securing reinvestment and that the finances were in worse shape than he had thought. He didn't give any specifics, but he left no room for doubt we weren't going to recover and he issued the directive to halt production with immediate effect and inform the staff we were to close."

"He's not a one-man band, fella. He can't do that without Adrian Quinn approving." Macpherson had taken a perch on the edge of the table.

"That's what I said." Seawright pulled a finger around the collar of his shirt. "He told me he had executive power as Adrian wasn't coming back."

"He said that?" Macpherson's face darkened as he shared a look with Taylor.

"Or words to that effect."

"Had he been speaking to Adrian?" said Taylor, trying to see beyond Seawright's flustered anxiety.

"Not as far as I'm aware. He made a more general comment about the news of your search in Drumkeen Forest finding something. A… a… a body."

Taylor tapped her fingernail against her front teeth.

"While I can't divulge anything regarding what was found last night, Mr Seawright, I can tell you this remains a missing person's investigation."

"So Adrian's alive?" For the first time since they had walked into the room, Richard Seawright's tone was imbued with a sliver of optimism.

For the sake of his three little kiddies, I hope so, thought Taylor but as she looked around the room at the scattered lists of debts and listened to the angry calls outside she couldn't help but wonder that if Quinn was to be found alive, aside from the physical embrace of his family just what exactly would be left to return to.

Chapter 18

"JUST A SECOND." There was a scrape of keys across wood and then a rattle as the contents of the keyring jangled against the door lock. "Oh... it's yourselves. Is something wrong?"

Laura Roberts recovered her shock quickly enough and presented Reilly and then Chris Walker with one of her beaming smiles.

"We're sorry to drop in on you at home, Miss Roberts," said Reilly, returning the smile. "We tried at the forest park but it was shut up."

"There didn't seem much point opening up; your colleagues are still there and the paths are closed to the public. I've some work I can be getting on with from here." Roberts looked relaxed, her hair was loose, and she was barefoot, wearing a pair of skinny blue jeans and a cream cowl necked tee shirt under a cardigan in the same shade. She toyed with a chain around her neck, waiting with patience tinged with a little curiosity for the police officers to explain their trip to her home.

"We're sorry about that, it's an inconvenience, I'm sure. Could we come in?" said Reilly.

Roberts hesitated for a fraction of a second and then took a step back.

"Sure, but please ignore the mess." She skipped up the hallway ahead of them, taking a right turn into the lounge.

The trip out to Roberts' house had taken only half an

hour or so. With the sun shining it had made for a pleasant journey, heading east across the Queen Elizabeth Bridge and quickly leaving behind the city and the suburbs as they headed for the commuter town of Newtownards then skirting around the A20. Under the watchful eye of Scrabo tower they continued into the countryside proper, hugging the peninsula with emerald green fields on one side and the shimmering waters of Strangford Lough on the other.

Reilly had expected Roberts' statement to be the polite and modest aside people generally made when accepting unexpected visitors into their home but as she entered the lounge, to her surprise she found that her hesitation was warranted and likely stemmed from embarrassment.

The homeowner pulled aside a set of drapes to let in sunlight, offering a view of the lough at the end of her garden, "Grab a seat, I'll be two seconds," she said, passing Reilly to stoop and gather up an ashtray in one hand and a wine bottle and glasses with the other. Walker raised an eyebrow as he moved to take an armchair. Roberts had opened a window, but the breeze hadn't killed the smell of marijuana.

"Drink?" she called from the kitchen. Reilly noted a tightness in her voice and pictured the woman looking at her reflection and swearing inwardly to herself at the awkwardness of the situation.

"We're grand, thanks," said Reilly. "And sorry, I promise we won't take up much of your time." She hoped her tone gave some comfort that they weren't about to haul her in for possession.

The coffee table displayed some official-looking paperwork and a collection of gold foil chocolate wrappers, which Roberts swept up as she returned to the room. She balled the wrappers and tossed them atop the spent ashes of an open fire and set the other documents on top of a bookcase to the right of the chair which Walker had chosen. He blushed, averting his eyes as her top rode up, revealing a flat midriff and the lacy trim of her underwear. Roberts gave a small smile as she turned, adjusting her clothes and her necklace.

"I heard on the news there was some kind of discovery, I hope…."

"It's still a missing person's case," said Reilly. Roberts nodded, acknowledging the pair weren't about to reveal too much more.

"So, you need some help?" she said.

Reilly removed a selection of photographs from the document wallet she carried.

"Could you have a look at these? The CCTV we initially viewed is helpful, but it doesn't give us much detail. We're trying to eliminate some people and vehicles from the enquiry." The DC brushed her blonde fringe from her eyes as she first laid out a catalogue picture of a dark blue Ford Everest.

"Is this the model of vehicle you saw boxing-in the BMW?"

Roberts leaned forward, studying the picture. She absentmindedly tapped her silver chain off her chin as she did.

"Could be?"

"But you're not sure?

"Not a car buff I'm afraid," said Roberts, sitting back.

"That's okay," said Reilly as she removed a half dozen

headshots. Among them were Adrian Quinn, Jackie Mahood and Raymond Kilburn.

"What about any of these men?"

Roberts' finger went straight to Quinn. "That's the man who drove the BMW."

"Anyone else? Specifically, the man you saw arguing with him?"

Roberts pored over the remaining pictures, her eyes drifting to Adrian Quinn now sitting apart. There was silence as she concentrated, the lough-side house creaking with the sort of noises associated with a smallholding exposed to the coast and the elements. Above, the floorboards groaned as though someone had shifted in bed or the central heating had come on and was expanding the old joists. Roberts finally broke the silence.

"Have you any idea where he is?" Reilly shook her head.

"That's why whatever help you can give us could be vital."

Roberts nodded slowly, her gaze drifting back from Quinn to the line-up. She reached out a finger, heading for Jackie Mahood until at the last second she slid out the photo of Raymond Kilburn.

"This one."

"Sure?"

"Pretty sure."

Reilly glanced up at Walker, who was watching Roberts with rapt attention.

Chapter 19

TAYLOR AND MACPHERSON had just exited the lift and were returning to the blue baize cubicles of CID when a familiar voice broke their stride.

"Inspector?"

"Chief Superintendent."

William Law looked like a man on a mission; his strides marked time along the hallway with a clipped beat, his boots were shined to parade perfection and the dress uniform he wore was unblemished with not so much as a blade-sharp seam out of place or an epaulette badge that wasn't exquisite in alignment or radiance. He carried his cap in his left hand, the peak gleaming like a curved black mirror.

"Helios and this Quinn business."

"Yes, sir?"

"I've had Charlotte Quigley on demanding an answer as to why nearly two hundred of her constituents have been made unemployed in the blink of an eye." He stopped at attention two feet from the two officers, Taylor easing a step between the two men, eager to avoid either Macpherson dropping an inappropriate comment or his appearance drawing any ire from their rigorous superior.

"Down Under has some cheek getting on the phone when she couldn't be arsed standing up for the freeze on our pay," huffed Macpherson, following up with a tut and a shake of the head. Law's face bled puce from his starched collar to his forehead, his eyebrows dancing like angry caterpillars.

"Sergeant, should you need reminding, Ms Quigley is an elected representative in an area where fifty per cent of the community still don't wholly trust us and the other half hold us in contempt. I don't think throwing her weight behind a campaign to ensure you can afford to go to Portugal instead of Portstewart on your holidays, aids the delicate balance of diplomacy."

"Maybe there wouldn't be so much contempt if she wasn't so keen on swapping handshakes and blank cheques with Gordon Beattie… sir."

"Chief Superintendent." Taylor jumped in, desperate to divert the conversation away from the notorious gangland figure turned business magnate and the memories and dark period of personal history he represented.

"We've just come from Helios. The firm is being handed to the administrators. Jackie Mahood gave instructions to his plant manager to break the news this morning. They've suffered significant financial impacts over the last quarter and the business, according to him, is no longer viable."

"They were winning awards and on the cover of the Business Eye not two months ago, where's the money and where is Adrian bloody Quinn?"

"We're just on our way to review where we are on that with DC Cook, sir, and we're waiting on forensic results from Seapark following last night's search. As soon as they're in, I'll appraise the DCI."

"See that you do, and see if you can make it sooner rather than later, Inspector."

Macpherson managed to refrain from saying anything

else as Law about-turned and marched back the way he had come.

❖❖❖

"…more interested in the larger transactions than the smaller quantities we are thinking link to Aoife Quinn on a spending spree."

Cook had once again rigged up the monitor in 4.12 and was giving Taylor and Macpherson an overview of the expense report supplied by Mahood and information she was able to glean from Companies House on the business and its official financial reporting.

"What have you highlighted those for?" Taylor pointed out a set of yellow cells.

"Those fifteen transactions do match with Aoife Quinn. They are withdrawals from forecourt ATMs at two filling stations along the A55. We struck lucky when ANPR picked up her car entering and leaving in a close time frame."

"How much in total?"

"Seven and a half grand."

"Not that much when you consider she dropped nineteen on a piece of tat." Macpherson nodded to the other information Cook had retrieved and printed in her search, including a printout of the white gold chain and pendant Reilly had discovered.

"So, where are we here? She's spending heavily on a company credit card, one that she wouldn't officially be entitled to use, and if her husband is paying it off through company accounts that makes it one for HMRC rather than us," said Taylor.

"Even if it's bleeding the business to the point of ruin?" said Macpherson.

"Bigger spends than that, Doc," said Cook, dragging up another set of financial documents and a list of trades.

"Mahood explained to you that Quinn was involved in R&D to enhance the capability of their PV products. Over the last year, he has made monthly deposits to three companies, each over the past few months has folded. The money out forms the basis of the crisis in Helios; look at the numbers."

Taylor did, and they were staggering. What was more incredible was how Quinn had managed to keep the extent of the outgoings secret from Mahood.

"Mahood had a report and told Quinn to cease and desist," said Taylor.

"Well, he didn't, and he continued to accrue personal and business debt."

"He was running the company into the ground," said Taylor, Quinn's duplicity faintly evident in the plethora of numbers up on the screen.

"Why?"

Taylor shook her head, losing the thread she had just grasped, the complexities of the accounts blurring her vision.

"Why risk all he had worked for? Mahood's an arsehole but surely he wasn't going to this extreme to out him?" said Macpherson, he had also looked away from the screen and was doodling, tap-tapping his pen as he eased across some of the paperwork, more comfortable with the tactile nature of sifting hard physical evidence than digital forensic accounting.

"All the testimony we have says Quinn put that company over everything, what could change that?" Taylor let the worm burrow, the question rhetorical and neither Macpherson nor Cook interrupted her thoughts.

"Guv?" Erin Reilly entered 4.12, closely followed by a glowing Walker.

"How'd it go?" said Taylor, nodding in greeting.

"Positive ID on Raymie Kilburn."

Macpherson thudded a closed fist on the table, giving his younger colleagues an approving wink as Reilly continued.

"Di Pearson's reports are also coming in," she said.

Macpherson pushed aside the documents as he, Taylor and Cook made room for their colleagues.

"Go ahead," said Taylor.

"Confirmation of blood on the log. Tests return it as O-Negative. Adrian Quinn is O negative. Also, a quantity of blood and fibres in the bag and on the clothes match those in the car identifying them as belonging to Adrian Quinn."

There was a release of breath around the table as the news sank in and wheels started spinning. Quinn's clothes had been dumped a few hundred metres from his vehicle, and it was now looking like he was never coming back from his run. So much for worrying about how much of his company was going to be left or why he had been burning the proverbial house down.

"Soil samples on the trainers confirm flora and soil type correspond to the path but not to the deposition site…" Reilly paused as she scanned the next line on the report. "The log also carried skin sample traces which are being run through DNA, however, the bin bag containing the clothing held further fibres and fingerprint matches to a nominal already held on the database." Reilly looked up. "Raymond Kilburn."

"Chris, advise Sergeant Harris to have his sections be on the lookout for Kilburn and when you get the nod, I want him in here. Carrie, I need more CCTV footage from in and around the estate and the park. It's going to be crucial in proving he returned after that initial fracas with Quinn."

Chapter 20

THE TEAM HAD moved from 4.12 to the section briefing room, which was small and now overcrowded with the addition of Sergeant Harris and two crews from section four. Cook had remained behind and was trawling the Drumkeen Estate CCTV and ANPR cameras along the A55 in an attempt to confirm Kilburn's movements and spot his return to the forest park.

The uniforms of Section Four stood at the back of the room facing Taylor, who had taken a seat on the edge of a table positioned at the front where, to her right, Erin Reilly tacked up a picture of Raymond Kilburn and neatly printed his details on a whiteboard.

"Raymond Kilburn, Flat 3C Drumkeen Walk. Evidence is building up that Kilburn may have knowledge or be behind the disappearance of Adrian Quinn and should now be considered a suspect." Taylor took the time to look each of the uniforms in the eye as she continued the brief. Macpherson had adopted an at ease posture, hands behind his back and rocking back and forth on the balls of his feet, the motion and the crunching of the last of his brandy balls bleeding off his impatience.

Reilly moved to her inspector's left beside Walker; both were wearing body armour and had fastened utility belts with holstered Glock sidearms, extendable batons and TETRA radios around their waists. Walker fiddled with his earpiece, trying to get the balance of comfort and snug fit.

"Sergeant Harris has been notified by Mike-Eight that the suspect is at home so the plan is to head over there and affect the arrest of Raymond Kilburn, returning him here to Musgrave Street for questioning." She turned to indicate her two junior colleagues.

"The arresting officers are going to be DCs Reilly and Walker. Any questions?"

Taylor waited a beat but no one raised any concerns and each nodded, eager to get the show on the road.

"Okay, you're all clear. Get your PPE on, and any issues or escalation at the scene, report asap. Section Four, two of you with DC Reilly and Walker at the front, two of you round the back. I don't want a runner. Everyone else, usual cordon positions. Good luck."

❖❖❖

Taylor pulled out her chair and sat. Behind her, Macpherson closed the door to the interview room and a moment later the magnetic lock engaged with a dull click; he took the seat to his inspector's right.

The arrest of Raymond Kilburn had gone smoothly. Reilly and Walker had presented at the door and he had come without a fuss. The suspect now sat in an open-necked black shirt and dark jeans, his expression under the maturing black eye and bruises slipped between amusement and curiosity.

The solicitor, sitting to his left, was the more on edge of the two men and it seemed to Taylor his call for service had interrupted a set at the tennis club. She had seen him before but couldn't recall the name. He was mid-thirties and smelled of shower gel. His dark hair was still damp and there was a redness to his face and a disorder to the paperwork he shuffled that suggested more haste and less speed was required. Hoskins or Hopkins, she thought, definitely no closer to a Christian name as she checked her notes. His name was entered in the attendance checkbox, Jeremy Hoskins. Hoskins shrugged off his casual jacket and a crescent of perspiration peeked from under the armpits of his light blue polo shirt. A self-conscious sixth sense made him look up and he offered a quiet nod of acknowledgement that he was ready.

Taylor gave Kilburn a few more seconds under her stare before she pressed the discreet button on the edge of the desk.

Along the hall, in the observation room, Carrie Cook and an officer from the custody team were gathered around the mixing equipment and the digital video and voice recorders monitoring interview room four. Reilly and Walker had returned to Drumkeen Walk to follow up on any forensic opportunities that may present inside Kilburn's residence and Taylor had just taken a follow-up call from Reilly prior to entering the interview.

The recording system's dual tone broke the silence, a flat tone followed by a higher pitch.

"Interview commences at four thirty-eight pm. Present in the room, Detective Inspector Veronica Taylor, DS Macpherson. Mr Hoskins, representing the suspect, and…"

"Raymond Kilburn."

"You know why you're here, Raymond?"

"Yous think I offed that Quinn fella." Kilburn's face was impassive, his demeanour calm. The experience was not a new one for him.

"I believe you may know more about the disappearance

of Adrian Quinn than the account you gave my officers yesterday," said Taylor.

"You can believe all you want, I don't know where he is."

"Pull the other one, Raymie, it plays the sash." Macpherson leaned forward, his expression saying he wasn't buying a word of it.

"Sure it was old, and it was beautiful." Kilburn sang the first of the lyrics to the popular loyalist ballad at Macpherson and then broke into a laugh, his eyes turning to linger on Taylor.

"Have you any evidence to corroborate your theory, Inspector?" said Hoskins, cutting over Kilburn's chuckles, everything about his manner saying he wanted the interview over with. Taylor gave the solicitor a nod and he scratched out a note he had made in a supermarket brand A4 spiral pad.

"We have an eyewitness who places you in Drumkeen Forest Park yesterday morning. They suggest you and Mr Quinn had a disagreement."

"I reported him for that," said Kilburn with a grin.

The monitor on the wall flickered, the rifle green background and PSNI logo replaced by a window showing a still image of the busy A55 dual carriageway.

"This is an ANPR image taken yesterday at seven thirty-seven am. Do you recognise the car?"

"Which one?"

"Raymie, we're not having a laugh here. A man's missing, a family man. He's three wee kids at home wondering why he hasn't come home to them."

If she thought appealing to his better nature would

work, she was wrong. Kilburn pulled a face.

"The car in the centre of the image is a blue Ford Everest. Registered to you." Taylor paused and Cook duplicated the image on her monitor, the screen now showing grainy footage from the entrance to Drumkeen Forest. Kilburn's vehicle caught as it rattled over a cattle grid.

"Seven thirty-nine am, you enter the car park which corroborates the eyewitness statement."

"So what, I was there same time as him. So were twenty other people."

"Nobody else had followed him up the road, boxed his car in and then chased him into the woods," said Macpherson.

"I didn't chase him."

"No?"

"No."

"What's your version?" said Taylor.

"I told the other two, he nearly ran me and my dog down, I wanted a word."

"Raymie, we've the benefit of having your record here. You're not the type to leave it with just a word."

"Mr Kilburn's previous convictions have no bearing on this case," said Hoskins.

"They give a quare account of his character though, don't they, Raymie?" said Macpherson with a wink

"No comment."

"When was this alleged hit and run?"

"I'm not exactly sure."

"You're not sure. Okay, so tell us about your injuries?"

Kilburn pointed to his face. "What's to tell."

"Quinn assaulted you?"

"I cornered him and put him straight on his driving and he lifted a log and hit me a thump."

"Image Bravo, seven, one, A."

In the observation suite, Cook dragged up the corresponding images taken at the scene and then at the forensic laboratory in Seapark.

"Is that it?" said Taylor. Kilburn shrugged.

"If you say so."

"You've two cracking shiners, big fella, but not much in the way of cuts," said Macpherson. Kilburn didn't answer and Hoskins had sat back in his seat, arms folded and looking weary.

"What DS Macpherson is telling you, Raymie, is that there was blood detected on the log. That blood belongs to the same blood group as Adrian Quinn."

She waited as Cook introduced the close-ups of the bloodied stump onto the screen, all eyes watching the images scroll from the branch in situ on the grass to a white and brightly illuminated bench in the lab, the item then framed with forensic measurement tape and notations.

"Do you want to tell me how it got there?"

Kilburn shifted in his seat, his expression darkening. Taylor could see him replay events in his head.

"Losing your touch, Raymie. You didn't see it coming, did you?" Macpherson laughed. "I'd have paid to be there to see your face when he whacked you."

"Aye, he thought he was the big lad…" Kilburn rocked his two closed fists together.

"You taught him otherwise?"

Hoskins sat forward to speak, but Kilburn got in first.

"Did you think I was going to let him get away with it?

With doing this to me?"

Kilburn again pointed at his face, his cheeks aglow, and his breathing heavy as the wash of his anger and aggression crashed over the table.

"What happened then?" said Taylor

"Once you started you couldn't stop?" added Macpherson.

Kilburn scoffed.

"You don't know what you're talking about."

"DC Cook?" said Taylor.

The image changed to the forest glade and a bag of discarded clothing, a close-up of a bloodstain, and a carefully snipped section of black plastic bin liner.

"These items were recovered from nearby where we believe an assault on Adrian Quinn took place. The items are identified as belonging to him."

"Never seen them before."

"There are multiple fibres which are currently being forensically processed. We'll run them against matches of clothing we have recovered from your flat that match those the eye witness described."

"Go ahead."

"Image Bravo, nine, two, C shows a section of bin liner that contained the clothing. Can you explain why your fingerprints are on the bag?"

Hoskins suddenly looked wide awake. Kilburn let out a loud, bellowing laugh.

"Piss off."

"You're in the system, big lad, the evidence doesn't lie," said Macpherson.

"Is this a fucking fit-up?"

Taylor shook her head. Hoskins was scribbling more notes. She caught his eye and played her ace.

"Raymie, following your arrest, officers searched your home and found a large sum of cash. Can you explain where you got it?"

"No comment."

Taylor had printed the images she received from Reilly from the flat in Drumkeen Walk. She drew them from a document folder she had on the table. First was the cash bundled in a black bin liner similar to that in which the clothes were deposited, and the next image was one of the notes laid out on what must have been Kilburn's dining table.

"That's twelve grand of cash. I need an explanation."

"No comment."

"Did you rob Adrian Quinn of that money?" said Taylor.

"What?"

"We know Mr Quinn had access to large quantities of cash, did you rob Adrian Quinn and in the process hurt or injure him so that he was left incapacitated?"

"No…"

"Inspector, might I confer with…" Hoskins blurted.

"Adrian Quinn was in debt. Had he approached you for a loan? Was he unable to pay back what he owed and as a result you hurt or injured him so that he was left incapacitated?"

"I fucking don't know where he is!"

"Did you kill Adrian Quinn and afterwards make attempts to hide his clothing and similarly his body in Drumkeen Forest Park?"

"I only gave him the bloody slap he deserved for doing

this to me!" shouted Kilburn.

"We have a witness who places you at the scene. Your prints on a bag of his clothes. Give us a few more days and we will find DNA and fibres relating to you on those articles, and the cash we will match to withdrawals Adrian Quinn was making from ATMs at nearby service stations each morning."

"It's not his bloody money." Kilburn had both fists on the table, his voice rising, drowning out Hoskins' protests for a break.

"Raymond Kilburn, up until this point you have been arrested on the suspicion of…"

"They're fitting me up! I didn't take his money…"

"You are now officially accused of…"

"She gave me the money to keep my trap shut!" bellowed Kilburn.

Taylor stopped speaking. Macpherson's eyes narrowed to slits.

"Who gave you the money?" said Taylor into the silence.

"His missus. Quinn's wife."

"What for?"

"So I wouldn't tell him that she was knocking off his bloody mate behind his back."

Chapter 21

AOIFE QUINN FLINCHED. The harsh metallic buzz that announced the unlocking of the security gate was enough to set the teeth on edge, let alone when it combined with the rasp of hinges in need of a good oil.

As Macpherson pushed the screaming gate aside, Taylor led Quinn into the custody corridor, her hand firmly on the forearm of the nervous woman. The lift had been straightforward and without incident. Taylor and Macpherson were waiting when the woman returned to Bladon Manor after the school run, her queries turning to incredulity and then quiet compliance when asked to accompany them to Musgrave Street.

Following Kilburn's revelation, Taylor had called time on his interview and had him placed in the cells pending further questioning, granting Jeremy Hoskins the reprieve he had been yearning for, and her team time to dig into the allegations.

As she guided Quinn along the corridor the echo of a dull sonorous bang sounded, just another background noise the two officers automatically filtered out but one which gave Quinn a start. The unmistakable metallic thud of a cell door slamming closed was hopefully enough to reinforce the mental image Taylor wanted in the forefront of Aoife Quinn's mind as she put her in the interview seat.

Along the corridor to the right, Raymie Kilburn resided behind one such heavy door. They had enough to hold him, and given the evidence Taylor expected Seapark to follow through with, it was likely by the end of the day she would have enough to charge. What she now needed to ascertain though, was whether he had acted alone and in retaliation to Adrian Quinn's objectionable driving or was there something more sinister afoot.

Up ahead, their images were captured on a trio of wall-mounted monitors hanging on metal arms above the custody sergeant's booking-in desk. Taylor felt Quinn stiffen as she caught sight of herself in the display and coming under the impassive gaze of the custody sergeant. He stood patiently, hands flat on the countertop, the panelling that boxed in his domain festooned with contact details for duty representation, department head phone numbers, warnings of CCTV in operation and the reminders of the official bureaucracy that needed to be followed by all who entered his domain.

As they approached the booth, another corridor fed from the right, ending in a similar metal gate to the one they had just entered.

"Aoife Quinn, attending for a voluntary interview," said Taylor. The sergeant nodded, reaching for a thick black book.

"Sign in, please." He pushed the open book across to Quinn. A black biro was attached to the cover with a measure of string and a wad of Sellotape.

"Are you carrying any of the following?" He pointed at a laminated card mounted to his left showing a selection of contraband items, and then a small white plastic basket. "If so, may I ask that you deposit them here until you're signing out."

Quinn took a glance, then shook her head, reaching out a trembling hand to take the pen, her scribble and attention distracted by the harsh buzz of the second access gate. Taylor suppressed a smile as Macpherson plucked the pen out of Quinn's hand and slid the book back to the custody sergeant.

Thirty metres away, Erin Reilly entered first. Behind her, Jackie Mahood reluctantly followed with Chris Walker's hand on his shoulder.

"Thanks, Mrs Quinn," said Taylor, loud enough to project to the ears of the approaching Helios director. "If you just come this way, we'll take your statement."

Quinn forced her gaze away from the approaching Mahood, his expression darkening at the sight of her.

As Macpherson held the door open, Taylor guided Quinn through and on towards the interview suite.

So far, so awkward. Mission accomplished.

Chapter 22

"DO YOU RECOGNISE this man?"

Having already fulfilled her obligations to the recording and ensuring Quinn was settled with a beaker of water and confirming her understanding she was there voluntarily and consenting to questions regarding her husband's disappearance, Taylor presented an eight by ten copy of Raymond Kilburn's mugshot taken a little under twelve hours before.

Aoife Quinn cut a forlorn figure. She had adopted a similar position to that from the sofa in her home, albeit made more uncomfortable by the hard, narrow chair on which she now sat, her eyes down and hands clamped between her thighs, Taylor suspected the former was to hide the shock of her recent sighting of Mahood, and the latter to better hide the nervous tension as she stared at the picture on the table.

"Mrs Quinn?"

Quinn glanced up, then back down, but made no answer.

"Mr Kilburn is in custody. We have reason to believe he was the last person to see your husband. When we spoke to you yesterday, we informed you of the recovery of clothes matching the description of your husband's. I can confirm after forensic analysis they are his," said Taylor.

Aoife Quinn sat stock still, the shallow rise of her breast and the slight flare of her nostrils the only movement.

"Do you know this man, Aoife?"

Quinn gave an almost imperceptible nod.

"You're nodding, that's good. Can you tell us how you know him?" said Taylor.

"What about Adrian? Have you found him?" Quinn's voice was small. Taylor shook her head.

"No. We still don't know Adrian's whereabouts. I need to be clear here, Aoife. We found blood on Adrian's clothes and an eyewitness places this man with your husband on the morning of the disappearance so it's imperative you tell us how you know him."

"I…" Quinn's eyes dropped to her lap. Macpherson nodded to Taylor, indicating the document wallet in front of her. The inspector drew out the list of Helios expense transactions.

"We followed up on the twins' hospital appointment. It checked out." Taylor laid a finger on a line item that had been highlighted blue. Quinn followed the finger and then looked into Taylor's eyes as she continued.

"However we are able to say, based on CCTV evidence and the balance of probability, these other fifteen transactions were carried out by you."

Quinn remained silent, her eyes falling unfocused on the damning document.

"We know your husband was in financial difficulty. Did he approach this man for a loan?" said Macpherson, attempting to break the spell.

"Aoife, what were the ATM withdrawals for? Was Adrian paying this man off, or were you?" said Taylor.

A single tear fell from the corner of Quinn's left eye. Taylor pulled Reilly's photo of the cash from Kilburn's flat.

"This a significant sum of cash recovered at Raymond

Kilburn's flat. It matches the sum withdrawn, by you, across various ATMs over the past few weeks." Macpherson spoke gently, trying to tease a reply.

"Aoife, help us understand why? It won't take much for us to match this cash to the batch that was issued from the ATM. You do understand how this looks?"

Quinn blinked away more tears. Taylor pulled a packet of tissues from her pocket and passed them across. Quinn took one and dabbed her eyes, taking a ragged breath and shaking her head.

"He approached me."

"This man?" said Taylor, eager to hear it.

"Yes."

"When?"

"Eight, ten weeks ago?"

"Where?"

Quinn shook her head and snorted in derision.

"At the kids' school. I was waiting in the car."

"And what did he say?"

"He told me he knew Jackie." Quinn's voice cracked as she spoke his name. She covered up the discomfort with a blow of her nose.

"And he told you he knew about the affair?" said Taylor, watching Quinn keenly as the words sank in. For a long moment, she said nothing and then her chin dropped, and she uttered a quiet hiss of affirmation.

"Kilburn says this cash came from you. Can we establish right now that is true?"

Quinn nodded, dabbing more tears.

"Was he blackmailing you?"

"He said he would tell Adrian," she said with a nod. "It

was a stupid, stupid mistake."

"Did you tell Jackie?"

Quinn was still shaking her head in bitter regret as she answered. "He said he would sort it."

"How?"

Quinn shook her head, a memory etched on her face.

"Did he offer him money?"

"Jackie wouldn't spend on Christmas, and he certainly wouldn't be blackmailed."

"Are you saying he threatened your man?" said Macpherson, making a note to the list of follow-ups they would need to ask Kilburn.

"Whatever he did, it didn't work. He came to me again, and I told him I'd pay him to shut up."

"Aoife, are you and Jackie Mahood still having a relationship?" said Taylor. Quinn's face cracked, and the tears began to flow with abandon.

"It just happened… I was angry… angry about Katherine… angry about Aido putting the business first, again…"

"Aoife, do you know where Adrian is? Do you know if anything has happened to him?" Taylor leaned forward, her words landing with sobering clarity on the woman opposite.

"No…" The denial was abrupt, her face surprised. Taylor slid out an image of her husband's running gear. The one shoe and a snapshot of blood.

"You knew Adrian's route, his routine," she said.

"What? Why is that…"

"Did you conspire with Raymond Kilburn to kill your husband to conceal your affair and claim life insurance to secure the debts Adrian had accrued against your family home?"

Quinn looked horrified. She swallowed, her face blanching a peculiar shade of pale green and Taylor thought she might be about to vomit.

"No…"

"Did Jackie Mahood?"

Chapter 23

TAYLOR SIPPED A coffee, and Macpherson sucked the remnants of an iced finger from his thumb and forefinger. They had withdrawn from Aoife's interview and returned to the adjoining observation suite to join Carrie Cook.

She had drawn up two screens on the large observation monitor which they now watched; one showing Aoife Quinn and the other, Jackie Mahood. While the former had an expression wracked with tension and looked fragile, worn out and on the fringe of breakdown, Mahood, by contrast, was as bullish as ever. His demeanour was contemptuous, arms folded high on his chest, legs akimbo and leaning back in his seat, the front two legs beating a rhythm as he rocked back and forth.

"Not as naïve as Mrs Quinn," observed Cook. Macpherson snorted, taking a slurp of tea and shaking his head impatiently, Mahood having stalled the process in his request for having his solicitor present.

"No sign of the brief yet?" said Taylor, looking at her watch. Cook responded with a shake of the head.

"Should we pull Kilburn out again?" said Macpherson.

"Wait until we've had a crack at him," said Taylor, aiming her cup at the screen. Mahood stared back as though he were the one watching them.

A series of short beeps emitted from the observation suite code lock and the door opened. Reilly entered first, followed by a smiling Chris Walker.

"Great timing, Guv," he said, beaming from ear to ear. "Couldn't shut the bugger up until he saw you and heard Quinn was about to spill."

Taylor returned his enthusiastic smile and Macpherson slapped his younger colleague on the back as he sat down.

"Just what we wanted, son. Well done, the pair of you."

"How did you get on?" said Reilly. Taylor pursed her lips.

"She's admitted to the affair and for paying off Kilburn. One of which isn't a crime, and the other makes her the victim."

"What about smiler?" said Macpherson, nodding to the screen.

"Mr Personality?" said Reilly. "You weren't wrong. He went off on one and the first person he pointed the finger at was…." Reilly pointed her index finger at the screen showing Aoife Quinn.

"And they say chivalry is dead," said Cook.

"What did he say?" said Taylor.

"What you'd expect. He doesn't know where Quinn is and if anyone does, it's his missus. Then we took a healthy dose of slabbering about how to conduct our investigation and how he gave us evidence they were thieving from the business and nothing has been done."

"You kept a lid on Kilburn and the affair."

Reilly and Walker nodded in unison.

"Good," said Taylor. "I want to go through what we have again. All actions, those we covered and anything either just in or that remains outstanding."

She jettisoned her empty cup into an overflowing wastepaper basket and sat to Cook's right. Her train of thought had coalesced over the last twenty-four hours to form the opinion something untoward had happened to Adrian Quinn.

It wasn't a huge leap of deduction considering they had his clothes and evidence of his altercation with Kilburn, but the reasoning behind it was now more complex and troubling. All the information and verbal testimony had initially pointed to a meticulous and intelligent individual with the world at his feet, but what had caused the deterioration in his attitude towards his business partner, the excessive risks he had taken to drive that business forward and the compilation of massive debts threatening his home sat just outside her grasp.

Had the wool been pulled by Mahood and Quinn; were they behind the company's dwindling fortunes? Aoife Quinn certainly had been bashing the plastic, and Mahood by his own admission had put a noose on Adrian Quinn's spending, but it was he who had ultimately called time on the business. Had the adulterous couple tried to push Quinn out for their own gain, and if that hadn't worked or if he had found out would they have had the guts to make a final, brutal bid to ensure they stayed together and became wealthier as a result? Despite it looking like Helios was falling into administration, Chief Superintendent Law's simple query continued to burrow into her ear; where is the money?

"We need to link these three and we need to establish if Kilburn returned to the forest park. Any joy on CCTV first?"

"I've trawled the ANPR and CCTV available in and around the Drumkeen Estate," said Cook, her tone somewhat deflated. "Other than what we have of the morning, I've no images of Kilburn returning by vehicle, so the supposition is he returned on foot from his flat on Drumkeen Walk. We've nothing in the way of coverage if that's the case."

"Erin?"

"Laura Roberts gave a positive ID," said Reilly.

"And she's offered to supply the rest of the footage from the RSPB headquarters building. I've made arrangements to recover it," added Walker.

Macpherson chortled. "I'm sure you have. This doll must be something? You've been running about like a puppy with two tails since you first went over there. First, it's conservation and petitions, then you're dickied up like you fell out of Millets window…"

Walker blushed. "Millets doesn't…"

Macpherson waved the protest away.

"That's good, Chris," said Taylor. "We need something that places Kilburn back at the scene to establish him as being behind the dumping of Quinn's clothes so any CCTV of him on foot will be gold."

"What about any other eyewitnesses?" said Cook.

"None from the appeal," said Taylor.

"Laura didn't mention any further sightings?" said Macpherson with a pointed look at Walker.

"Nothing from her or the ground staff," confirmed Reilly, sparing Walker his blushes.

"We're going to struggle without a body," said Taylor.

"Search teams have scaled back but we're still combing the forest park. That being said, it's a huge area." Reilly shrugged.

Taylor thought for a moment.

"Did we ever get the GPS back on Quinn's motor?"

Cook nodded.

"Yes. It arrived at the park on the morning he went missing, the route matches ANPR and it didn't move until we had it towed." Cook's fingers darted across her keyboard and she pulled up a report and map showing the built-in GPS data attributed to Adrian Quinn's BMW. Attached to the report from technical services was a map of recent and regular locations, each pinpointed by geo coordinates.

Taylor nodded, the consideration that perhaps Quinn had been moved in his own car after the sighting now defunct.

"Okay, where are we on financials?"

Cook killed the GPS screen and launched a new window of transactions, one Taylor recognised and another she didn't.

"Jesus, I'll be seeing those numbers in my sleep," said Macpherson. "I'm away to get another round in. Same again?"

"I'll go," said Walker standing. He collected his mobile phone and shrugged at Macpherson. "Call of nature."

"Call of the naturist more like. You give her a call while you're out and rustle up the CCTV, oh, and see if you can get another one of those iced fingers while you're at it." Macpherson rubbed his eyes as Walker left the room and he returned his attention to the monitor. "Go on then, but remember maths isn't my strong suit."

Cook chuckled as she drew out the data, giving a nod to Reilly.

"We consolidated the information we got from the card and the complaint Mahood issued. A good proportion of that spend is ATM withdrawals, the transactions we can link to Aoife Quinn and her spend across the city."

"It was burning a hole in her pocket alright," said Macpherson. "Mahood wasn't going to need to be a forensic accountant to spot his money was being spent on shoes and jewellery."

"Up until now, we've assumed Quinn had issued her the card. What if it was Mahood? A perk for the mistress?" said Reilly.

Taylor nodded, considering the viewpoint. It was one way Quinn may have stumbled on his wife's indiscretions, and if he had and challenged them, it would be the simple answer to how a conflict developed.

"The transactions on that card all fall within a geographical boundary that runs along the A55 for ATM withdrawal and in and around the city centre for spend," said Cook, a map superimposed now on the screen and she used the cursor to point out the broader area and locations. "We have found another card linked to the Helios business account that has also been active during the same period and following the same pattern of activity as the first."

The desk phone rang. Taylor picked up the receiver, returning it a few moments later after a short conversation.

"Mahood's brief is delayed. He's finishing up in court now so it could be another hour," she said. Macpherson looked at his watch and groaned. That would mean any interview would be cutting into dinner time.

"Sorry, Carrie, crack on."

"The second card follows a similar pattern of ATM

withdrawals although outside the other card's geographical boundary; in saying that, it does share one common retail hit. A high-end jewellery store. Callan's of Ann Street."

The name was familiar to Taylor and she could place the black shop front where it sat on the corner of the main pedestrian precinct, but not how it related to the case. Cook shifted the map view and again used the cursor to point out the broad scope of the card's travels. As the cursor cut east across the suburbs, she highlighted four locations they knew to be ATMs. A Sainsbury's store at a retail park off the main A2 carriageway, a filling station on the A20 close to the Ulster Hospital and several others at retail parks further outside the city. Taylor's train of thought caught, crashing to a stop as suddenly as a head-on collision.

"Carrie, go back," she said. Cook glanced at her sharply, the sudden impetus in the inspector's voice crystal clear.

"To the other card…?"

"No back, back. The tech services report on Quinn's GPS data."

The door to the observation suite opened, and Walker entered.

"For God's sake you're asked to do one job—" said Macpherson, his words tumbling to a halt as he caught the younger man's expression. Walker carried no cups and no iced finger. His complexion was as white as the wall.

Cook clicked back through the screens until she had the technical service report and the map of Quinn's locations.

Taylor spotted the pattern now she knew what to look for.

"Guv…" Walker's voice caught with a block of emotion, and Macpherson stood fearing he was about to fall. Walker held out his phone.

Taylor looked at the display and then back to the details Cook had put on screen. She gave a short nod, the single image embedding a hook in what seconds ago might have been conjecture. She handed the phone to Macpherson.

"Ack, Christ," he said with a sad shake of the head, glancing up before looking back down at the screen to confirm what he was seeing, a case of innocent Facebook stalking gone horribly wrong. He shook his head again. "You poor bugger."

Chapter 24

THE CLOUDS THAT obscured the low-lying sun painted a purple palette across the sky above Strangford Lough, while below, the cold waters of the inlet were rippled by strong currents and eddies that earned the beguiling and beautiful stretch of water its dangerous reputation.

Macpherson negotiated the narrow lane from the main Portaferry Road towards a stony car park that clung to a rocky cove on the water's edge, as the car crunched down the track. Both his own and Taylor's eyes were drawn beyond an old sea wall where, rising from the gloom of the waves and trailing a white plume of water, stood the world's first commercial tidal stream power station.

"I didn't even know this was here," said Macpherson, the Volvo taking a crunching dip as it entered the car park and he eased the car to a stop.

"I've a vague memory about it launching, but yeah, it's still a bit of a surprise to most I guess."

SeaGen loomed out of the water like the bulbous periscope from a Bond villain's lair or the conning tower of a futuristic submarine. The underwater tidal electricity generator took advantage of the fast tidal flow of the lough to drive its powerful turbines and in turn generate enough electricity to power thousands of the surrounding peninsula's homes.

"I said it once and I'll say it again, I'm some mentor." Macpherson ratcheted on the handbrake and gave Taylor an approving nod. She smiled sadly.

"It's easy when it's staring you in the face." She raised the image they had printed from Walker's phone.

Taylor pulled her jacket and scarf tighter as she exited the car. The wind that whipped off the sea inlet was cold and the waning sun would do little to oblige them with any heat from behind its impressionist canvas.

The dog's head snapped up sharply at the sound of Macpherson closing his door, the small terrier uttering a series of staccato barks at the strangers.

Macpherson fell into step beside Taylor as they approached, the small dog dancing in excited circles around the feet of its owner.

"Ms Roberts?"

Taylor raised a hand as they got closer. The dog's low rumbling was audible over the keening of the wind.

Laura Roberts squinted into the breeze, plucking a hair from her mouth as she stooped to secure the dog on its lead. As she stood back up, Taylor caught the gleam of white gold under her unzipped gilet. A long chain lay against the dark material of her sweater, on the end of which hung a distinctive pendant.

"I wondered how long it would take." Roberts shushed the growling dog and turned towards the low sea wall and the spectacle of the tidal generator. "I have to admit, when your colleagues called to the house I thought that was it."

Taylor fell into step to the woman's right, the terrier's little brown face staring up as it trotted along, a bit more calm but still straining against the lead. Its interest in the newcomers and what treats they had, if any, piqued.

"It took a bit of putting the pieces together but we

usually get there in the end," said Taylor.

Roberts gave a small huff of laughter but there was a sadness in her eyes. She gave the dog a measure of leash as they approached the edge of the car park. The wall was broken by a set of pillars offering a way to a crescent of stony beach and the water's edge beyond, and as they neared, they saw a figure casting off, standing at the water's edge, another fishing rod sitting on a tripod to the left beside a dark tackle box.

As her feet hit the stony shale and crushed shell, Taylor watched the figure turn, a sudden shaft of light breaking from the edge of the clouds to frame him in a golden spotlight.

She stopped ten feet away. Macpherson—as always—was at her shoulder. The mystery solved but a hundred questions yet to be answered.

"Adrian Quinn?" she said.

Epilogue

TAYLOR WATCHED FROM the end of the hallway as Reilly escorted Aoife Quinn from the custody sergeant's desk to the noisy gate that led to the car park and freedom. She turned at the sigh from behind.

"Is that it then?" said Walker.

Taylor nodded up at the monitor which showed Macpherson and Cook in deliberation with Kilburn and his solicitor. Mahood had already gone.

"Soon will be," she said.

Walker hung his head, and she felt a pang of sympathy for the young man but also a swell of contentment in knowing that a rough edge had been knocked off and he would, in time, reflect on a lesson learned. He wouldn't be the first and he wouldn't be the last to fall for the charms of a pretty young witness.

"Come on," she said, putting an arm around his shoulder and guiding him back up to 4.12.

Macpherson and Cook entered close behind them with Reilly coming in last but not least, the tray of tea and coffee and selection of pastries and cream buns raising Macpherson from his seat like he'd been stung.

"That's mine, thanks very much," he said, claiming the lone iced finger before there was any time for objections.

"Kilburn away?" said Taylor as he took a huge bite. Cook answered.

"Released without charge."

Taylor nodded, Kilburn's involvement, it seemed, had been a contrivance by the man to shake down Quinn for more cash by offering him information that he already knew. Kilburn's bash to the head and hours facing a potential murder charge seemed a fitting punishment for being greedy and playing two ends off against the middle, but in the end, Taylor reckoned it wouldn't be enough to have taught him a lesson.

The wall behind held the image of the technical services map and the list of financial transactions and other Helios trades uncovered by Cook over the last days.

"What did he have to say for himself?" said Cook, tearing apart a fresh cream apple turnover, Macpherson made to speak but his mouth was still full.

"He wasn't one bit sorry for the damage he's caused," said Taylor, declining the plate and instead, stirring her coffee. "Although to be fair he did have some guilt at giving us the runaround."

She thought back to the beach and the knowing look that crossed Adrian Quinn's face when he realised his few short days of peace and isolation were up. He had apologised immediately, but any remorse that he might have shown for the suffering he had caused his wife and his former business partner was conspicuously absent.

"He knew of the affair," she explained. "It had been ongoing for some time and reading between the lines it wasn't the first time Aoife had strayed. He alluded to the fact that her infidelities were what drove him to Katherine Clark, although he confirmed her story that it was a one-off. He's filing for divorce and joint custody of the kids."

All heads bowed at the thought of the upheaval and the

impact on the three innocent lives.

"And Roberts?" said Reilly. She offered a sympathetic glance at Walker whose eyes remained fixed on the table. He hadn't taken a bite either, his pride damaged and the object of his crush suddenly plunged headlong into the arms of Adrian Quinn.

"Quinn and Roberts struck up a conversation at the forest park and one thing led to another. When the expansion deal was in full swing, Quinn found that Mahood had cut a deal without his knowledge to buy up the sites for the plant and the solar farms; he had Clark leak the news when Roberts informed him of an issue with one of the locations."

"The site acquired on the edge of Drumkeen Forest," said Walker. Taylor nodded. He had been doing his homework.

"The reason there were no building works on that site already was due to the nature of the substrate, it was sand based and a known area of flood risk because of its proximity to the River Lagan. Bad for development but five-star hospitality for migratory birds." Taylor took another sip of coffee. "Roberts had been trying to overturn the development order for years, designating the area as a protected wetland and pressing for specific status as it was a known breeding ground for the curlew."

All eyes now stared at the picture of the white gold chain and its pendant of the wading bird with the long curved beak. "According to Quinn, Mahood knew about him and Roberts and bought the land as a means to strong-arm him into handing over the majority share of Helios in exchange for release of the ground to the park trust."

"What Mahood didn't know was Quinn was a step

ahead," said Macpherson sucking the icing off his fingers. Taylor continued.

"When Jackie Mahood bought into the business, Quinn had a non-compete drawn up. He knew Mahood had a habit of buying into firms, asset stripping and then setting up as a competitor but at the time he needed the finance. Quinn then found himself bound by the agreement, so he found a way around it."

Cook considered what they knew about Quinn's financials, his Helios trades both fair and foul and the state of the company as he had left it.

"He was stripping out the liquid assets…" she said

"To reinvest away from solar…" continued Reilly.

"And into tidal. He has secured a position with SeaGen to advance their tidal power capacity with the technical advances he made in Helios and offered to bring those advances and the key individuals essential to their integration across with him."

Macpherson shook his head. "You've got to hand it to him. Any wonder Mahood thought the money he was burning through was wasted. It wasn't meant for Helios in the first place."

"What will happen to him?" said Walker. "To Laura?"

Taylor smiled, the expression mirrored by her two female colleagues, as Macpherson rolled his eyes.

"Given the way Quinn went about things, he'll likely be struck off as a company director. Were his actions criminal? Probably not. Were they morally questionable? Definitely, although he believes all staff pensions are secure and any debts remain manageable through the administrators' sale of the remaining PV assets and his own intellectual properties. He was quite happy when he mentioned it wouldn't leave much for Mahood or his wife, though. As for Laura Roberts, other than her questionable taste in men, she answered the questions we asked and corroborates Quinn's side of the story. Yes, she ditched his bag of clothes but other than having the council issue her a fine for fly-tipping…."

"Lucky escape, son," said Macpherson, pushing back his chair and standing to ease out the cricks in his back. "Take it from me…"

"Brace yourselves for a lesson from the relationship guru," said Reilly, rising and stacking the cups.

"What are you talking about?" Macpherson scowled. "Twenty years I'm married. If I can find a woman to stick with me that long, I must have some tips to offer. Chris, come on and I'll tell you about the time…"

"Never mind him. Chris, give us a hand and we'll get these sorted and go for a drink. I'll buy," said Reilly.

Taylor shook her head in mirth as Macpherson's mouth dropped open.

"I'll buy," said Cook. "You can tell me about that petition. My dad was quite taken with it when I was telling him about the plight of Belfast's starlings."

"I'm not sure if I'm in the mood…"

"Right, fella." Macpherson pointed a finger and blustered. "There's two fine wee girls offering to buy you a drink and if you don't get up off your arse and take them up on it you're more of a buck eejit than I thought you were."

"Go on, the three of you," said Taylor. "We'll square up here and see you in the morning."

Reilly and Cook offered their thanks and Walker followed suit, rising with just a little reluctance, but seemingly brighter at the prospect of roping in Carrie, or at least her father, to his newfound passion.

"And I thought we only dispensed the good cop, bad cop routine on the villains?" said Taylor.

"You're too soft," said Macpherson, gathering some of the files and watching them go.

"I blame my mentor," said Taylor with a smirk. "Speaking of which, when are we going to discuss your transfer to the training college with the chief super?"

She ducked the flying files with a raucous laugh, the sound of it and Macpherson's swearing reaching far enough along the corridor to put a grin back on the face of a retreating Chris Walker.

❖

AFTERWORD

THANK-YOU FOR READING 'THE BELFAST CRIME CASE-FILES Vol.1'

I sincerely hope you enjoyed this collection. If you can **please** spare a moment to leave a short review it will be very much appreciated and helps immensely in assisting others to find this, and my other books.
Follow Detective Inspector Veronica Taylor and her team in my Debut novel:

'CODE OF SILENCE' and in the upcoming novel 'THE CROSSED KEYS'

You can find out more about the books in the series so far by signing up at my website:
www.pwjordanauthor.com

AUTHORS NOTE

I AM GRATEFUL now that the dark days known as the troubles are in the distant past and as a society, while not perfect, we have moved on.

My books explore these new times where the police and law enforcement face dynamic changing threats and challenges while still dealing with the shadow of the past.

I hope that my version of the city and my novels and characters can open this great place up to a new audience who will love its flawed uniqueness as much as I do.

Belfast and Northern Ireland as a whole has so much to offer and when we come together to showcase our diversity, shared love of friendship, family and strangers for a small speck of green in a very big world we shine very brightly indeed.

I hope in the aftermath of recent difficult times those who can visit will, and as the world gets back to normal and global pandemics return to their place in dystopian fiction novels and films, many more international travellers can experience the world renowned craic and hospitality of this once troubled but always welcoming island we here know as :

'The Land of the Giants.'

❖

ACKNOWLEDGEMENTS

ALTHOUGH THE WRITING of a book is largely a solitary affair getting it to the point where the baton can be passed across into the hand of readers is very much not.

I was incredibly fortunate as I started on my path to publishing to count on a community of like-minded individuals who generously shared with me their road map and were willing to share their experiences and pitfalls as they pursued their own writing ambitions.

First and foremost then, thanks to those at the '**Self Publishing Formula**' who have answered the questions of a naive newbie and been patient and kind enough to offer critique on covers and blurbs while offering encouragement and constructive criticism.

Without the incredible generosity of **Mark Dawson** and his team, hundreds if not thousands of people, like me, would still be scratching around in the dark.

To **Suzy K. Quinn,** the '*How To Write A Bestseller*' course fell into my lap at the right time and not only offered an incredible insight into the writing process but reassured me I was on track even though I didn't quite know what I was doing.

But for that lightbulb moment none of these books might have made it out of my imagination and for that I'll be forever grateful.

As the writing community has been a massive part of the team so have the readers, bloggers and book groups who have read the series so far and been hugely encouraging.

My sincere and heartfelt thanks to all the admin's at **UK Crime Book Club** for the support, interviews and promotion of the books. Not just for myself but all the authors they champion. Thank-you **David Gilchrist** and **Caroline Maston** for founding such a warm, welcoming and safe space for readers and writers to share their love of crime stories, and to **Kath Middleton**, a fantastic author herself, who unselfishly offered notes to improve each of the books you have just read.

To the bloggers (to namedrop a few- **Deb Day, Nicki Murphy, Lynda Checkley, Nigel Adams, Donna Morfett**)- thanks for taking the time to indulge this particular debut author, offer such great feedback *and* tirelessly promote and support the author community.

There's a quote attributed to Samuel Johnson: *'A writer only begins a book. A reader finishes it.'*

To the readers, **THANK YOU!**

I am so grateful that my books have passed through the hands of thousands of readers, something I could only dreamed of happening when I typed the first words, so to each and every one of you, thanks for taking that chance on a newcomer.

To have someone reach out and express their joy at reading your book, or to offer unsolicited feedback is both overwhelming and incredibly humbling.

There have been several people who maybe don't know the positive effect their words have had so thank-you: **Laura Hamilton**, the kind critique and encouragement of a stranger made sure this journey didn't end at the first hurdle. **Steve Munoz**, as a reader I always valued your insights and thoughtful book reviews. To hear mine were being read across the Atlantic and then for you to reach out personally really cemented my desire to keep writing at a time when imposter syndrome was at a premium and I just wasn't sure if I was up to it.

Last but not least (and by no means a lone wolf) thank you so very much to **Maureen Webb**. Not only is she one of my fantastic advance reading team but Maureen never misses an opportunity to sing the praises of **The Belfast Crime Series** across social media. I'm indebted to you for your eye to detail and continued championing of each book.

And finally, thanks to my incredible and very patient editor, **Melanie Underwood**. It is your work that makes these books shine.

- Phillip Jordan- January 2023

GET EXCLUSIVE MATERIAL

GET EXCLUSIVE NEWS AND UPDATES FROM THE AUTHOR

Building a relationship with my readers is *the* best thing about writing.

Visit and join up for information on new books and deals and to find out more about my life growing up on the same streets that Detective Inspector Taylor treads, you will receive the exclusive e-book 'IN/FAMOUS' containing an in-depth interview and a selection of True Crime stories about the flawed but fabulous city that inspired me to write.

You can get this **for free,** by signing up at my website.

Visit at www.pwjordanauthor.com

ABOUT PHILLIP JORDAN

ABOUT PHILLIP JORDAN

Phillip Jordan was born in Belfast, Northern Ireland and grew up in the city that holds the dubious double honour of being home to Europe's Most Bombed Hotel and scene of its largest ever bank robbery.

He had a successful career in the Security Industry for twenty years before transitioning into the Telecommunications Sector.

Aside from writing Phillip has competed in Olympic and Ironman Distance Triathlon events both Nationally and Internationally including a European Age-Group Championship and the World Police and Fire Games. Taking the opportunity afforded by recent world events to write full-time Phillip wrote his Debut Crime Thriller, CODE OF SILENCE, finding inspiration in the dark and tragic history of Northern Ireland but also in the black humour, relentless tenacity and Craic of the people who call the fabulous but flawed City of his birth home.

Phillip now lives on the County Down coast and is currently writing two novel series.
For more information:
www.pwjordanauthor.com
www.facebook.com/phillipjordanauthor/

COPYRIGHT

A FIVE FOUR PUBLICATION.
First published in Great Britain in 2023
FIVE FOUR PUBLISHING LIMITED
Copyright © 2023 PHILLIP JORDAN

The moral right of Phillip Jordan to be identified as the author of this work has been asserted by him in accordance with the Copyright, Designs and Patents Act 1988.

All the characters and events in this book are fictitious, and any resemblance to actual entities or persons either living or dead is purely coincidental.

All rights reserved. No part of this publication may be reproduced, stored in a retrieval system or transmitted in any form or by any means, without the prior permission in writing of the publisher, nor is it to be otherwise circulated in any form of binding or cover other than that in which it is published without a similar condition, including this condition, being imposed on the subsequent purchaser.

Cover Images- Coverkit

THE BELFAST CRIME CASE-FILES Vol.1

FIVE FOUR PUBLISHING

Printed in Great Britain
by Amazon